spy school
secret service

Also by Stuart Gibbs

The FunJungle series
Belly Up
Poached
Big Game
Panda-monium

The Spy School series
Spy School
Spy Camp
Evil Spy School
Spy Ski School

The Moon Base Alpha series
Space Case
Spaced Out

The Last Musketeer

STUART GIBBS

spy school
secret service

A spy school NOVEL

Simon & Schuster Books for Young Readers
New York London Toronto Sydney New Delhi

SIMON & SCHUSTER BOOKS FOR YOUNG READERS
An imprint of Simon & Schuster Children's Publishing Division
1230 Avenue of the Americas, New York, New York 10020

Library of Congress Cataloging-in-Publication Data
Names: Gibbs, Stuart, 1969- author.
Title: Spy School secret service / Stu Gibbs.
Description: First edition. | New York : Simon & Schuster Books for Young Readers,
[2017]. | Series: Spy School | Sequel to: Spy ski school. | Summary: Thirteen-year-old Ben
Ripley is assigned to protect the president from an assassination attempt in his first solo
mission, but he may be in over his head.
Identifiers: LCCN 2016037360 | ISBN 9781481477826 (hardback) |
ISBN 9781481477840 (eBook)
Subjects: | CYAC: Spies—Fiction. | Assassination—Fiction. | Presidents—Fiction. |
Friendship—Fiction. | Schools—Fiction. | Washington, D.C.—Fiction. | BISAC:
JUVENILE FICTION / Action & Adventure / General. | JUVENILE FICTION /
Mysteries & Detective Stories. | JUVENILE FICTION / Humorous Stories.
Classification: LCC PZ7.G339236 Spq 2017 | DDC [Fic]—dc23
LC record available at https://lccn.loc.gov/2016037360

For Dashiell, the best son anyone could ever ask for

acknowledgments

Turns out, it isn't very easy to get into the White House. It used to be a bit easier: you could arrange for a tour shortly before visiting Washington, DC. But these days, you have to call your congressman's office months ahead of time, and even then, there's no guarantee you can get in. I couldn't. So I called my good friend Nani Coloretti instead. Nani is the kind of person who gets invited to the White House, rather than having to take the tour. She gave me all sorts of fascinating info about the White House, which was invaluable in writing this book. I couldn't have done it without her. In fact, I probably learned more from Nani than I would have from the tour, because the official tour doesn't even take you to the West Wing or the Eisenhower Executive Office Building, while Nani has been to both. (I should point out that, if I got anything wrong in my description of the White House, that's not Nani's fault; I may have screwed some things up.)

For the record, the White House does have a website that gives some info about the place, and you can even tour it on Google maps, so that was all helpful too.

In addition, I owe thanks, yet again, to my good friend Larry Hanauer. For those of you who have been carefully reading the acknowledgments to every one of my books, you will certainly have seen Larry's name come up before. In fact, this is the third series Larry has helped with, making him the first person to get the coveted Stuart Gibbs Trifecta Award. Larry's contribution this time was to tell me what an insane place the Pentagon was—and to point out that, even though it's almost impossible to get into the White House, pretty much anyone can take a tour of the Pentagon. (Including me, it turns out.)

Also, thanks to my editor, the great Kristin Ostby, who sadly left the publishing world after this book. (Not because of it, mind you. She simply had other things she wanted to do more.) Kristin oversaw a lot of my books and left some pretty big shoes to fill, but my new editor, Liz Kossnar, has stepped up to the challenge. And huge thanks to my publisher, Justin Chanda, for making the transition happen smoothly and always supporting my work.

Thanks also need to be given to my eternally excellent agent, Jennifer Joel, without whom Spy School wouldn't exist, and to her extremely clever nephew Maverick Satnick, who came up with the title for this book.

Finally, I need to thank my wonderful wife, Suzanne, for her constant support, enthusiasm, and cheerleading—and the world's greatest test audience, my children, Dashiell and Violet. I love you all to infinity and beyond.

spy school
secret service

contents

February 9

2100 hours

Mr. ████████

Since my last dispatch, I have continued to monitor various channels used by SPYDER for their communications. I regret to report that, in the last twenty-four hours, there has been an enormous increase in chatter concerning a ██████████████████████. Given this, I think we can only assume that you are in imminent danger. This is a Code Red situation. We need to activate Operation Pungent Muskrat immediately.

To that end, I stand by my recommendation of agent-in-training Benjamin Ripley for the job. I have worked with Benjamin on three previous (albeit unauthorized) missions and he has proven himself on each, displaying intelligence, cleverness, and moral fiber. The only drawbacks are his ████████████████████████ and his severe crush on ████████████████, neither of which should affect this mission. I have attached his dossier for your approval.

Of course, this mission will also require the cooperation of your son, ██████. I know you two have had your issues lately, but please impress upon him that ████████████████████████████████████. Your life—and the fate of this entire country—is in his hands.

Please let me know if we are clear to proceed at your earliest convenience. I am prepared to initiate this operation at a moment's notice. Although, for your safety, the sooner it happens, the better.

Sincerely,

████████████

P.S. Given the highly risky nature of this mission, please do not discuss it with anyone at ████████████, not even ██████ and ██████. In addition, burn this message and the dossier and then, if possible, flush the remains down the toilet.

RESURGENCE

Vandenberg Library

Nathan Hale Building

CIA Academy of Espionage

February 10

1500 hours

"SPYDER is back!"

Zoe Zibbell's exclamation rang out through the spy school library. In her excitement, Zoe had spoken a bit too loudly—and since we were in the library, it was quieter than any other place on campus. The cavernous room was four stories tall, ringed by three mezzanines on which thousands of books were shelved. Zoe's words seemed to echo off every last one of them: "SPYDER is back . . . SPYDER is back . . . SPYDER is back. . . ."

Zoe winced, realizing her announcement had been a lot more public than she'd intended. Then she quickly sat down at the table where she had just interrupted my homework.

The library was far more crowded than usual. On most afternoons, my fellow students and I would have probably been studying in the school dormitory, but on that day the freshmen had their first homework assignment in Introduction to Explosives: Each was assigned to defuse a small bomb. The bombs weren't supposed to be strong enough to level a building, but where explosives were concerned, things could always go wrong, so it made sense to play it safe and steer clear of the dorm. More than a hundred students, ranging from second to seventh years, were hunched over tables throughout the library. They all tried to act like they weren't interested in Zoe, as we'd learned in Intermediate Clandestine Observation: Seeing Without Being Seen, but I could tell they were desperate to hear more.

Until recently, SPYDER's existence had been extremely classified: Only a few highly ranked people at the CIA had known about the evil organization. But in the past year, SPYDER had caused some major trouble, like trying to blow up the very building I sat in, attacking a busload of students near the school's wilderness training facility, and attempting to destroy a large portion of Manhattan. After that there was no hope of keeping SPYDER confidential at the Academy of Espionage. Everyone there was training to be a spy; it was their job to know things. Almost all of them had sussed out the truth by now.

I made no attempt to hide my own interest in Zoe's news. SPYDER had attempted to recruit me twice—and then tried to kill me when I'd refused—so I had a vested interest in knowing what they were up to. I looked up from my cryptography homework and asked, "How do you know?"

Zoe slid into a seat across the table from me and whispered, "Chameleon and I overheard. We were doing our eavesdropping project for Advanced Covert Ops, and we figured the higher-placed our target, the better our grade would be. So we went after the Idiot."

Zoe was into nicknames. Chameleon was Warren Reeves, who excelled at camouflage (but was lacking in most other spy skills). The Idiot was our school principal, who was an idiot. A big one.

"And you pulled it off?" I asked.

"Yeah." Despite her worried state, Zoe flashed a proud smile. "We slipped two X-class wireless transmission bugs into his office last night."

"His office?" I repeated, impressed. The principal wasn't an easy target. True, he wasn't a very intelligent person—his job was basically to handle paperwork and administrative issues that no one else wanted to—but the CIA *knew* he wasn't intelligent, so he had far more security around him than a capable person would have required. His office was on the top floor of the building we were in, five floors above us, and entry to it was protected by an advanced network of cameras and armed guards. "How'd you get past all the security?"

"I distracted the guards while Chameleon did the infiltration."

"And he did it without any problems?"

"Why do you sound so surprised?"

"Because Warren's a lousy spy. The last time he tried to infiltrate a room, he got stuck in the air vent. We had to call the fire department to get him out."

Zoe frowned. "Chameleon's been working hard to improve his skills lately."

"That doesn't mean they've actually gotten better."

"Yes, they have," snapped a nasal voice behind me.

I wheeled around to find Warren standing three feet away. Although if he hadn't spoken, I might not have noticed him. His camouflage was even better than usual. He was wearing a set of clothes and face paint that exactly matched the ancient oak furniture of the Hale Building, allowing him to blend in perfectly at the end of a row of shelves.

I wasn't the only one who'd failed to notice him. Most of the nearby students were caught by surprise as well. A fourth-year girl who'd been pretending to browse the books behind us while furtively listening to our conversation was so startled by Warren's sudden appearance that she yelped in fear and dropped a heavy volume of Caldwell's *Pictorial Guide to Poisons and Antidotes* on her foot.

Warren sat down beside me, gloating smugly. This was disconcerting, as he'd done such a good job with the face paint that he didn't really look human. Instead, it was like sitting next to an extremely obnoxious ventriloquist's dummy. "You're no better a spy than I am," he declared. "The only reason you've had all these missions is that you've just been lucky enough to have SPYDER attack you."

"I wouldn't exactly consider that lucky," I said.

"Whatever. The point is, if I'd been there, *I* could have saved the day instead of you."

"Chameleon, you *were* there," Zoe pointed out. "And you *didn't* save the day. In fact, you nearly killed Ben by accident. Twice."

Warren recoiled like a puppy who'd been caught piddling on the carpet, the way he always did when Zoe hurt his feelings. While Zoe was developing into a very good spy, she somehow remained completely oblivious to the fact that Warren had a massive crush on her.

"Hold on," I said to Zoe. "Did you say you infiltrated the principal's office *last night*?"

"That's right," Zoe replied.

I looked back at Warren. "Then why are you still camouflaged?"

"The paint won't wash off," Warren said morosely. He looked as though he might have turned red if he hadn't been painted brown. "I couldn't get the perfect oaken tone with standard face paint, so I had to use wood stain instead. Now I can't remove it."

Zoe snickered despite herself.

"It's not funny!" Warren whined. "Today in self-defense class, Professor Simon mistook me for a table and set a book on my head."

Zoe laughed even harder.

"We're getting off track," I reminded her. "What'd you hear in the principal's office?"

"Oh, right." Zoe returned her attention to me while Warren sulked. "We've been monitoring the bugs ever since we placed them last night, but we didn't pick up any intel until just now."

"Was the principal out of the office all day?" I asked.

"No, he's been in since oh-nine-hundred," Zoe reported. "He just hasn't been doing anything important. He spent most of the day filling out ammunition-request forms and playing games on his smartphone. And it took him an hour to decide what to order for lunch. But then, about thirty minutes ago, he got a phone call about SPYDER."

"From who?" I asked.

"I don't know," Zoe admitted. "We didn't tap the phone. We only bugged the room, so we could only hear the Idiot's side of the conversation."

"What did he say?"

Zoe glanced around the library before answering. All the other students who'd been eavesdropping made a show of pretending to read their textbooks. Zoe removed her cell phone from the pocket of her jacket and slid it across the table to me.

A set of earphones was wound around it. I stuck the buds in my ears. Warren gave me a jealous look, as if I were the luckiest guy on earth because I might have come into contact with some of Zoe's earwax.

Zoe's phone was already cued up to the proper audio file. I pressed play.

The file began with the principal muttering what sounded like nonsense. "Stupid hedgehogs!" he yelled. "Stop stealing my flapjacks!"

I looked to Zoe, intrigued. "Is this some sort of top secret code?"

"No," Zoe replied. "It's about the game he's playing on his phone."

"It's called Flapjack Frenzy," Warren explained. "You try to make as many pancakes as possible and these hedgehogs try to steal them. So you have to fight them off by shooting them with maple syrup. . . ."

"The rules of the game really aren't important right now," Zoe told him.

Warren frowned sullenly.

On the recording, the principal's phone rang. He let it ring ten more times while he apparently tried to finish the level of the game, before finally giving in and answering. "This is the principal," he said curtly. "This had better be important. I'm in the midst of something very serious." Then he gasped in surprise and asked, "SPYDER? Really? How do you know?"

This was followed by a period during which the principal was obviously listening to a lot of information that the person on the other end of the phone line was giving him. For the most part, it seemed he was trying to sound interested, saying things like "Hmmm" and "Fascinating" and "Wow," although I could also hear the distinct sounds of the game continuing: tinny music punctuated by the occasional squelch of maple syrup and squeal of pixelated hedgehogs. Suddenly, the principal said, "No, I'm not playing a game on my phone! I'm listening to you!" And then the tinny music shut off. Afterward, the principal continued to make interested sounds, as if trying to prove that he was rapt with attention.

At the entrance to the library, Mike Brezinski slipped through the doors.

My fellow students regarded him with almost as much surprise as they had given Zoe's announcement that SPYDER had returned. Mike was well known on campus as the newest recruit to spy school. Until only a few weeks before, he'd been my best friend from the outside world. Up until that point, I had tried to keep my enrollment at the Academy of Espionage a secret from him—as well as everyone else I knew, including my own parents. The school's very existence was classified: The rest of the world thought we attended St. Smithen's Science Academy for Boys and Girls. But Mike hadn't merely figured out that I was attending a top secret spy school; he'd also played a crucial part in thwarting some bad guys on Operation Snow Bunny, after which the CIA had recognized his potential and recruited him. However, even though Mike was my age, he had been forced to start as a first-year student. Which meant he should have been dealing with his explosives homework, not sauntering into the library.

"What's *he* doing here?" Warren hissed.

"Maybe he finished his homework already," Zoe suggested.

"There's no way," Warren said. "They only started the

timers fifteen minutes ago. Even Erica Hale didn't defuse her first bomb that fast."

Mike spotted us, waved happily, and hurried over, pausing to smile at a few attractive girls along the way.

Most of the girls smiled back. That's the kind of guy Mike was.

The recording on Zoe's phone was still playing. On it, the principal suddenly spluttered, "Benjamin Ripley?" He sounded extremely annoyed. "What do you want with him this time?"

I stiffened, surprised that he'd just used my name.

Unfortunately, nothing else was said. The principal returned to listening again, only now his occasional grunts and interjections sounded much more aggravated than they had before.

The principal wasn't a big fan of mine. Shortly after my arrival at spy school, I had insulted him to his face in order to further an investigation, and at the beginning of the current school year, I had accidentally blown up his office with a mortar round. That hadn't entirely been my fault, but no matter how many times this had been explained, the principal refused to listen. He was still using a broom closet as his office, and he hated me for it.

Mike reached my table, spun a chair around, and sat in it backward, resting his arms on the backrest. "What are you listening to?" he asked.

"Class lecture," I replied quickly. I didn't know if Mike had learned about SPYDER's existence yet (he had missed all my previous confrontations with them), but I certainly didn't have clearance to tell him about it.

Mike gave me a sideways glance, like he didn't believe me and wanted me to know it.

"What happened to your explosives homework?" Zoe asked, trying to distract him. "Did you defuse it already?"

"No," Mike said.

Warren gasped. "You mean you left a ticking bomb in your dorm room?"

"Calm down, Salamander," Mike told him. "I didn't do that either."

"My nickname's 'Chameleon,'" Warren said testily. "Not 'Salamander.'"

Mike shrugged. "They're both lizardy things."

"So what'd you do with the bomb?" Zoe asked.

"Well, I started to try to defuse it," Mike explained, "but it was ridiculously complicated. So I figured, what's the point? I mean, suppose some bad guy had really left this bomb for me. Defusing it wastes valuable time. While I'm dorking around with it, the villain escapes. So why not just forget about it and let the villain *think* I'm busy defusing it? He drops his guard, figuring I'm out of the picture—and that's when I nab him!"

"So you're going to let the bomb go off?" Zoe pressed.

"Yes," Mike said, then thought to add, "Although I left it in a safe place where it won't hurt anyone. I also moved the timer up so it'll detonate earlier than expected."

"Why would you do that?" Warren demanded.

"Diversion," Mike told him. "The bomb explodes, and the bad guy thinks, 'Aha! He's dead!' and then *really* lets his guard down."

Zoe and I shared a look, realizing that, while unorthodox, Mike's plan actually had some merit. This was where Mike had already stood out at spy school. Unorthodox thinking often earned you high grades here, and Mike didn't merely think outside the box; he rarely even noticed there was a box in the first place.

Warren, however, was one of those kids so rigid about proper procedures that he could barely brush his teeth without consulting a manual. Mike's refusal to play by the rules always exasperated him. "In exactly what sort of safe place did you leave this bomb?"

"Out in the quad," Mike replied. "It's far from any innocent bystanders—and I placed a nice heavy pot from the kitchen over it to cut down on shrapnel. I also taped up some signs warning people to keep their distance."

"Signs?" Zoe repeated. "What'd they say?"

"'Live bomb in area,'" Mike replied. "'Beware of explosive debris.' Things like that."

"You can't do that!" Warren spluttered. "It's against the rules!"

"The bad guys aren't going to play by the rules," Mike countered. "Why should we?"

This was exactly the sort of thinking that tended to get A's at the academy.

The distant bang of a small explosion echoed from the quadrangle. The books shuddered on the library shelves. All the students who hadn't been close enough to overhear Mike's plan leapt from their tables and ran to the windows to see if any large pieces were now missing from the dormitory.

"See?" Mike said proudly. "The perfect diversion."

Zoe grinned, impressed. Warren glowered even more.

On the recording I was listening to, the principal finally stopped grunting, indicating that whoever he was talking to had finished speaking. "Fine," he said petulantly. "I'll approve his activation." Then he hung up.

The recording ended.

I looked to Zoe and Warren, disappointed. "That's it?"

"That's all there was," Zoe replied. "What more do you need? He confirmed that, uh"—she glanced at Mike warily—"what we were discussing before is actually happening."

"Wait," Mike said. "Are you guys talking about SPYDER?"

We all turned to him, surprised.

"SPYDER," he repeated. "The international consortium of bad guys committed to causing chaos and mayhem for a price?" He looked to me. "Don't pretend like they don't exist. They've tried to kill you a few times."

"How long have you known about SPYDER?" Warren asked suspiciously.

"Oh, for a while now," Mike said. "It's not like its existence is a secret."

"Actually, it is," I said.

"Really?" Mike asked. "Well, it's not a very well-kept secret."

"Apparently not." I sighed, then slid Zoe's phone back to her. "Though I'd love to know what they're up to now."

"You'll find out soon enough," Zoe said brightly. "They're activating you!"

"We don't know that for sure," I said. "I know the principal mentioned my name, but that was a couple minutes back. For all we know, he's activating Warren."

"Warren?" Zoe laughed. "Don't be ridiculous! He can't handle SPYDER!"

"Um . . . I'm right here," Warren pointed out gloomily.

"The Idiot was obviously talking about you," Zoe told me. "He sounded really upset. He wouldn't be that peeved about activating most people. But he hates you with every last fiber of his being and will until the day he dies."

"Well, that's reassuring," I said.

"You blew up his office," Warren told me.

"Because *you* put a live round in a mortar!" I reminded him. "If I hadn't aimed it toward this building, a bunch of innocent people would have died!"

Warren shrugged, as though this argument wasn't convincing.

"If you're getting activated," Mike said eagerly, "can you pick me as your partner?"

"No!" Zoe squealed, raising her hand. "Pick me! He's only a first year."

"This is an undercover mission, not a kickball game," I informed them. "I don't get to pick teams. And I'm still not completely convinced I'm the one being activated."

"You should be," a voice said.

We all jumped in our seats.

Erica Hale was leaning against a bookshelf only a few feet away. Unlike Warren, she hadn't gotten close to us by camouflaging herself. Instead, she simply moved with a stealth and grace that would impress a tiger. Erica was only a fourth-year student, but she was still the best spy-in-training at school by far. Much of this was due to having exceptional natural talent, but she was also a legacy: Her family could be traced all the way back to Nathan Hale and had worked as spies ever since. Her grandfather had trained her since she was a baby. There were rumors that at age three Erica had thwarted a trio of bank robbers with only a juice box and a Slinky.

Erica was dressed in her standard way: a tight black outfit that allowed her the freedom of movement to steal through the night or pummel enemy agents while still looking extremely stylish. But then, Erica was beautiful enough that she would have made a potato sack and a clown wig look stylish. I had a serious crush on her, as did almost every other guy on campus. However, I was the only student who had really spent any time with Erica. Erica was so determined to be an elite agent that she considered friendships to be liabilities, which led her to be distant and reserved. (Zoe called her "Ice Queen.") I'd only gotten to know her because she'd been my partner on my previous missions.

In the process, Erica's chilly demeanor had thawed around me now and then. In fact, near the end of our most recent mission, Erica had even kissed me. Afterward, however, she had told me it didn't mean anything, claiming that she'd merely been trying to calm me down, as we were about to be annihilated in a nuclear explosion. Ever since then, she'd grown even more distant than usual, avoiding me like the plague. This was the first time she'd spoken to me in weeks.

"Get your coat," Erica told me. "It's time to move out."

"Wait," I said. "Am I being activated right now?"

"This is a crisis situation," Erica said flatly. "There's no time to waste."

"How about bathroom breaks?" I asked. "Is there time for one of those? Because I should probably go while I have the chance."

Erica sighed, like needing to go to the bathroom was something that only happened to other people. Now that I thought about it, though, this might have been true. I couldn't recall her ever needing to make a pit stop. "Fine," she said. "You can go. But make it quick."

I started to grab my books and backpack, but Erica said, "Don't bother. You won't need those." She looked to Mike. "Can you take those back to Ben's room?"

"Sure." Mike flashed her his standard winning smile. "Anything else you need me to do?"

"No. By the way, that was good thinking with the explosives homework."

Zoe and Warren gaped in astonishment. Hearing Erica give anyone a compliment was almost as unlikely as spotting a unicorn.

"Good thinking?" Warren spluttered. "What he did was reckless and dangerous and against the rules!"

"Yes," Erica agreed. "It's exactly what *I* did on that assignment." She shifted her attention back to me. "Why aren't you in the bathroom already?"

"I was waiting for you," I said.

"Why? I don't need to go."

"I just thought it was good manners to not run off. . . ."

"There's no room for manners in the spy game," Erica told me.

"Your father has excellent manners," Zoe pointed out.

"My father's the worst spy on earth," Erica countered.

"Good point," Zoe conceded.

I waved good-bye to everyone and hustled out of the library, slipping my winter coat on as I went. I could feel the eyes of every other student on me as I exited. Most had returned from the windows, having confirmed that Mike's explosion hadn't caused any damage, and were now watching me jealously.

It was exceedingly rare for a student to be activated for a mission while at spy school. In fact, it was rare for *graduates* of spy school to be activated for missions. Normally, only the cream of the crop was approved for fieldwork; the rest became analysts and desk jockeys. Meanwhile, this was my fifth assignment (albeit only my second official one) and I'd barely been at the academy a year. I had ended up on my first missions mostly due to bad luck, but I'd proven myself on each, figuring out the enemy's plans and helping thwart them each time. That had earned me the right to participate in Operation Snow Bunny. Apparently

I'd performed well enough on that to merit being activated again.

Despite this, I was still awfully nervous. I did my best to put on a good show, holding my head high and striding confidently through the library, but inside I was a mess. I was worried about what lay in store and how dangerous it might be. I was concerned that I might not be up to the task and feared that I might fail—or die.

And, to be honest, I was pretty disturbed by how Erica was behaving around Mike.

There were certainly other things I should have been concentrating on, but this one kept gnawing at me: Erica had given Mike a compliment. She'd barely ever given me a compliment—and I'd helped her prevent the nuclear devastation of Colorado. Yes, she had kissed me, but she'd then insisted she hadn't felt any emotion toward me. Meanwhile, Mike had a way of winning over girls.

I glanced back toward my friends, trying to be subtle about it, fearing I might catch Erica giggling at something Mike had said, giving her hair a coy flip, or batting her eyes at him. None of that was really Erica's style, but then, neither was complimenting people.

Thankfully, Erica was on her way up the aisle behind me.

Although, she was *also* looking back toward Mike.

He waved good-bye.

And Erica, to my astonishment, waved back.

Which made me feel even worse than being assigned to a potentially life-threatening mission did.

I shoved through the big oak library doors into the soaring entry foyer of the Hale Building, ducked into the boys' room, quickly took care of business, then emerged to find Erica waiting impatiently for me. She checked her watch, as though the fifty-three seconds I'd taken to pee had been fifty-three seconds too long. (I have an unusual gift for math, and one of the side effects is an uncanny sense of time. I always know exactly how long it takes me to do anything, right down to the second.)

Erica strode toward the main doors of the Hale Building.

I dutifully followed her. "Where are we going?"

"We?" she said icily, though her annoyance didn't seem directed at me. "*We* aren't going anywhere. Only you are."

I froze in astonishment. "You're not on this mission?"

"No. I'm just the messenger." Erica barged out the doors, allowing a blast of cold air to knife into the foyer.

I suddenly felt even more worried than before. My success on my earlier missions was due, in large part, to Erica. She had always been close by to help me out, determine what to do, and, more often than not, clobber a few bad guys. The idea of being activated without her was terrifying. She was smarter than me, calmer than me, more confident than me—and a hundred times better at combat than me.

I emerged from the Hale Building to find Erica standing by the driveway that circled past the entrance. It was nasty cold out. The grounds of the academy were a carpet of dead grass encrusted with ice.

A large black SUV was idling in the driveway.

A stoic driver sat behind the wheel, her eyes shielded by sunglasses.

The rear windows were tinted, so I couldn't see who was in the back.

Erica opened the rear door and said, "Here he is," to whoever was inside.

I looked to her, hoping for some hint of what was going on, but she didn't give me one. "Have fun," she said, though she didn't sound like she really meant it.

I climbed into the SUV and Erica shut the door behind me.

The interior of the vehicle was unusual. It was designed more like a limousine. The middle row of seats faced backward, toward the last row, so you could face whoever you were riding with. There was a plate of soundproof glass between the middle seats and the front, so the driver couldn't hear anything if you didn't want her to. There was a small bar built into each of the side panels, with rows of glasses and an ice bucket.

But the most unusual thing about the SUV was the two other people inside it.

The first was Cyrus Hale, Erica's grandfather and one of the finest spies the CIA had ever produced.

The other was the president of the United States of America.

ASSIGNMENT

Covert Transportation

En route through Washington, DC

February 10

1530 hours

President David Stern was tall and handsome, with a square jaw, perfect hair, and a chin that appeared to have been professionally dimpled. He wore a blue three-piece suit with an American flag pin affixed to the lapel.

I was so surprised by his presence, I didn't sit down right away. Instead, I stood crouched in the back of the SUV, facing the rear seat, gaping at the president in amazement. So when the driver hit the gas, I pitched forward.

The very first thing I did in front of the leader of my country was sprawl facedown at his feet.

Cyrus Hale rolled his eyes.

Cyrus was even harder to please than his granddaughter; although I'd been on three successful missions with him, I still felt I had yet to earn his respect. Now that he was an "emeritus agent" (meaning he was unofficially still working for the CIA), he had stopped wearing suits. Today he wore sweatpants with a matching fleece and a fanny pack.

President Stern graciously leaned forward to help me up. "Oopsie," he said, somehow even making that word sound dignified. "Guess we caught you off guard."

I tried to say "yes" but was still so surprised, all that came out was a squeak of air.

The president pressed an intercom button built into the armrest next to him and spoke to the driver. "Careful, Courtney. Our guest isn't buckled in yet."

Courtney reflexively hit the brakes. Now that I'd made it halfway to my feet, I was pitched backward into the rear-facing seats.

Courtney checked to make sure I was all right. "He's fine," Cyrus told her, and Courtney started driving again.

I quickly buckled myself in.

The SUV pulled out of the front gates of the academy and headed downtown. We made it a whole sixty feet before getting stuck in traffic. Washington traffic is about the worst in the country. There are times when snails move faster.

I stared at the president and finally managed to form some actual words. "How are you out in the world like this? Without a motorcade?"

The president laughed. "Motorcades draw a lot of attention. If I want to be incognito, I travel this way." He pointed out the window.

Sure enough, none of the pedestrians or fellow drivers gave our car a second glance, completely unaware of who was inside. Black SUVs were as commonplace in Washington as lampposts, constantly shuttling low-level diplomats around.

"Without the Secret Service?" I asked.

"I doubt we'll encounter any trouble, but should it happen"—President Stern nodded toward the driver—"there's nothing Courtney can't handle."

I glanced over my shoulder through the glass partition, which I now took to be bulletproof. Courtney was of slight build and didn't look particularly dangerous, but then, neither did Erica Hale, and she was capable of wiping out a platoon of mercenaries.

Courtney's eyes met mine in the rearview mirror. There was something in her gaze that said that if I tried to do anything to the president, she would kill me without a second thought. Then she went back to inching forward in traffic.

I returned my attention to the president. "So you do this often?"

"No. In fact, I almost never do. But I needed some privacy and, frankly, the White House isn't necessarily the best place to get it. No one except those of us in this car even knows I'm here. My staff thinks I'm taking a nap."

"A nap?" I echoed.

"I need them on occasion. It's not easy being the leader of the free world—and I'm always getting woken up in the middle of the night to deal with some crisis or another. Anyhow, Cyrus and Courtney arranged for me to sneak away. So here we are. I have to admit, it's interesting to be out here, moving around in the world like a normal person."

"Do you miss this?" I asked.

"Heck no," the president said. "I haven't had to stop for a red light in years. Being stuck in traffic like this sucks."

The president spoke in a genial, fatherly way that made me feel extremely comfortable. I had already forgotten all about being awed by him and was about to make more pointless small talk when Cyrus held up a hand, silencing me.

"I apologize for interrupting, Mr. President, but we have far more important things to discuss than traffic."

"Of course." David Stern gave me a grave stare and said, "Benjamin, a tremendously serious matter has been brought to my attention and Agent Hale here assures me that I can trust you to help take care of it."

I glanced toward Cyrus, surprised he had said anything remotely nice about me at all. Instead of confirming this, he merely handed me a dossier.

It was stamped FOR YOUR EYES ONLY: OPERATION PUNGENT MUSKRAT. It also had a thick wax seal embossed with the logo of the CIA.

My heart pounded. It was always exciting to get an FYEO dossier. And yet . . . "Operation Pungent Muskrat?" I asked, failing to hide the disappointment in my voice.

"I know, it's a lousy name," the president said. "But I assure you, this is an extremely important mission. From what I understand, the Agency used to give their all missions very exciting names like Operation Cobra Strike and Operation Lightning Blast, but by now all those have been used up and we're kind of left with the dregs. Trust me, it could be worse. The last mission I was party to was called Operation Zesty Walrus."

That made me feel a little better. I tried to crack open the secure seal on the file. Only, the seal turned out to be a lot more secure than I'd expected. I struggled with it for a few seconds but made no progress.

"Oh, for Pete's sake," Cyrus muttered, then snatched the dossier back from me and tried to open it himself. It turned out he couldn't do it either.

President Stern put a hand over his mouth, trying to hide the fact that he was laughing.

Cyrus threw the dossier on the floor. "You know what? We don't need to open this blasted thing anyhow. I know everything that's in it. The headline being this: We have reliable intel that SPYDER is planning to assassinate the president."

I sat up in my seat, worried for the president; if any organization could determine how to get around all his security and take him out, it was SPYDER. I was also worried because I was *with* the president. If SPYDER decided to kill him right then, they'd have killed me, too. "What kind of intel?"

"We've picked up chatter on various channels we've been monitoring," Cyrus explained. "Enough to make us believe this is a credible threat."

His tone indicated he expected me to be satisfied with that answer and not pester him with any more questions. However, there was still one I had to ask: "Who's *we?*"

"My team," Cyrus said.

"Who is . . . ?"

"Classified."

"I mean, is this an official CIA operation?" I asked. "Or is it another unauthorized mission?"

Cyrus lifted his eyebrows, apparently surprised I had dared to ask this.

The president chuckled and gave Cyrus a sly smile. "You did say he was sharp."

"Too sharp for his own good sometimes," Cyrus grumbled. Then he turned back to me. "As you know, I have expressed concerns before about the degree to which SPYDER has infiltrated the CIA. With the exception of you and Erica, I don't believe there is anyone at the Agency we can fully trust."

"Not even your son?"

"There are two definitions of trust," Cyrus explained. "You can trust someone not to be a traitor—and you can trust someone to handle things competently. I know my son isn't working for SPYDER. But as far as his competence is concerned, I'd rather rely on a monkey."

I knew this to be true—although Alexander Hale had managed to fool the entire CIA into thinking he was actually a good spy for years. His single greatest skill was lying about how great his other skills were. In practice, Alexander was well meaning but inept, careless and prone to knocking himself unconscious. "Do you trust the principal?" I asked. "He was just informed that I was to be activated."

"How do you know that?" Cyrus asked suspiciously.

I thought about telling the whole story, but then decided to go with the answer Erica always gave me instead. "I'm training to be a spy. It's my job to know things. Does the principal know what's going on?"

"The principal wouldn't know what was going on even if he was here with us right now," Cyrus said. "Yes, I told him SPYDER was active so he'd authorize your mission without any delay, but I lied to him about everything else. He thinks you're infiltrating a prep school in Bethesda. And if SPYDER's tapped his phone lines—which they probably have—then hopefully they bought it too."

"So, this mission isn't authorized?" I asked.

"The priority of this mission is to protect the president at all costs," Cyrus said, deftly avoiding answering my question.

"Are we working with the Secret Service?"

"No," Cyrus replied. "SPYDER may have infiltrated them as well. As far as I'm concerned, every single government security agency may be compromised."

I looked to the president, wondering if Cyrus might be overstating things. The president shrugged. "Agent Hale believes SPYDER may already have a mole in the White House—either on my staff or in my security detail—and that this mole may be part of the assassination plot."

"Can't you just swap out your staff, then?" I asked.

"The White House has far more employees than most people realize," the president answered. "On an average day, there are more than one thousand Secret Service agents on the property, not to mention hundreds of staffers in the West Wing, plus cooks, butlers, landscapers, and who knows what else. I have three full-time florists working there, for Pete's sake. And every one of those people is a government employee, which means it'd take a ton of paperwork to boot even one of them."

"Plus, it's still only a hunch that there's a mole in the first place," Cyrus added. "All I know is that SPYDER is plotting to assassinate the president. I have no idea how they're planning to carry it out. Having someone inside— or several people—merely seems like a good way to do it. And heaven knows they've infiltrated the CIA before. Which is where *you* come in, Benjamin."

I glanced out the window. We were moving slowly through traffic at Dupont Circle. *Very* slowly. Dupont Circle was one of the worst intersections on earth, where ten streets met at one place, and traffic there often moved at a speed that made glaciers seem fast. Still, we seemed to be heading directly toward the White House, which gave me an idea as to what Cyrus's plan might be. "You want *me* to spy inside the White House?"

"Exactly," Cyrus replied. "As we found with Operation

Snow Bunny, no one expects a child to be a secret agent."

"*Leo Shang* didn't expect me to be a secret agent," I corrected. "But SPYDER might. They know who I am! I've thwarted them before."

"True," Cyrus admitted. "That's why we're going to keep your profile at 1600 Pennsylvania as low as possible. Hopefully, SPYDER won't notice. After you helped destroy their headquarters last fall, SPYDER isn't quite the organization it used to be. Its leaders have scattered around the globe and their intelligence operations are fractured. If we're careful, there's a good chance they'll have no idea you're on the case."

"How?" I asked. "Won't I be obvious as the only kid inside the White House?"

"You *won't* be the only kid inside," the president reminded me.

With that, I realized exactly what my mission was going to be.

President Stern had two children: a fifteen-year-old daughter named Jemma and a thirteen-year-old son named Jason. Although the family tried to keep them out of the spotlight, they were still two of the most famous kids in America, if not the world. I'd seen them on TV a few times: standing behind their father as he was sworn in, attending the White House Easter Egg Roll, waving as they boarded

Air Force One. They always appeared to be well mannered and cheerful.

"I'll be posing as a friend of your son?" I guessed.

"Correct," the president replied. "Jason is your age. He has friends over on a regular basis. It won't seem the slightest bit unusual to have you in the house."

"Of course, you'll need to stick close to Jason to sell this," Cyrus added. "However, Jason himself has been briefed and is eager to help out. After all, his own father's life is on the line. You will present yourself at the White House today—"

"Today?" I repeated.

Cyrus frowned, annoyed by the interruption. "SPYDER's plans are already in motion. When did you *think* we were going to start investigating? Next month?"

"No," I said. "Sorry. This is all just happening so fast. . . ."

"A good agent must always be prepared for activation, anywhere, anytime," Cyrus informed me. "Your cover story is that you and Jason met through online gaming and hit it off. So he has invited you over to the White House for a playdate this afternoon."

I cringed. "Agent Hale, I'm a little old for playdates. Can we call it something else? Like 'hanging out'?"

Cyrus gritted his teeth. "You have a date to play together. It's a playdate. End of story. Now then, all visitors to the White House present themselves at the Eisenhower Executive Office Building on the west side of the property. Jason has already placed you on the guest list. I trust you have your student ID with you?"

"Yes, sir." I took it from my wallet and showed it to him. It said I was a second-year student at St. Smithen's Science Academy for Boys and Girls, which was a front for the Academy of Espionage. All spies-in-training pretended to be students at St. Smithen's. The ID looked very official, although my photo on it was one of the worst I'd ever taken. But there was something that concerned me even more: While the school's name on the ID was a fake, my own name wasn't. It still said "Benjamin Ripley."

"I don't get an alias?" I asked.

"Why would you get an alias?" Cyrus asked grumpily.

"I got one last time. On Operation Snow Bunny."

"That was different," Cyrus informed me. "On Operation Snow Bunny, you were trying to fool a thirteen-year-old girl. To get into the White House, you need to be vetted by the U.S. Secret Service. It would take months of work to create a fake background good enough to trick them, and we don't have that kind of time. The academy has been using St. Smithen's as a front for more than fifty years, so it's well established. As for you, the Service has already combed through your records, verified your social security number, and called your parents to confirm you're not a threat."

"My parents know I'm going to the White House today?" I asked, surprised.

"Yes," Cyrus said. "And they're very excited about it."

I pulled out my phone. I had been so distracted that afternoon, I hadn't checked it in an hour. During that time, I had missed four phone calls from my parents and received three dozen text messages from them as well. My mother wanted me to get a selfie with Jason Stern and my father wanted to know if I could get any cool White House swag.

We were still stuck in Dupont Circle traffic. It seemed to be agitating the president far more than the knowledge that a secretive evil organization was plotting to kill him. "This traffic is insane," he groused. "If we go any slower, we'll be moving backward."

Cyrus pressed the intercom button so he could speak to Courtney in the front seat. "Pull over. Ben will take the subway to the White House from here."

"I will?" I asked.

"You certainly can't show up with the president," Cyrus said. "The president doesn't chaperone *playdates*. You need to approach the White House the way a normal teenager would. The subway shouldn't take too long."

"Given this traffic, it'll be a heck of a lot faster than

driving," the president said. "Maybe I could take the subway too?"

"Negative," Courtney replied, edging the SUV toward a red zone. "May I remind you, sir, that people are trying to kill you? It would be incredibly unsafe for you to be on public transit."

"Maybe no one would think it was actually me," the president suggested hopefully. "Who would ever expect the president to be on the Metro?"

"I'm afraid that can't be done, sir," Courtney said. "We're going to have to drive back like normal commuters."

"Ugh." The president frowned and slumped back in his seat. "Being normal stinks."

Cyrus told me, "Once you're through security at the White House, you'll meet up with Jason, and he'll take you around from there."

"If there's anywhere you want to go, just ask him," the president said. "He's been told to do anything you need to help."

"Keep your eyes and ears open," Cyrus ordered. "The moment you learn any actionable information, I want you to contact me. I trust you still have my cell number memorized?"

"Yes." My gift with numbers was my one great asset in the spy game. There had been plenty of times when I would have preferred better fighting skills—or the ability to shoot straight—but being able to remember every phone number or location coordinates I'd ever heard and do complex computations within seconds had come in handy on occasion.

Courtney finally reached the red zone and pulled over.

"I'll expect a report once you're done at the White House today," Cyrus told me, then reached to unlock the door.

"Wait!" I said. "Is there anything else you can tell me about SPYDER's plot? Who you *think* the mole might be? Or if it's a man or a woman? Anything at all . . . ?"

Cyrus groaned, as though I were being unreasonable with this request. "If I had more intel, I would have shared it with you already. We're deep down the mineshaft on this one."

"Down the mineshaft?" I repeated.

"In the dark," Cyrus explained. "Anyone anywhere could be the mole. And if SPYDER senses we're onto them, this whole thing could go very bad very quickly. So don't screw anything up."

Cyrus might have been a great spy, but when it came to giving pep talks, he was awful.

"Good luck," the president told me.

"Thanks," I said. After that, there didn't seem to be any other option except to get out of the car. So that's what I did.

Hundreds of pedestrians swarmed the sidewalks around

Dupont, but none seemed remotely interested in the black SUV. The only person paying any attention to it was a meter man from the Department of Parking Enforcement, who stormed toward it with the zeal of a Navy SEAL team, already writing a ticket. "You can't park that here!" he barked. "It's a red zone!"

Courtney lowered her window and glared at him. "I'm not parked. I'm idling! That's allowable."

"Not on my watch," the meter man huffed. "According to District Code 46a, subsection D, there is to be no blocking of the red zone for any amount of time for any purpose at all. . . ."

"How about national security?" David Stern asked, rolling down his window. "You see, I'm the president of the United States."

"And I'm the queen of Sweden," the meter man declared sarcastically. Unaware that he was facing the actual president, he dramatically ripped off the ticket and handed it to Courtney.

"Jerkwad!" Courtney yelled at him, then pulled back into traffic.

I headed for the Metro station, trying to stay calm. Less than an hour before, I had been in the midst of another normal school day. Or, at least, as normal a day as there was at spy school. And now, suddenly, I was being sent undercover on another unauthorized mission against the very same evil organization that had attempted to kill me multiple times. Without the backup of Erica Hale.

It sounded extremely difficult, daunting, and dangerous.

And it was going to turn out even worse than I'd feared.

SECURITY

The White House

1600 Pennsylvania Avenue

Washington, DC

February 10

1700 hours

It took me only ten minutes to ride the Metro to the closest station to the White House and then walk to the Eisenhower Executive Office Building.

It took me another whole hour to get through security.

This wasn't because of any trouble with my alias. As Cyrus had said, the Secret Service had already examined my files ahead of time. Now the agents on duty simply confirmed I was on the official "playdate" list for Jason Stern and checked my fake school ID. The problem was that lots of other people were trying to gain access to the White House as well. There was a large crowd of senators, congresspeople, diplomats, ambassadors, military officers, and other assorted muckety-mucks, all of whom had at least one aide, if not two or three, and every single one of them insisted that they ought to have higher priority than everyone else going in. As the only person still in middle school, I kept getting pushed to the side.

The worst part was that the security was all outside the EEOB, in the cold. Apparently, the building predated increased modern-day security protocols, and there wasn't enough room inside for it all. Instead, the security operations were all arranged at a metal gate in front of the building.

Given the long wait, I had plenty of time to scope out everyone in the crowd, trying to determine if any of them might be working for SPYDER. No one seemed particularly evil—although most appeared quite irate about the security lines. Two of the aides to a French diplomat seemed extremely uneasy, however. And there was one businessman who seemed downright shifty: A short, swarthy man in a heavy fur-lined coat, he kept glancing at me suspiciously, as though trying to figure out what I was doing there. Under the guise of pretending to check my e-mail, I took some pictures of him—and everyone else in the waiting area—with my phone.

Eventually, the crowd dissipated and it was finally my turn to enter the EEOB. I was given another ID card, this one much fancier, with all sorts of holograms and built-in sensors, to wear on a lanyard around my neck. Then I passed through a magnetometer, like they had in airport security, and was followed by a pair of bomb-sniffing dogs. The dogs looked a lot like German shepherds, but I knew they were actually a breed known as the Belgian Malinois, which were famed throughout law enforcement for their incredible noses.

The dogs got one whiff of me and went berserk. Both started barking as loud as they could, straining at their leashes, going after me like I was a stray cat who had rolled around in raw meat. Every Secret Service agent instantly went on alert, snapping their weapons from their holsters and aiming them my way. I raised my hands over my head, desperate to show my innocence, and yelped, "Don't shoot! I'm only here for a playdate!"

This did not put the Secret Service at ease. They kept their guns trained on me while one of the canine agents—a wall of muscle with a crew cut and a permanent scowl—came closer, allowing his snarling dog to home in on whatever had set it off. The dog seemed particularly focused on my winter jacket.

"Take the jacket off," the agent ordered.

"Okay," I said, quickly shrugging it off and handing it over. It was freezing outside without it, but given the circumstances, it didn't seem like a good idea to make any trouble.

"Hey! Hey! Hey!" someone yelled. The voice was sweet and high-pitched, like that of a Disney princess. A young woman in a pantsuit with her hair pulled back in a ponytail slipped through the crowd of men aiming guns at me. "At ease, guys. This kid isn't a terrorist. He's here to see Jason."

"Cagney and Lacey say otherwise," the hulking canine agent informed her, nodding to the dogs. "And if they're suspicious, *we* need to be suspicious." He passed the jacket on to another, equally imposing agent, who began searching through it. "For all we know, this kid's a sleeper agent set on blowing up the White House."

"He's a kid set on playing Ping-Pong with Jason," the young woman informed them. Then she turned to me and said, "You can put your arms down, Ben. I'm Kimmy Dimsdale, one of the White House aides. Sorry about this." She glared at all the agents aiming their guns and said, "You guys want to lower your weapons and focus on looking for *real* terrorists?"

All the agents now looked kind of embarrassed, but they didn't holster their guns. Instead, they turned to the canine agents, wondering what to do.

I noticed the names on the canine agents' badges. Agent Fry was the big guy holding the dogs at bay. Agent Nasser was the one going through my jacket. Nasser was now wiping my jacket with a white cloth, which he then placed in a small machine the size of a microwave. It beeped a bit, then glowed green.

"No explosives residue reported," Nasser announced.

Fry frowned, like this somehow made me *more* suspicious, rather than less. "The dogs wouldn't be acting like this unless they smelled something."

"Well, maybe they smell something that *isn't* explosives residue," Kimmy suggested. "Like meat."

"Why would a kid have meat on his jacket?" Fry demanded.

"Why would a kid have explosives on his jacket?" Kimmy countered.

"Because he's a covert terrorist," Fry said.

"Or maybe he's a normal kid who ate some meat while wearing that jacket at some point," Kimmy told him. "He had a hot dog at a cart, or he went to a barbecue, or he put a piece of beef jerky in his pocket."

"My father's a grocer," I said, which was the truth. "I've worn this jacket into his meat locker plenty of times."

"The dogs aren't supposed to get this excited about meat," Fry said. "They're only supposed to respond like this to explosives."

"But there are no explosives," Nasser said.

"I *know* there are no explosives!" Fry exclaimed. "I'm just saying that our response here was justifiable, given our duty to protect the president."

"Oh yeah," Kimmy agreed sarcastically. "The president is much safer now that you've intimidated a seventh grader. Could you give him back his jacket before he freezes to death?"

Nasser quickly handed me my jacket. "Sorry."

All the other Secret Service agents finally lowered their guns, looking a bit ashamed.

I quickly slipped my jacket back on. The dogs kept barking at it, though. "Maybe there's still a tiny piece of jerky that got stuck in my pocket," I suggested.

Fry glowered at me, as though I had somehow ruined his day, then spoke to the dogs. "Cagney, Lacey, *Geluidsarm!*"

I figured that was Dutch for "be quiet." The Belgian Malinois were all trained using Dutch, as it was the native language of Belgium. Also, most American criminals didn't speak it, so there was less of a chance they'd know the commands to back down.

The dogs obediently stopped snarling at me and sat.

Kimmy quickly escorted me beyond security and into the blessed warmth of the Eisenhower Executive Office Building. "I am *soooo* sorry about that," she said. "I know those agents are only doing their job, and that POTUS is the prime target of enemy organizations all over the world, but sometimes I think they get a little *too* paranoid. Anyhow, it's nice to meet you." Now that the incident with the dogs was behind us, Kimmy was exceptionally cheerful. She didn't seem the slightest bit disappointed to be saddled with a friend of the president's son while her fellow aides got to shepherd far more important people around. "Have you ever had a chance to visit the White House before?"

"No," I said. I hadn't grown up very far from Washington, and the White House did offer tours, as well as hosting public events like Christmas tree lightings and Easter egg rolls, but my parents had never managed to get tickets to one.

"Oh!" Kimmy said, sounding thrilled that she had someone new to share White House facts with. She instantly went into tour-guide mode. "Well, this is a very fascinating place. The building you're in right now, the Eisenhower Executive Office Building—or 'EEOB'—was originally built in 1871 to house the state, war, and navy departments, although today it serves mostly as office space for the executive branch of the government. It has more than two miles of hallways! Up until 2001, it was located outside the White House fence, but security concerns led the Secret Service to expand the perimeter of the

White House property. So you are now within what we refer to as the 'Twelve Acres'—the secure zone around the president's home."

We passed directly through the EEOB and right back outside again, onto what had once been the street that ran along the western side of the White House property. Now it was parking for high-ranking officials. A line of black SUVs that looked exactly like the one I'd ridden in earlier were parked there. Most had a driver sitting in the front seat, reading the paper or playing with a smartphone.

There was also a herd of reporters gathered under a canopy nearby: video camerapeople and photographers and a few reporters I recognized from the national news. They were all milling around, stomping their feet in the cold, apparently waiting for something exciting to happen.

"Are all those people here for something important?" I asked Kimmy, trying to sound like your standard inquisitive teenager and not a covert agent doing reconnaissance.

Kimmy looked their way, surprised, as though she had taken their presence for granted for so long that she had forgotten they were all actual people, rather than something more permanent, like landscaping. "Not really," she said. "They're pretty much here all day long. There's always *something* going on at the White House."

"Even if the president isn't here?"

"Oh, sure. There's lots of important people with offices here besides the president." Kimmy leaned in and whispered, "In fact, there's quite a few who think they're even *more* important than the president."

I couldn't tell if she was joking or not. "Like who?"

Kimmy suddenly seemed to realize that this might not be the best thing to discuss on White House grounds, so she blatantly changed the subject. "The presidential basketball court is over that way," she said, pointing toward a clump of trees on the South Lawn. "Jason likes to play down there sometimes. Do you like basketball, Ben?"

"Not really."

"Oh. Well, there are lots of other fun things to do here as well. Did you know the White House even has its own bowling alley?"

"Really?"

"Yes!" Kimmy exclaimed excitedly. She seemed quite pleased to have distracted me from the political issue she'd brought up before. "I believe it was installed by Harry S. Truman, who was an avid bowler. In fact, he once bowled a perfect game against Dwight Eisenhower. Well, here we go. The White House itself!" She pulled open the doors with a triumphant "Bum da da bum!"

I entered the most famous home in America for the very first time.

It was a complete letdown. I had expected a grand entry foyer, with marble pillars and fancy carpets and portraits of famous Americans. Instead, we were in what appeared to be a regular office building, and an outdated one at that. Every available space was crammed with cubicles, and all of those were overflowing. The walls were lined with extremely small offices, from which people were constantly coming and going. There were far too many people for the space, so it was loud and crowded. It felt like being inside an anthill. An anthill that had been furnished at a discount office store.

Kimmy instantly picked up on my disappointment. "This isn't the *real* White House," she assured me. "This is only the West Wing. It's the headquarters of the executive branch of our government."

"*This* is the West Wing?" I asked. I had heard of it, of course. But I'd imagined that it would be far less ordinary. "This is where the Oval Office is, right?"

"Correct!" Kimmy agreed enthusiastically, as though I were a kindergartner who had just said my alphabet correctly. "The president's office is right over there." She pointed to a corner of the West Wing that looked a bit more impressive, but not a whole lot more.

"Is he there right now?" It seemed to be something a normal person who hadn't recently been secretly talking to the president would ask. Plus, I wondered if the president had actually made it back through traffic yet.

"No," Kimmy replied. "The president is in one of the ceremonial rooms in the White House. I believe he's hosting the teachers of the year. Or maybe the premier of Canada. It's so hard to keep track of his schedule. Come to think of it, I wonder where Jason is. He usually comes down to meet his friends here when they arrive."

"Oh." I wasn't quite sure what else to say. I was also distracted by all the people around me. When Cyrus had told me to keep an eye out for possible assassins, it hadn't occurred to me that the White House would be so crowded. There were more than fifty people swarming about the warren of cubicles around me, and those were merely the people I could see. I could also hear the murmur of conversations from behind the doors of several offices, and even more people were rushing in and out of the cubicle area at every moment. If any one of them could have been an assassin, it would take me *weeks* to investigate them all.

I instantly felt extremely overwhelmed. On each of my previous missions, I'd had Erica backing me up. We'd usually kept in contact via radio, so she could offer advice, suggest what I should do next—and, on more than one occasion, question my competence. Still, even that had given me a sense of security. Now I was completely on my own.

Meanwhile, despite Cyrus's assurance that as a kid I wouldn't stick out, I couldn't help feeling that I did. I was the only thirteen-year-old in the West Wing, and though everyone was carrying on like the fate of the free world was at stake—which might have truly been the case for some of them—most of them stopped to watch me, as though surprised I was there. They probably assumed I was a friend of Jason's, but if anyone *was* a covert SPYDER agent, my presence was so obvious, I might as well have been banging cymbals together.

Suddenly, Cyrus's plan seemed far less thought out than I'd hoped. "Do you know where Jason might be?" I urged Kimmy, wanting to get out of the West Wing as quickly as possible. "It took longer than I expected to get through security. I have less time with him than I'd hoped."

"He's probably up in his room, playing video games," Kimmy said. "That's where he usually is. C'mon. That's in the *real* White House. I think you'll be far more impressed by that." She led me through the cramped maze of cubicles.

A group of people in military uniforms exited through a door marked SITUATION ROOM in front of us. Given the large number of medals arrayed on their chests, I figured they were all of high rank. I caught a glimpse of the Situation Room itself as we wove through them. To my surprise, it was smaller than my living room at home, and crammed full of electronic equipment that all looked to be at least ten years out of date.

A hallway passed out of the West Wing and hooked right toward the more famous part of the White House, the part with the huge portico in the front and the sprawling gardens in the back; I got a glimpse of it through the hallway windows as we approached. I could also see several more Secret Service agents outside: Some were patrolling the South Lawn; some were posted along the fence line; one was lurking in the Rose Garden. And those were merely the ones out in the open; I figured there were probably plenty more hidden from sight.

The hall was wide, but it was crammed full of filing cabinets and other storage units that had spilled out of the West Wing, giving the feel of passing through the most securely protected attic in the world.

Two more Secret Service agents waited at the end of it, guarding a more formal set of doors than any we had passed through so far.

"Hi, guys!" Kimmy said with a cheerful wave. "This is Ben Ripley. He's here for a playdate with Jason."

The agents snickered at this.

I held up the badge I'd been given and smiled nicely for them. "It's not really a 'playdate.' We're gonna hang out and chill. . . ."

"Whatever," one said, then checked a list on a clipboard and grunted approval. "He's on here," he informed the second agent.

With that, they held open the doors, revealing the true White House beyond.

It still wasn't that impressive.

We entered what seemed to be the basement level. A long central corridor ran the length of the building, flanked by rooms on both sides. The hall was lined with presidential portraits, although since this was a less visited area, they were the portraits of lousy presidents most people had forgotten, like James Buchanan, William Henry Harrison, and Millard Fillmore.

Kimmy went back into full-on tour-guide mode, pointing out items of interest. Or items that she *thought* were of interest. "We are currently passing the White House kitchen," she said, indicating a set of doors, from behind which we could hear the clanging of pots and pans. "There are five full-time chefs here, meaning that the kitchen is capable of making a five-course dinner for up to one hundred and forty guests—or hors d'oeuvres for one thousand people. Frankly, they make a shrimp puff to die for."

Farther down the hallway, yet another pair of Secret Service officers flanked yet another set of double doors. Given their presence and the muffled sounds emanating from the room behind, I got the impression that something important was going on there.

Before we reached it, though, Kimmy ducked left and led me up a staircase. "This is one of eight staircases in the White House. There are also three elevators, twenty-eight fireplaces, one hundred and thirty-two rooms, and four hundred and twelve doors."

"Why are there so many more doors than rooms?" I asked.

"Er . . . ," Kimmy said, thrown. "I have no idea. But I *do* know that it takes five hundred and seventy gallons of paint to cover the entire exterior!"

We reached the first level, which seemed to be the main level of the White House, where all the formal events occurred. We spent exactly three seconds on it, heading right up the next flight. All I got to see was a small marble-lined foyer with a window that looked out across the front lawn toward L'Enfant Plaza. As usual, a crowd of tourists was gathered at the White House fence. A few were protesting, waving signs and chanting, though most were taking selfies with the White House in the background.

Erica Hale stood among them.

She was staring directly at the White House, wrapped in a black winter parka. Despite the cold, she wasn't wearing a hat or scarf, allowing me a clear view of her ice-blue eyes, her sculpted cheekbones, and her raven hair.

My glimpse of her was so quick, however, that her presence didn't even register until I was a few steps up the next staircase. I froze in mid-stride, wondering if it would be okay for me to retrace my path and take another look.

As if answering my question, Kimmy deftly took my arm and led me onward. "The marble on this staircase was originally selected by Dolly Madison, wife of our fourth president, James Madison. . . ."

It occurred to me that Kimmy's litany of interior decorating facts was probably designed to distract me from what was *really* going on at the White House, although I didn't read anything sinister into it; it was most likely standard White House tour procedure. Guests were led through the building all the time, and it made sense that they would be told things about paint color and floral arrangements rather than "In the room behind us, the president is currently meeting with military advisers about thwarting a top secret cabal that is plotting World War Three. . . ."

Kimmy had no idea I was there for national security issues. She thought I was there for a playdate. So she was probably under orders to shepherd me through the official areas as quickly as possible and get me to the private quarters. Not wanting to make waves, I let her lead me up to the top floor.

"You are really quite lucky, Ben," she told me. "Very few members of the public ever get to see this portion of the White House. Only those whose presence is requested by the first family . . ."

What was Erica doing there? I wondered. Had it even really been her? I'd seen her for half a second, if that, and she'd been quite far away. Furthermore, Erica usually excelled at *not* being seen. The only reason I could imagine that she'd have posted herself right out in the open, without a hat or sunglasses, was that she *wanted* to be seen.

Though I had to wonder, was she hoping *I* would see her—or hoping someone else would?

We arrived at the top floor of the White House. The residential area. Compared to the rigidly formal first floor, it was surprisingly homey. It was cleaner than any of my friends' homes—there was doubtlessly a large domestic staff at the White House—and the décor was over-the-top patriotic, with lots of historic prints and carved eagles, but there was a lived-in feeling to it. The carpet was worn, the walls all looked as though they'd been beaned with a baseball now and then, and I could hear folk rock emanating from behind Jemma Stern's bedroom door, as well as Jemma chattering away on the phone with a friend. Close by, the door to the kids' bathroom hung open, revealing toothbrushes and acne medication lined up on the sink, towels embroidered with an official White House logo, and a surprisingly cheap-looking plastic shower curtain.

"Well, here we are!" Kimmy announced, stopping outside the door to Jason's room. I could tell it was his, because there was a handmade sign taped to it proclaiming JASON'S ROOM. KEEP OUT!

From behind the door came the sounds of gunfire and ominous action music, the telltale soundtrack of a first-person shooter video game.

Kimmy knocked. "Jason!" she called out. "Ben's here!"

"Cool!" came the reply. "Send him in!"

"Looks like my work here is done!" Kimmy said. Ignoring the homemade warning sign, she opened Jason's door and ushered me inside.

The room was that of a quintessential teenage boy, albeit a teenage boy with access to pretty much anything he wanted. The walls were plastered with posters of professional athletes and rock bands (all autographed) and the floor was covered with sports equipment and dirty laundry. The shelves were stacked high with books, games, and model airplanes. There was a small air hockey table, a keyboard, two electric guitars, and a large television, currently displaying the video game I'd heard. I recognized it as *Target: Annihilation*, a game in which you were supposed to be a spy. It was nothing like my experience of being a spy had been. Jason's avatar was running through a rail yard filled with heavily armed enemy agents, mowing them down with a gun the size of a small cannon. Jason himself was slumped in a tatty beanbag chair, his back to me, the game controller clenched in his hands.

If it hadn't been for the stellar view of the South Lawn and the Washington Monument out the window, I might have forgotten I was even in the White House.

"Have fun!" Kimmy exclaimed, then closed the door to give us privacy.

Jason was so engrossed in his game, he didn't turn around. All I could see of him was a mop of unkempt black hair.

"Uh . . . hi," I said.

Jason didn't respond. He kept blowing away enemy agents.

I tried again. "What are you playing?"

There was still no answer.

"Mind if I play too?"

"Yes, I mind!" Jason snapped angrily. "My father might be able to force me to hang out with some loser I've never met, but he can't make me like it. So sit down, shut up— and don't touch any of my stuff."

"Hey now . . . ," I began.

"What part of 'shut up' did you not understand?" Jason

yelled. "I don't want you here, okay? The sooner you leave, the better, get it?"

I sighed, realizing that the friendly, smiling kid I'd seen by the president's side on TV apparently was an act. Instead, the real Jason Stern was a raging jerk—and now I was stuck with him.

CONFRONTATION

The White House

Second Floor

February 10

1730 hours

I gave Jason a minute to calm down before I tried speaking to him again. "You know why I'm here, right?" I asked. "It's for your father's safety. We think his life is in danger."

Jason snorted, annoyed. "People *always* think he's in danger. They think all of us are. I can't even go to the bathroom without having sixteen Secret Service agents follow me."

"This time is different," I said.

"Yeah, this time it's screwing up my life worse than

usual." Jason blasted a few enemy agents indiscriminately. "I was supposed to have a *real* friend come by today. But now that's been canceled and I have you instead."

I looked around for a place to sit but couldn't find one. The bed and the only chair were buried under Jason's things. A pair of rancid socks was slung over the back of the chair; they reeked so badly, they could have killed a canary.

So I remained standing awkwardly in the middle of the room. "Look, I'm not thrilled I have to be here either. . . ."

"Yeah, right. I'll bet they really had to twist your arm to get you to hang out with me at the White House."

"If you don't want me here, the fastest way to get rid of me is to help me find whoever is after your father."

Jason blew a few pixelated birds out of the sky just to watch them explode into clouds of red mist. "If there really was some evil organization smart enough to get an assassin into the White House, how is some lame dork in second-hand clothes supposed to find him when the entire Secret Service can't?"

I looked over my clothes, which were indeed mostly secondhand. I was dying to tell Jason exactly what I'd done before, so he'd understand what I was capable of: I had saved his own father's life from a missile attack; I had engineered the destruction of SPYDER's headquarters; I had prevented half of Colorado from being nuked. Only, I couldn't tell him any of that, because all that information was classified. Sometimes security protocols really blew.

Instead, all I could offer was, "They wouldn't have sent me if they didn't think I could help."

Jason gave another snort of disgust, then returned his full attention to his game, done speaking to me. His secret agent avatar was now moving through an abandoned warehouse, trading potshots with bad guys.

I was starting to get quite warm. The heat was cranked up to subtropical temperatures and I was still wearing my winter jacket. I shrugged it off and set it gingerly on the bed.

"I SAID DON'T TOUCH MY STUFF!" Jason roared. He threw his controller aside and whirled around, allowing me to see his face for the first time since I'd arrived. He was at an awkward spot in puberty where his nose had ballooned, his hair was getting greasy, and his skin was blotchy with pimples. "Are you too stupid to understand English?"

A year before, I probably would have turned tail and fled the room. But I'd learned a few things at spy school. First and foremost: When in an uncomfortable situation, imagine what Erica Hale would do.

So I stayed rooted to my spot and fixed Jason with as hard a stare as I could muster. "I know you're very busy pretending to be a spy, but I actually *have* to be one. And real-life espionage isn't anything like that game you're playing. In the first place, no evil organization worth its salt would set up shop in an abandoned warehouse. And they're not going to sic three hundred minions on you without teaching them to shoot straight. Meanwhile, any agent idiotic enough to run blindly into a place like that without backup would last thirty seconds tops before he got blown to pieces, no matter how lousy his opponents' aim is. A real enemy organization is clever, elusive, and always trying to be three steps ahead of you, so if you want to beat them, you have to be smarter than they are. Which is why I've been sent in. I might not be the best shooter or the best fighter at the CIA, but I am *not* stupid. I have level-sixteen math skills, I can speak three languages fluently, and frankly, compared to me, you have the IQ of a hamster."

Jason's jaw dropped open. "Urk" was all he could manage. I couldn't tell if he was cowed by my response, or stunned because people usually didn't talk to him like this. Either way, I appreciated the effect.

"So," I went on, "I'd really appreciate it if you'd can the pathetic 'woe is me' attitude and help me out. I could give a hoot about a stuck-up brat like you, but I'd really like to prevent these guys from killing your father."

In response to this, Jason appeared to think about his behavior. He took a moment to consider how he'd treated me—and then went right back to being a jerk again. "That makes one of us," he spat. "If anyone whacked my father, they'd be doing me a favor."

With that, he picked up his controller again and resumed the game.

I walked out of the room. I wasn't turning tail, though. I was just so annoyed at Jason Stern that I didn't feel like being anywhere near him. Plus, I had to use the bathroom. It had been nearly two hours since I'd gone back at school.

Unfortunately, I was so distracted by Jason's obnoxious behavior that I didn't notice that something very important had changed about my surroundings.

The bathroom door was now closed.

It wasn't locked, either. So the door opened when I turned the knob, and I barged right in on the fifteen-year-old daughter of the president of the United States as she sat on the toilet.

Jemma Stern was an awkward, gangly girl who had often seemed ill at ease when I'd seen her on television, so interrupting her in the most personal of moments didn't go over well at all. She promptly screamed at the top of her lungs, a shrill, bloodcurdling shriek more attuned to someone who'd been physically attacked than merely caught with her pants down. Every Secret Service agent within earshot promptly came running. The closest one, a thickly built fireplug of a woman who'd been posted outside the presidential bedroom, charged around the corner and, before I could even try to explain what had happened, nailed me with a flying tackle.

We sailed into the wall by the stairs, hitting it hard enough to fracture the plaster and dislodge a stuffed eagle mounted there. The eagle toppled, landing on the Secret Service agent, piercing her back with its beak. Now *she* screamed. Then, perhaps mistaking the strike as an attack from behind by another assailant, she whipped around, grabbed the eagle, and flung it into the wall, where it burst into a cloud of stuffing and feathers.

Unfortunately for Jemma, all of this prevented me from doing what she probably wanted most: simply closing the bathroom door. It now swung all the way open, so that Jemma was still fully visible on the toilet when three more Secret Service agents came charging up the stairs. All of them had their weapons drawn, ready for action.

Jemma screamed again, then kicked the bathroom door shut in their faces.

The agents now shifted their attention to me, yanking me off the floor and shoving me up against the wall. Several pairs of hands roughly frisked me at once. I tried to explain what had happened, but the first Secret Service agent had knocked the wind out of me when she'd tackled me. All that came out was a wheeze of air.

"Miss Stern?" the biggest of the agents called through the

bathroom door. "Miss, is everything all right in there?"

"No, everything isn't all right!" Jemma yelled back. "That little pervert walked in on me!"

"It was an accident," I gasped. "She hadn't locked the door."

"I shouldn't have to lock the door in my own house!" Jemma cried. "This is the most secure building in the country! I wasn't expecting a pervert to be on the loose here!"

The Secret Service agents all looked at me accusingly.

"I'm not a pervert," I said quickly. "I'm a friend of Jason's, here to hang out."

This didn't seem to convince the agents of anything. "I wasn't informed of any playdate today," the big agent said.

"It's not a playdate," I said quickly. "And it was kind of last-minute. Maybe they forgot to tell you."

"Or maybe you're a pervert who snuck in here to see Jemma Stern on the toilet," the agent replied suspiciously.

The agent who'd tackled me was massaging her back where she'd been gouged by the stuffed eagle. She pounded on Jason's door and said, "Jason, could you please come out here?"

"I'm busy!" Jason shouted back. I figured he had certainly heard all the commotion in the hall but was willfully ignoring it.

"It's a matter of national security," the wounded agent said.

Jason groaned, and then the sound of his video game paused. His footsteps slowly thumped across the floor.

"Could you all possibly handle this somewhere else?" Jemma asked through the bathroom door. "I could really use some privacy."

"We're taking care of this as quickly as we can, miss," the female agent informed her. "Feel free to go on with your business."

"You have got to be kidding me," Jemma groaned.

Jason yanked open his door dramatically, as though we'd been asking a great deal of him to walk all the way across his room. "What?" he demanded.

The big Secret Service agent pointed at me. "We just caught this young man attempting to peep on your sister while she was on the toilet. . . ."

"I wasn't peeping!" I protested. "I needed the bathroom and the door wasn't locked!"

The agent ignored me and spoke to Jason. "He claims he's a friend of yours, rather than an intruder. Can you confirm that?"

Jason looked at me, then turned to the agents and shook his head. "Never seen him before," the little creep said. "Looks like a pervert to me." Then he gave me a quick, smug smile and shut the door, leaving me at the mercy of the Secret Service.

POSSIBLE SUSPECTS

Eisenhower Executive Office Building

February 10

2000 hours

I got to see another part of the White House that people on the regular tour normally miss: the holding cell. In fact, I got to spend two solid hours there, while all the confusion was resolved.

Ultimately, Kimmy Dimsdale was tracked down to explain that I *was* actually a friend of Jason Stern's, rather than some young, psychotic Jemma Stern fanatic who'd somehow infiltrated the White House with the intention of catching her on the toilet—and that Jason had merely pretended not to know me to cause trouble.

This didn't seem to be much of a surprise to the Secret Service agents. Apparently, Jason Stern had a reputation as a nuisance around the White House. (His Secret Service code name was Hades.) Furthermore, my visit *had* been listed in that day's official memo, but some of the agents had missed it. By this point, however, it was nearly eight o'clock on a school night. Even if I had actually wanted to continue my playdate—which I didn't—it was time for me to go home. There was a formal dinner at the White House that night to honor the teachers of the year, and Jason Stern, being a student, was expected to be there on his best behavior. So Kimmy called "Grandpa Cyrus" to come pick me up.

I was allowed to leave the White House holding cell and wait in the lobby of the EEOB with Kimmy, who spent most of the time making lame excuses for Jason's behavior, apparently worried that I might blab to the press that the president's son was a jerk—or worse, that I'd seen the first daughter's panties. "Jason has been under a lot of pressure lately," Kimmy explained weakly. "It's tough to be a kid when the public is watching you all the time."

"Know what else is tough?" I asked. "Getting falsely accused of being a pervert in front of the Secret Service."

"Er . . . yes," Kimmy conceded. "I suppose it would be. Would a souvenir White House key chain make you feel better?"

"A little," I admitted.

By the time Cyrus arrived fifteen minutes later, I had scored an additional four White House key chains, three White House reusable water bottles, a model of *Air Force One*, a set of fancy pens with the presidential seal on them, and three dozen packets of official White House jelly beans. I figured my father would be thrilled.

There were many people still at work, either in the EEOB, or funneling back through it from the White House. Overall, a staggering number of people had access to the "Twelve Acres" of the White House property. The Secret Service probably kept most of them at a distance from the president, but if anyone was a SPYDER agent, they could still probably find an opportunity to get close enough to take a shot at him.

I spotted the shifty businessman from when I had come in that afternoon now leaving with several high-ranking military men. The businessman grew nervous when he noticed me, as though surprised to see a kid in the lobby of the EEOB so late at night. Or maybe he was a covert SPYDER agent who knew my true identity and was unsettled to see me.

My phone buzzed with a number I didn't recognize. I cautiously answered it. "Hello?"

"Hey, hey! Is this my big-shot grandson who got to

visit the White House today?" The voice was definitely Cyrus Hale's—although the tone caught me by surprise. He sounded like an actual doting grandfather, rather than his usual cranky self. I assumed he was acting for the benefit of anyone who might overhear the call—or be eavesdropping on it.

"Hi, Grandpa!" I said cheerfully, doing a bit of acting myself. "Are you close?"

"Approaching the building right now."

"Okay. I'm coming out." I hung up and informed Kimmy, "My grandfather's here."

"Great!" she said, then thought to add, "In the interest of national security, I hope I can trust you to not share certain stories about what transpired here today?"

"You don't have to worry about me," I assured her.

Kimmy heaved a sigh of relief, then ushered me out the door. Cyrus was pulling up in front of the building in a well-worn sedan that looked exactly like the sort of car a normal grandfather would drive. The Secret Service agents were going on alert when Kimmy yelled to them, "He's okay! He's just picking up a friend of Jason's!"

Cyrus rolled down the window and shouted, "Hey there, champ! Did you have fun?"

"Sure did, Gramps!" I replied, then slid into the passenger seat.

Kimmy waved good-bye enthusiastically. "So long, Ben! Hope to see you again soon!"

Cyrus rolled up the window, drove away, and immediately dropped the kindly old grandfather act. "You didn't waste any time screwing up this mission, did you?"

I sank back in my seat. "It wasn't a total loss. . . ."

"From what I understand, you were with Jason Stern a whole three minutes before everything went sideways. You were supposed to lay low and keep an eye out for trouble, not make a ruckus and spend the whole afternoon in the lockup!"

It suddenly occurred to me that, although I'd been on several missions with Cyrus Hale, I hadn't spent more than thirty seconds alone with him. Cyrus was as curmudgeonly as anyone I'd ever met, but I'd either had Erica around to calm him—or Alexander to draw his disdain. Now that it was only the two of us, the ride back to school promised to be as much fun as dental surgery.

Luckily, the traffic had lessened considerably since that afternoon. Campus wasn't too far from the White House and Cyrus was driving like a maniac, so hopefully, the ride itself wouldn't be that long.

"You didn't warn me that Jason was the world's biggest jerk," I said.

"What was I supposed to do, say right in front of the

president of the United States that his son's a scumbag? Part of your training is to be ready for anything. If you can't handle some thirteen-year-old punk, how can you be expected to handle a high-stakes criminal organization like SPYDER?"

"I *have* handled SPYDER," I reminded him. "Plenty of times. The people who work there might be evil, but they were still generally nicer to me than Jason Stern was."

"SPYDER tried to kill you," Cyrus pointed out.

"Yes, but that was business. Jason was mean for no good reason. He actually said that anyone who killed his father would be doing him a favor."

Cyrus's eyebrows rose slightly. When he spoke again, he sounded intrigued, rather than irascible. "He did? To a total stranger? You think it's possible he's SPYDER's man inside?"

"Jason?" I asked, incredulous. "He's only a kid."

"*You're* only a kid. And you've met other folks your age working for SPYDER."

"Yeah, but that was different."

"How? You said yourself this kid was a class-A scumball."

"I still can't imagine him plotting to assassinate his own father. In fact, I can't imagine *any* kid wanting to do something like that."

"Just because you get along with your father doesn't mean everyone does. Believe me, there are plenty of people out there who'd be more than happy to bump off their daddies."

Like your *son?* I thought, although I didn't say it out loud. I wondered if Cyrus was thinking it himself. His relationship with Alexander was among the worst I'd ever encountered. I didn't really think Alexander would ever be reduced to patricide, but he certainly had some serious issues with his father.

Cyrus wove around a few cars and shot through a traffic light a good three seconds after it had turned red.

"There were plenty of other possible suspects at the White House," I said.

"Like who?"

"There was this businessman who seemed pretty suspicious of me." I brought up the picture I'd taken of the shifty man on my phone, then handed it to Cyrus.

He took a quick glance, then said, "Forward it to Erica; see what she can dig up. Anyone else?"

"A couple aides to a French diplomat looked kind of squirrelly." I flashed Cyrus their pictures as well.

"Send them to Erica too," he said.

I wondered if I should mention that Erica had been lurking outside the White House that afternoon, then decided against it. If Cyrus had asked Erica to be there, then this wouldn't be news to him. But if Erica had decided to come down and check on me without his permission, Cyrus would probably be livid at her.

Instead, I said, "Then again, maybe these are the people we should be the *least* concerned about."

"How's that?" Cyrus asked.

"Well, these guys were kind of nervous and awkward, but that's natural, isn't it? They're going into the White House. That's a big deal. But if SPYDER really has someone on the inside, they'd probably be trained to *not* look nervous and awkward. I mean, there were hundreds of people there today, and these were the ones whose behavior caught my attention."

Cyrus met my eyes, which was a bit disturbing given that he was driving at fifty miles an hour. He probably should have been watching the road. "So you think the people we should really be suspicious about are all the people who weren't acting nervous?"

"Right."

"Even though there were hundreds of them?"

"Yes. I realize it sounds kind of crazy, but you know SPYDER. What makes more sense to you: that they'd send in someone who looked nervous and shifty to kill the president—or that they'd co-opt someone on the inside to handle the job? Someone who'd look cool and confident and not stand out at all?"

Cyrus drummed his fingers on the steering wheel thoughtfully while he careened through an intersection. "So, after all your undercover work today, your deduction is basically that *anyone* in the White House could be the mole."

"Er . . . yes."

"You do realize that the whole point of sending you on this mission was to narrow the list of possible suspects down? It makes my job a lot easier if I only have to investigate one or two people, rather than every single person who set foot in the White House today."

I sighed, feeling extremely ineffectual. "I understand."

"There isn't a single person you feel confident you can rule out?" Cyrus asked.

"Not really."

"The Secret Service agents, for example? Given that the whole point of their job is to protect the president?"

"Actually, they seem like they'd be the perfect targets for SPYDER to turn into assassins. They can go anywhere they want on the property and they're allowed to carry weapons."

"How about that nice young gal who brought you to the car? You think she's possibly a sleeper agent?"

"Kimmy?" I considered her. She was so sweet, she'd probably scoot a cockroach out the door instead of stepping on it. But then, Ashley Sparks had seemed awfully sweet as well, and she'd been a full-bore SPYDER agent. "It's possible. Acting like the nicest person in the White House would be an awfully good way to deflect suspicion."

"How about the landscaping staff?" Cyrus asked, annoyed. "Or the chefs? Or the florists? You think every single one of them could be a potential assassin?"

"Yes," I agreed. "Them, and every staffer and every aide and every single person who works for the president. If SPYDER could corrupt enough people inside the CIA that even *you* don't trust your own agency, what's to say they couldn't corrupt one person who works inside the White House? Or more than one? Maybe they've corrupted five or six people. Or twenty. So if we actually catch one or two of them, the others are free to go on with the job."

Cyrus muttered under his breath. He seemed even more annoyed now than he had when he'd picked me up. Only, he didn't seem annoyed at me so much as at the entire situation.

We arrived at Dupont Circle. Instead of being chock-full of cars as it had been earlier that day, now it was merely moderately crowded. This didn't slow Cyrus down at all, however. He appeared to be venting his frustration through aggressive driving. Despite the presence of other vehicles, he sped around the circle so fast that the centrifugal force threw me against the door of the car.

I was beginning to think that it might have been safer to stay back at the White House surrounded by potential assassins.

Cyrus veered from Dupont onto one of the northbound

roads, forcing other cars to slam on the brakes to avoid him. I heard the soft crunch of two minor accidents behind us.

"All right," Cyrus said finally. "You have a point. Any one of those people in the White House could be a potential killer. Which means your job just got a whole lot harder. And to make matters worse, our timetable has shrunk."

"What do you mean?"

"The chatter I've been monitoring increased this afternoon. SPYDER is looking to hit the president soon."

"How soon?"

"I don't know. But I'd say sometime in the next few days." Cyrus zoomed through a stop sign, prompting a bicyclist to shout a lot of very bad words at us.

I swallowed hard, daunted by the thought of this. "So, I have almost no time to vet hundreds of people and figure out which of them might be potential assassins? Without drawing any attention to myself?"

"No one ever said the spy game was easy."

"Which means I'm going back for another visit with Jason."

"After school tomorrow. And you're gonna keep going back every day until you get to the bottom of this."

"But Jason made it awfully clear he didn't want me there."

"Then figure out how to make it work. And figure it out fast. Because if you don't . . . the president is going to die.

And it will all be on your hands." Cyrus roared through an intersection. A car swerved to miss us and ended up in someone's front yard.

I slumped in my seat, feeling overwhelmed by my mission and wondering if I really had what it took to succeed.

We raced onward into the night.

PHYSICAL EDUCATION

Obstacle Course

CIA Academy of Espionage

February 11

0900 hours

I didn't hear back from Erica about the photos I'd sent her until the next morning. That was unusual. Erica wasn't a big fan of human contact, but when she had a mission, she never wasted any time following a lead. In fact, there had been several occasions when she had felt it was perfectly reasonable to wake me in the middle of the night to discuss something, rather than wait until the morning. However, there had been only silence from her until she caught up to me on the school obstacle course during PE.

At my old, normal middle school, physical education had generally meant running laps around the school track. At spy school, we ran a gauntlet of potentially harmful obstacles, pitfalls, and booby traps that our sadistic trainer, Coach Macauley, regularly altered for maximum torment. The administration claimed this was to prepare us physically and mentally for the strenuous and unpredictable demands of being a field agent, but I was quite sure that, in reality, the administrators simply enjoyed watching us get pummeled. Quite often, I caught glimpses of our professors laughing at us from the sidelines.

To make matters worse, PE was always the first class of the day, when it was freezing outside. This was a major concern, as a large number of the obstacles on the course involved mud. Crawling through mud at two in the afternoon on a sunny day was bad enough; doing it at nine a.m. in the winter was repugnant.

All classes had PE at once, although Coach staggered our starting times for the obstacle course so that no one got trampled—and so he had plenty of time to enjoy each student's humiliation. When Erica found me, I was scrabbling through one of the course's many mud wallows on my hands and knees with Zoe and Warren. The mud was the consistency of slightly melted ice cream, which allowed it to ooze into our clothing and refrigerate our various body parts. Our dull gray academy tracksuits were now stained brown—as were our faces. As if this weren't bad enough, Coach had rigged a devious set of sensors only two feet above the pit; anyone who raised their head too high and tripped one would be immediately blasted with a paintball gun. The entire experience was awful—and I wasn't the only one who thought so.

"Honestly, what is the point of this?" Zoe was griping. "The CIA does most of its work in cities. I don't know of a whole lot of cities with mud pits in the middle of them."

"There's a pretty big mud pit in the middle of downtown Mogadishu," Warren pointed out. He was so covered with mud that he was camouflaging himself without even trying. I could barely see him except for the whites of his eyes.

"Maybe so," Zoe said, "but the Mogadishans still don't *crawl* through it. They go around it. We ought to be learning useful stuff, like how to do car chases on city streets and have knife fights on the tops of speeding trains, not this garbage."

"No CIA agent has had a knife fight atop a moving train since Kennedy was president," Erica said, catching us all by surprise. As usual, we hadn't even known she was near us. She was simply there beside us in the mud, as though she'd spontaneously popped into existence. "And it wasn't even a speeding train. It was only a freight hauler moving at five miles an hour."

Zoe, Warren, and I turned to Erica, stunned by her sudden appearance—and by the fact that she was engaging in normal conversation.

"I need to talk to you," she told me.

"Now?" I asked. *"Here?"*

"National security is at stake," she said.

"It was at stake this morning, when I was having waffles in the cafeteria," I pointed out. "We couldn't have discussed this then?"

Erica didn't answer me. Instead, she turned to Zoe and Warren and said, "This is a sensitive issue. Could you two give us some space?"

Zoe and Warren didn't look pleased to be cut out of the conversation, but they understood Erica's reasons and obediently squelched toward the far side of the mud pit to let us talk in peace.

Erica and I continued wallowing through the muck. Erica lowered her voice to a whisper and said, "I looked at those photos you sent me last night. The sketchy business-man you were suspicious of? He's Vladimir Gorsky."

I hesitated before responding. I had no idea who Vladimir Gorsky was but was worried that Erica would judge me harshly for this gap in my knowledge.

Unfortunately, Erica knew exactly why I'd hesitated. And then she judged me harshly for the gap in my knowledge. "Don't tell me you've never heard of Vladimir Gorsky."

"I haven't," I admitted.

Erica sighed disdainfully, like I'd just told her I didn't know the capital of America. "Really? Because he's only one of the world's most powerful men."

"Oh!" I said, trying to cover. "Vladimir *Gorsky*! Of course I know who he is. I thought you said Vladimir *Borsky*. . . ."

"Stop trying to cover," Erica told me.

"Okay." I grimaced, not merely because of Erica's curt tone, but also because frigid mud had just seeped through my sweatpants and into my underwear.

"Gorsky is a Russian arms dealer," Erica explained. "He's made billions funneling weapons to pretty much every war waging in the world right now, often to both sides at the same time."

"And he's meeting with the president?" I asked, incredulous.

"First of all, his being at the White House doesn't mean he's meeting with the president. A thousand other people work in the West Wing and the EEOB. Second, just because he's an arms dealer doesn't make him a criminal.

No one has ever been able to prove that he's done anything wrong . . . yet. There are plenty of reasons someone in the administration might want to be meeting with him. We might want him to arm some rebels who support a cause of ours—or to *stop* arming some rebels who are fighting a cause of ours—or heck, maybe we even want to buy some weapons from him ourselves."

"So, then, you don't think he's working for SPYDER?"

"I never said that. Gorsky's as sleazy as they come. Grandpa's pretty sure he's a front man for Paul Lee."

I grimaced once again, only this time it had nothing to do with the mud in my underpants. I knew the name Paul Lee. "The guy who sold SPYDER the missiles they tried to blow up New York City with?"

"The guy who *allegedly* sold them the missiles, yes."

"And the guy who sold Leo Shang the nuclear bomb we had to defuse?"

"Ditto."

"This guy Gorsky's working for him?"

"That's what Grandpa suspects, at least. No one has ever confirmed Lee and Gorsky are connected, but if it's true, then you can easily connect Gorsky to SPYDER."

We finally reached the edge of the mud pit. To get out of it, we had to scramble over a ten-foot-high wooden wall while Coach Macauley and some other professors took potshots at us with paintball guns. Erica vaulted over with the ease of an Olympic gymnast, landing gracefully on her feet.

I vaulted over it with the grace of a diseased elephant. I tried to stick the landing but lost my balance and face-planted in the dirt.

I still did better than Warren, though. While clambering over the wall, he caught his pant leg on a shard of wood, leaving him at the mercy of the paintball brigade. His rear end might as well have had a target painted on it. The professors shot him again and again before he finally managed to free himself—although to do it, he had to wriggle out of his pants altogether. He landed with a painful thud on our side of the wall in only his tighty-whities.

"Reeves, that was pathetic!" Coach Macauley shouted. "Do that in the real world and you'll get your legs blown off! Put your pants back on and start over!"

Warren whimpered at the mere thought of having to go through the mud patch once more.

Zoe hopped down from the wall and handed him his pants, which she'd dislodged. "It's not your fault," she said encouragingly. "Exactly when in real life are we ever going to exit a mud pit by climbing a wall? Even if there *was* a wall next to a mud pit, wouldn't we just go around it? The whole concept for this course is preposterous."

"Maybe, but I'm still flunking it." Warren glumly took

his pants from Zoe and slouched back toward the starting line.

Erica proceeded onward. The next obstacle was a three-inch-wide balance beam that stretched over yet another mud pit. The beam was covered with a slick of grease. Almost everyone who'd gone before us had slipped off and splatted into the muck. Erica calmly sauntered across it, as though it were a city sidewalk. Under most circumstances, she probably would have darted across it in seconds, but she took her time because I was following her and she still needed to talk to me.

At least, I was *trying* to follow her. The best I could do was edge slowly across the beam, desperately windmilling my arms to keep from toppling into the mud.

"So you think Gorsky's the one targeting the president?" I asked.

"It's possible. Or maybe it's one of the underlings who accompanied him yesterday."

"But they were there *yesterday*. If they're targeting the president, they kind of missed their chance."

"Not necessarily. Maybe yesterday was the setup for a Bombay Boomerang."

"A what?" I asked. The Hale family often dropped arcane spy jargon into conversations as if everyone in the world knew it.

"It's an old espionage ploy," Erica explained. "You don't schedule only one meeting with your target; you schedule several over a few days. The first time you come in, the Secret Service is really on guard around you, because they don't know you or trust you. So they go over you with a fine-tooth comb, scrutinizing everything you're carrying, everything you're wearing, and so on."

"Right," I said, recalling how aggressively the Secret Service had gone through my coat the day before.

"But then you come back again and again. By the second time, the Secret Service isn't quite as concerned about you, and by the third or fourth, it's getting routine, so they drop their guard around you. . . ."

"And that's when you can sneak in a weapon?"

"Exactly. You convince someone that you're not dangerous—and *then* you hit them." Erica stepped onto the solid ground at the end of the balance beam.

I still had a few feet to go.

Behind me, Zoe was also edging her way along, muttering sarcastically the whole time. "Balance beams. That makes sense. I'm sure our guys in the field confront greased balance beams every day."

Erica checked her watch impatiently, as though I were going slowly for no good reason.

"There's one big problem with Gorsky," I said. "Why

would he do this? You said he's a billionaire. Going after the president inside the White House is practically a suicide mission. What could SPYDER possibly offer him to get him to do that?"

"Maybe he doesn't care about the money," Erica replied. "Maybe he's willing to do whatever SPYDER wants. Or maybe they can *make* him do whatever they want. He could be a sleeper agent."

"You mean, someone who doesn't even know he's working for SPYDER until they activate him somehow?"

"That's right."

"Those really exist?"

"Yes. Are you ever going to get off that balance beam, or should I have your meals delivered there today?"

"I'm almost done." I finally sidled off the end of the beam. "What about those other two people I sent you pictures of? Who were they?"

"Only aides to the French ambassador. They're nobodies."

"So? SPYDER likes nobodies. They don't draw any attention. I'll bet those guys are in and out of the White House with the ambassador all the time. Don't you think SPYDER would rather pick them than some sketchy billionaire arms dealer?"

"It's possible." Erica set off on the course again, and I followed her. A narrow trail plunged into a thick copse of trees. "But I think there's something significant to the fact that SPYDER's plotting a hit on the president exactly when Gorsky shows up."

"It could be coincidence."

"There's no such thing as coincidence."

"Speaking of which, I happened to notice you in front of the White House yesterday."

Erica gave me a sidelong glance as we darted through a maze of undergrowth. "You didn't 'happen' to notice me. I *wanted* you to notice me."

That explained why she'd been right out in the open. "Why?"

"So you'd know I was keeping an eye on you. In case you ended up in danger."

I was quite sure that wasn't the whole story. Knowing Erica, she probably thought I couldn't handle the mission on my own. Even though *I* wasn't sure I could handle the mission on my own, I still felt insulted, and this combined with my annoyance at having to run through a dangerous obstacle course with frozen mud in my underwear. Before thinking better of it, I said sharply, "You mean, you were keeping an eye on me in case I screwed things up."

"No. I was there to protect you."

"I was inside the most secure building in the United States! I had the entire Secret Service there to protect me."

"The job of the Secret Service is to protect the president, not you. If anything goes wrong on this mission—and when SPYDER's around, things always go wrong—the Service won't give you a second thought. Heck, they'd throw you on top of a bomb like a human blast shield if they thought it would save the president."

I clammed up, realizing Erica was probably right—as usual. Although I still wasn't completely convinced she believed I could handle the job. "Does Cyrus know you were down there?"

"No. And you'd better not tell him I was."

"Why not?"

Before Erica could respond, we exited the copse of trees to find the final obstacle on the course. It was a doozy. Yet another balance beam stretched over a watery pit, only this time Coach Macauley had rigged six enormous logs to pendulum back and forth across our path. Not one student had made it to the other side safely. As we watched, my friends Jawa O'Shea and Chip Schacter, both among the better athletes at school, got clobbered by logs simultaneously and went flying into the water.

Even Erica seemed daunted by this. She actually appeared to forget about my question so she could focus on navigating the obstacle. Or maybe she was simply using the obstacle as an excuse to not answer me. Whatever the case, she cautiously headed out onto the beam, ducking around the first swinging log.

Zoe emerged from the woods behind me and gasped in dismay. "Okay, this is completely ridiculous! There is no possible scenario where we are ever going to have to face giant pendulums! What's Macauley think, someday we'll to have to fight the enemy inside an enormous cuckoo clock?"

Below us, Jawa and Chip scrambled out of the pit, shivering from the glacial water, then staggered across the finish line and raced for the locker room, where they could towel off and change out of their soaking tracksuits.

I summoned my courage and set off after Erica.

The obstacle was even more terrifying than I'd expected. The logs were the size of tree trunks and whizzed past with surprising speed. There was barely any room—or time—to rest on the beam between them. I dodged the first with an inch to spare, then slipped past the second with even less leeway.

Ahead of me, Erica was being careful but still exuding incredible calm, as though she were merely avoiding feather pillows, rather than hurtling tree trunks. She strolled casually past one pendulum, paused briefly, then ambled past the next and reached the end of the obstacle course.

"Nicely done, Hale!" Coach yelled.

There were no other students at the finish line. Erica was the only one who'd made it through the entire course unscathed.

Erica looked back at me. There seemed to be a challenge in her gaze, as though she didn't believe I could make it through the final obstacle on my own. The same way she didn't believe that I could handle my mission without her. I steeled myself, determined to prove her wrong on both counts. I watched the pendulums carefully, using my gift for mathematics to assess the exact speed each was moving and deduce the timing I'd need to get past them. Calculating quickly, I realized that if I waited six seconds and then ran full out, I'd be able to avoid the remaining four pendulums without even having to stop.

I counted the six seconds, then bolted down the beam. The first pendulum whooshed right behind my back as the second swung out of my way. I squeaked past the third, then ran for the finish line.

And tripped over my shoelace.

My calculations had been perfect, but they didn't mean squat if I couldn't stay on my feet. I stumbled, nearly pitched off the beam, struggled mightily to regain my balance—and found myself directly in the path of the final pendulum as it raced toward me. It nailed me dead-on, sending me pin-wheeling off the beam and into the icy water.

I emerged stunned, sputtering, and chilled, but surprisingly all right.

At which point, Zoe—who had also been clobbered by a pendulum—fell right on my head.

Zoe wasn't that big, but she came in fast, driving me so far down in the water that I hit the squelchy, muddy bottom of the pit.

We both resurfaced, gasping for air, and floundered to the edge of the pit. As I clambered up the side, someone reached out to help me up.

Mike Brezinski. He, too, was at the end of the obstacle course, only unlike Erica, he was completely clean, unsullied by even a drop of mud.

"How . . . ?" I gasped. "How'd you get here?"

"I ran," Mike replied, helping me out over the edge.

"Through the course?" I asked.

"Of course not!" Mike laughed. "I went around it. Why on earth would I go *through* the course? It's dangerous."

"But . . . ," Zoe said, as startled as I was, "that's what our mission was."

"No," Mike corrected. "Our mission was to get to the end of the course. No one said *how* we had to get here."

"That's not true!" Coach Macauley stormed over,

looking extremely peeved at Mike. "This is my class, and I gave everyone a direct order to do this obstacle course."

"Well, those orders were questionable," Mike informed him. "If this were a *real* mission and our lead agent told us to take an incredibly dangerous route to a destination when there was a perfectly safe alternative, that agent would probably get booted out of the Agency for recklessly endangering our lives. Following orders doesn't do us any good if they're going to get us all killed. I realized there was another way to achieve the objective without putting myself in harm's way, took the initiative to act on it, and successfully completed the mission."

"Yes, but . . . ," Coach began, but then seemed unsure how to argue his point any more. "You can't . . . I mean . . . The whole point of this class is to get some exercise!"

"Oh, I did," Mike said. "I had to run at a good pace to circle all the way around the course. I got my heart rate up and my endorphins flowing. Nice work."

"Er . . . thank you," Coach said, and then, not knowing what else to do, he wandered back to the obstacle course to yell at some other students who'd actually followed his orders and been knocked off the balance beam.

"Interesting thought process," Erica said, and gave Mike one of her rare smiles.

I was instantly overcome with jealousy again. On

Operation Snow Bunny, Erica had definitely been intrigued by Mike, and now it appeared to be developing into something more serious. I had just done everything I could to impress her and ended up looking like a nincompoop, while Mike had simply broken the rules and won another compliment and a smile. It didn't seem fair. I found myself shaking violently, although I wasn't sure if it was anger or hypothermia kicking in: I was soaked to the bone and it was below zero outside.

"Uh, Ben," Zoe said. "You're turning blue."

Apparently, it was anger *and* hypothermia.

"You'd better go dry off," Mike told me. "You too, Zoe."

Zoe raced for the locker room before her fingers and toes froze off. I probably should have done the same thing, but I didn't want to leave Mike and Erica alone together. Instead, I turned to Erica and said, "You never answered my question."

"What question?" she asked, even though I was quite sure she knew exactly what I was talking about.

"The one I asked you right before the final obstacle."

Erica weighed her options for a moment, then grabbed me by the arm and marched me toward the locker room. The moment we were out of Mike's earshot, she lowered her voice and said, "I don't want you to tell Cyrus I was at the White House because Cyrus doesn't want me on this mission."

"Why not?" I said, my teeth beginning to chatter. "He thinks you're a way better spy than I am. He could have just as easily sent *you* in instead of me. He could have arranged a playdate between you and Jemma Stern. . . ."

"He thinks it's too dangerous," Erica said coldly, like she was offended.

"Too dangerous?" I repeated. "For you? Cyrus thinks you can handle anything."

"Not this. Ben, Cyrus believes this mission is far more dangerous than he told you. He's pretty sure you can handle it, but if you can't . . . Well, you're . . ." Erica turned away suddenly. "You're expendable."

Even though I was desperate to get into the warmth of the locker room, I stopped walking and stared at Erica. "You mean he thinks I could die?"

"Yes." Erica seemed to realize how upset I was and made an attempt to comfort me. "Look, it's not like he *wants* you to die. And if it happened, he wouldn't be happy about it. . . ."

"Gee, that's reassuring."

"It's the nature of the business. This mission is crucial to national security."

"But not so crucial that Cyrus is willing to risk *your* life?"

"I'm his granddaughter," Erica said bitterly. It was

probably the first time I'd ever seen anyone angry about having their life *not* be in danger. "He's always told me to never let emotions cloud my decisions, and now he's doing it. I'm completely capable of handling this mission, but he's refusing to activate me."

"So you're activating yourself? Without authorization?"

"I'm not sitting on the sidelines while you get all the glory. Now go inside and warm up, will you? You're not going to be any use to this mission if you catch a cold." With that, Erica shoved me through the doors into the locker room.

It was blessedly warm inside. In truth, it probably wasn't really that warm at all—the heaters at spy school were barely functional—but it was still considerably warmer than it was outside. Plus, steam from the showers created a nice humid fog. Jawa and Chip were already cleaned up and happily swaddled in their school clothes.

I still felt chilled, however, and in a way that had nothing to do with the cold weather outside or my wet clothes.

The revelation of how dangerous the mission was had clarified things for me. What had seemed like the biggest flaw in Cyrus's plan suddenly made sense. Cyrus had never suspected that I could actually move about the White House without SPYDER's man inside noticing. In fact, he was probably counting on my being noticed. If SPYDER's agents tried to get rid of me, then they'd reveal themselves.

I was being used as bait to flush out the enemy.

And bait was usually dead meat.

BOOMERANG

The White House

Washington, DC

February 11

1530 hours

"Oh, it's you again," **said the Secret Service agent** posted outside the EEOB.

I was back at the White House for my second "playdate." Cyrus had even arranged for me to get out of my Advanced Self-Defense homework so that I could resume my mission as early as possible. He'd met me at school, given me a quick debriefing, then put me on the Metro down to the White House.

There was a crowd at the security checkpoint again—a

new gaggle of politicians, bureaucrats, and aides—but today the Secret Service agents recognized me. They all seemed quite surprised I had returned. "I thought Jason didn't like you," said the one manning the magnetometer. "Seeing as he got you thrown in the holding cell yesterday."

"That was just a prank that got out of hand," I explained. "He didn't realize you guys were going to lock me up. He felt really bad about it, so he invited me back today."

That was the cover story. The truth was that President Stern had been livid to hear what Jason had done. (After all, it had derailed the mission designed to locate his potential assassin.) So Jason had been told that if he didn't play nice with me, his spring break in Florida would be canceled in favor of digging latrines in Haiti as part of a Stern reelection publicity campaign. As further punishment, Jason was no longer allowed to hang out in his room playing video games until I arrived. Instead, he had been ordered to greet me personally at the EEOB—with Kimmy Dimsdale making sure it happened—which meant I was getting priority service. All the politicians, bureaucrats, and aides had to let me pass through security first, as the Secret Service didn't want to keep a member of the first family waiting too long.

I was quickly checked off the official list, issued my White House ID card, and hustled through the magnetometer. However, the dogs didn't understand protocol. Once again, they went nuts when they smelled me, barking and snarling like mad. The canine agents, Nasser and Fry, reacted with annoyance.

"Why are you wearing that stupid jacket again?" Nasser asked me angrily. "You know the dogs don't like it."

"It's the only warm jacket I have," I said truthfully. "And I washed it last night, I swear." After I'd returned to campus, I'd used one of the two balky washing machines in the dorm to clean the jacket, and even combed through the pockets for any rogue pieces of beef jerky. The best I could figure was multiple trips to my father's meat locker over the years had ingrained the smell of meat in it far more than any human could detect.

"Yeah, right," Fry said skeptically. "My sons don't even know what a washing machine is. They've worn the same clothes so many times in a row, the clothes could probably walk around on their own by now."

The dogs were still snarling at me, teeth bared, saliva dripping ominously from their lips, signaling that they'd happily maul me if given the chance. "Can you get them to back down?" I asked nervously.

"If you don't like the attention, maybe you should've gotten a new jacket," Nasser replied. He seemed to find my fear amusing.

He probably would have happily kept me there a lot

longer if one of the senators behind me in the security line hadn't spoken up. "Can you move things along, please?" she asked. "Some of us have actual governing to do here!"

"Sure you do," Fry mumbled sarcastically. But he jerked a thumb toward the EEOB and said, "Move it, kid." As though I had been the one stalling.

I hurried toward the building.

"Next time you visit, wear something else!" Nasser yelled after me.

Kimmy and Jason were waiting on some benches right inside the doors, where it was still warm. Jason was slumped over an iPad, playing another video game. Kimmy leapt to her feet with a big smile, while Jason made a point of ignoring me.

"Hey there, Ben!" Kimmy said warmly. "It's good to see you! Jason was really happy to hear you were willing to come over again after how awfully he treated you yesterday, weren't you, Jason?"

Jason didn't even look up.

Kimmy kicked his bench to get his attention. "Jason, your friend is here. I'm sure your father would like you to treat him nicely today." She then whispered, "Unless you like digging latrines."

Jason looked up and pasted a fake smile on his face. "Hi, Ben. I'm so glad you're here," he said, in a way that made it very clear he wasn't.

"That's better." Kimmy started through the EEOB toward the White House. I fell in beside her, while Jason plodded along behind us, returning his focus to his iPad once again.

"I am sooooo sorry about what happened with Jason yesterday," Kimmy whispered to me. "And so is the president. He's well aware what a"—Kimmy paused to think of the proper word—"rascal his son can be. In fact, he and the first lady are very concerned about it. They're hoping that a nice, well-behaved kid like you might be a good influence on Jason."

I figured this was the cover story the president had given Kimmy to explain why he had gone through so much trouble to get me back there. "I'm just hoping Jason doesn't send me to jail again," I said.

"Oh, he won't," Kimmy assured me. "The president asked me to stay closer to you today to ensure we don't have any more unpleasantness. But there are lots of fun things for you and Jason to do together. How would you like to check out that White House bowling alley?"

If I had really been there to hang out, with a person who actually liked me, I would have immediately said yes. But I wasn't there to hang out. And Cyrus had given me explicit orders to avoid the bowling alley at all costs. "It's the worst possible place to keep an eye out for suspicious characters," he had told me that afternoon. "It's way down in the basement, and you won't see another soul down there. Plus, the pinsetter never works properly. I think Nixon broke it."

Then again, Cyrus didn't want me getting stuck in Jason's room watching him play video games all afternoon either. So he'd suggested something that would put me in the midst of everything. "Would it be possible to get a tour of the White House?" I said.

"A tour?" Jason looked disgusted, as though I'd suggested we spend the whole afternoon bashing ourselves in the heads with rocks.

"Yes." I looked to Kimmy. "You told me so many fascinating things yesterday. I'd love to hear more."

Kimmy broke into a huge smile, flattered by my praise—and thrilled to go back into tour-guide mode. "Why, that sounds like a great idea!" she announced. "Is there anything in particular you're interested in?"

"Oh, I'm interested in *everything*," I replied. "The history. The architecture. The décor. No detail is too small."

"You've come to the right place!" Kimmy exclaimed. "I know a million small details about the White House! For example, did you know that the house was first painted white in 1798? They used a lime-based whitewash to keep the stone from freezing."

Jason groaned. It seemed he was beginning to think that maybe digging latrines in Haiti over spring break would be preferable to a minutely detailed tour from Kimmy.

We passed out of the EEOB and across the blustery outdoor corridor toward the White House. I cased the area while pretending to sound interested in Kimmy's recitation of each president's favorite type of tree.

Once again, the photographers and press were camped under their canopy and the chauffeurs were all in their SUVs. Sadly, I didn't have Erica's photographic memory, but it seemed to me that there were many familiar faces from the day before. Erica's explanation of the Bombay Boomerang came back to me. I wondered how many times each of those people had passed through White House security. Hundreds? Thousands? Did the platoon of Secret Service agents around the property even bother to consider that one of those people might be a threat? If SPYDER had turned any one of those reporters or chauffeurs, they could probably access the grounds with little inspection. Or perhaps none whatsoever. After all, I was only on my second day here and I'd waltzed through security pretty easily. Someone who was there day after day after day might get waved right in. . . .

Something about this line of reasoning worried me, as though I'd hit on something important but hadn't quite grasped it. I glanced around the White House grounds, wondering what it was that had set me on edge.

At which point, Jason tripped me. He lashed out his foot

for no good reason and sent me sprawling into a hedge.

"Jason!" Kimmy yelled.

"What?" Jason asked innocently. "It was an accident!"

I staggered back to my feet and glanced at all the photographers. Most of their cameras were now aimed my way. They had recorded my fall, probably because they had little else to do. Looking at all the enormous lenses, I had an unsettling thought: A weapon could probably have easily been smuggled in with all that equipment on any given day.

"I'm so sorry for that," Kimmy said, coming to my side. "Although, if you're curious, Ulysses S. Grant planted that hedge you just fell into."

We continued on toward the White House. I locked eyes with Jason. He gave me a hateful glare that indicated I probably had many more stumbles to look forward to. I decided to not get anywhere near a staircase with him, then ran back over what I'd been thinking about before he'd tripped me, trying to pinpoint what it was that had worried me so much.

Two more Secret Service agents nodded obsequiously to Jason as we neared the White House, then held open the doors as we entered the West Wing.

If anything, it was even more of a madhouse than it had been the day before. Staffers and aides were racing about, shuffling papers and texting furiously on cell phones. Each of them had an ID on a lanyard around their neck, each had probably come and gone from the White House a hundred times or more, each had probably stopped being scrutinized by the Secret Service long ago. Any one of them would have been a perfect sleeper agent for SPYDER, determined to kill the president—and me, should I get in their way.

And yet . . .

Every time I had come up against SPYDER, they had always caught me—and the CIA—off guard by undermining our expectations. They never did what we were expecting them to. Instead, they were always several steps ahead of us. Which meant that if we *thought* they were going to have a mole inside the White House assassinate the president, then that was probably the last thing they were going to do. True, that logic was quite warped, but SPYDER's own logic often seemed to be as twisted as a Möbius strip.

"Did you know that every year White House staffers eat more than ten thousand bags of pretzels?" Kimmy asked me.

"Big whoop," mumbled Jason.

Across the West Wing, Vladimir Gorsky exited the Situation Room. He was with several high-ranking military officers. Since I'd actually had time to prepare for my mission that day, I had spent much of the afternoon boning up on important government employees, trying to memorize their names and faces. So now I recognized some of the people with Gorsky. There were the secretaries of the army, the navy, and the air force, along with their boss, the chairman of the Joint Chiefs of Staff, as well as the secretary of defense and a dozen aides and assistants.

Gorsky was shaking hands with all of the top brass, as though a deal had been concluded—but when he noticed me, he recoiled in alarm, as if my appearance had shaken him somehow.

I looked at the lanyard hanging around his neck, wondering how much scrutiny he'd been subjected to by the Secret Service that day and whether it was as lax as mine had been. . . .

Then I stopped in my tracks, suddenly struck by a terrifying thought.

"The staffers also use more than six million Post-it notes every year," Kimmy announced cheerfully. "That's enough to cover Rhode Island!"

Gorsky stepped back, away from me—and thus, from the military officers as well. Several of them seemed confused or concerned by his reaction, then looked toward me curiously, wondering if I could have possibly been the cause of his alarm.

A second later, not far ahead of us, the door to the Oval Office opened. Everyone in the West Wing immediately fell silent. Every Secret Service agent snapped to attention as President Stern himself entered the warren of cubicles, accompanied by an entourage of aides. Courtney, the tough Secret Service agent who'd driven our car, was posted right behind him, like a shadow. The moment Stern noticed Jason, he broke into a warm smile. "Son!" he exclaimed. "What brings you down here?" If there was still any tension between him and Jason, he did an impressive job of hiding it.

On the other hand, Jason put his anger on display for everyone to see. "You know exactly what I'm doing here," he said acidly. "I'm having that stupid *playdate* you insisted on."

President Stern's smile flickered, then returned to its usual full strength. Rather than acknowledge Jason's comment at all, Stern turned my way and greeted me graciously, pretending like we'd never met. "You must be Benjamin. I've heard so much about you. It's a pleasure to meet you." He extended a hand to me.

I shook it, doing my best to act as though this was one of the most amazing things that had ever happened to me. Normally, it would have been—even if I hadn't spent private time with the president the day before—but now my mind was awhirl with terrifying ideas.

My security had been lax. I'd been hurried through the magnetometer, and the canine agents had allowed me through even though the dogs had gone nuts when they smelled my jacket. . . .

But I hadn't been lying when I said I'd washed my jacket.

I *had* washed it, trying to remove whatever scent the dogs had picked up. And yet they'd still smelled something.

The entire West Wing remained focused on us. Because when the president was around, people stopped to watch him. Even people who saw him every day. They were all looking at me expectantly, except for Jason, who was staring at his shoes, making a point of letting his father know how angry he was. I tried to say something appropriately deferential, like "It's a pleasure to meet you too, Mr. President," but I wasn't really sure what I said, because I was putting everything together and, at the same time, hoping it couldn't possibly be true.

SPYDER never did what anyone expected. SPYDER was always several steps ahead of us.

So maybe SPYDER didn't just know that I'd been activated; maybe SPYDER had wanted me activated all along.

I had the mortifying feeling that *I* was the Bombay Boomerang.

The president said something else to me that must have been funny, because everyone around us laughed, but I had no idea what it was.

My winter jacket was thick and heavy. If anyone had stuffed an extra few ounces of explosive inside, I probably wouldn't have noticed. And now here I was, only a few feet from the president, easily close enough for a good-size blast to wipe him out.

Which would also wipe me out as well.

As I considered this, something clicked inside my jacket. Something very small. I barely felt it. If my senses hadn't been heightened, I would never have noticed it—and it was completely possible that I was so keyed up that I was merely imagining things—but I knew that if there was ever a time to trust my instincts, this was it, because if I didn't, then I wouldn't have much more time left, period. So even though almost every person in the West Wing was already looking my way, I had no choice but to behave like a total maniac.

I suddenly bolted past the president, shrugging off my jacket as fast as I could.

In any other building, I would have headed for a window, hoping to open it and toss the jacket outside. But I knew the windows inside the West Wing were made of bulletproof glass and probably didn't even open for security reasons. Meanwhile, there were too many people between me and the door I'd entered through to return that way, so the only real option—the only place in the West Wing that appeared devoid of people—was the room that the president himself had just exited.

The Oval Office.

There were Secret Service agents posted between me and the office, but they seemed perplexed by my sudden run, rather than concerned by it. After all, their job was to keep people from running *toward* the president and I was running away from him. So they, and pretty much everyone else, seemed to think I was sprinting toward the Oval Office because I desperately wanted to see it.

In their defense, this probably made much more sense than the idea that I was running there to dispose of a bomb that had been slipped into my jacket because I'd been used as a patsy by an international consortium of evil agents dedicated to causing chaos and mayhem.

So instead of tackling me or pistol-whipping me, they merely stepped into my path with their hands up, like school monitors. "Whoa there, kiddo," one said.

I didn't stop for them. I had my jacket mostly off by now—only my left wrist was still caught in the cuff—and I yelled, "Look out!" and plowed right through them.

"Ben!" Kimmy yelled. "Come back! That room isn't on our tour!"

The Secret Service agents grasped at me as I slipped between them, then spun around after me.

My stupid watch was caught on the cuff of the jacket.

I arrived at the Oval Office itself, catching a glimpse of the famous blue carpet and the red-striped couches and the big oak desk and the portraits of Lincoln and Washington.

It was smaller than I'd expected.

And yet it was still going to be a shame to blow it up.

At the moment, however, I was still far more concerned about blowing myself up along with it. My watch remained caught on the jacket. I yanked as hard as I could, ripping the jacket off my left arm, then flung it into the Oval Office, over the closest couch, and right onto the giant seal of the United States in the center of the carpet. Then I slammed the door shut just as the Secret Service grabbed me.

"Everyone get down!" I yelled, pulling free from them and diving behind the president's secretary's desk.

No one else took cover.

My jacket didn't explode, either.

Instead, there was an awkward, excruciating silence. Everyone in the West Wing, including the president of the United States of America, stared at me like I was a moron.

I had never been so embarrassed in my entire life.

Jason Stern seemed even more mortified than I was, given that I was supposed to be his friend. "Ben has mental problems," he told everyone. "I've only invited him here as an act of charity. You know, to help the deranged."

At which point, the Oval Office exploded.

There was a deafening blast, and the walls trembled as though an earthquake had hit. The office door tore off its hinges and flew into the West Wing, nailing both the Secret Service agents near me hard enough to knock them on their butts. A ball of fire rolled through the gap where the door had been.

Now everyone dove for cover. Four Secret Service agents tackled the president, knocking him to the floor. Two more tackled Jason Stern.

The fireball sailed over their heads, scorching the furniture, setting memos on fire, and singeing our hair.

The sprinkler system came on, dousing everyone with water and shorting out all the computers. Several exploded in sprays of electrical sparks.

I glanced toward the president. His face was blackened from smoke and one of his eyebrows appeared to have been charbroiled, but other than that, he was alive and well.

So was everyone else in the West Wing.

The Oval Office wasn't doing as well, though.

The windows had blown out, the furniture was decimated, and despite the gushing sprinklers, a fire was blazing in the middle of the room.

"Oh my God!" Kimmy screamed. "Jacqueline Kennedy picked out that carpet! And now it's ruined!"

Around the West Wing, people scattered every which way. Some were running for their lives, fleeing the burning building. Others were rushing toward the fire, hoping to help put it out. Secret Service agents were swarming the president. From my position, facedown on the carpet, I could no longer see Vladimir Gorsky. It appeared he had fled.

Jason Stern lay on the floor close to me, no longer

anywhere near as cocky as he had been before the explosion. Instead, he was crying like a baby.

I got to my feet, hoping to catch a glimpse of Gorsky, but I'd barely been up for a second before a team of Secret Service agents flattened me. They shoved me right back down into the soaked carpet and aimed a dozen guns at me at once.

"Stay right there, kid," one of them warned. "You're under arrest."

APPREHENSION

The White House
Washington, DC
February 11
1600 hours

This time I was deemed too big a threat to be left
in the White House jail. Instead, the Secret Service decided
to remove me from the property immediately. I was yanked
back to my feet and hustled away amid a scrum of agents.

"I'm not an assassin!" I protested. "I've been set up!"

"You just tried to blow up the president," an agent
growled in my ear. "That looked like an assassination attempt
to me."

I cased the West Wing desperately, searching for the

president, hoping he would come to my rescue and admit that he'd brought me on board as a covert agent, but Courtney and another set of Secret Service agents had already rushed him off somewhere else. Either they were concerned that another bomb might go off, or they simply didn't want him to get wet from the sprinklers and catch cold.

I was rushed outside, into the wind tunnel between the White House and the EEOB. The photographers and journalists were no longer merely lounging around. The explosion was big news, and they were doing all they could to record it. A hundred cameras were documenting the flaming wreckage, though they quickly shifted to me as the Secret Service dragged me past.

"I didn't try to blow up the president!" I argued. "Someone else did. I saved his life!"

No one responded. It was possible no one had heard. The agents were all talking among themselves and were now being barraged with questions from all the reporters: "What happened?" "Was that boy responsible?" "What's his name?" "Is the president hurt?"

One agent, an older woman who appeared to have some seniority, stopped to inform the reporters that the president was fine—"thanks to the brave actions of the Secret Service"—but that no further questions would be answered at this time.

A black sedan with tinted windows skidded to a stop in the driveway between the West Wing and the EEOB. I was tossed into the backseat and locked inside.

The car was quite luxurious, but there was no doubt that I was trapped in the back. There was that same plate of thick, impenetrable glass between me and the front seat, but this time there were no locks or handles on the inside doors for me to let myself out. I was basically in the world's fanciest squad car. After the cacophony outside, it was surprisingly quiet. The din of the reporters was now only a distant murmur.

In the new silence, I realized my ears were still ringing from the explosion. There was a low, constant hum inside my head.

A tough-looking agent in his mid-twenties with a crew cut and sunglasses, despite the fact that it was cloudy and gray outside, sat at the wheel of the car. Another agent, this one looking older and even tougher, slid into the passenger seat. "Go," he ordered.

The driver hit the gas and the car lurched forward. Two black SUVs, identical to the one I'd been in with the president, swerved into position in front of us and behind us. Sirens on them wailed and the traffic in the street obediently pulled over. Our small motorcade raced off the White House property.

I swiveled around to look out the back window. The Oval Office was still on fire, sending clouds of smoke billowing into the sky. A gaping hole had been torn in its famous curved white wall, like a handful gouged out of a wedding cake. A flaming footstool, flung out by the explosion, was lodged in the branches of a jacaranda tree.

Oh boy, I thought. *I'm really going to be in trouble for this one.*

The previous fall, I had accidentally blown up the school principal's office and had been punished with immediate expulsion from spy school. Now I'd blown up the most famous office in America. For all I knew, I'd get kicked out of the country for that.

Hundreds of passersby had become spectators. They crowded the sidewalks, taking pictures with their phones. Thousands more were coming, pouring out of office buildings and rushing over in waves from the nearby monuments to see what had happened. Some paused to photograph my motorcade, thinking it might be important, then went right back to photographing the burning Oval Office again.

I scanned the crowds, hoping that Cyrus or Erica might be among them, but I didn't see a single familiar face.

The motorcade raced past the Ellipse to the south of the White House grounds and hooked a right onto Constitution Avenue, skirting the edge of the National Mall.

"I didn't try to kill the president," I said to the agents in the car. "I was only used as a pawn by people who *did* want to kill him."

I figured they probably wouldn't believe me, but it couldn't hurt to try. I didn't even know if they could hear me through the glass barrier between us.

They could. The older agent in the passenger seat turned to face me. Despite the dreary day, he was wearing sunglasses too, but I could tell he was glaring at me from behind them. "Who are you working for?" he asked.

Unfortunately, I couldn't tell him the truth. My mission for the CIA was unofficial, my status as an agent-in-training was classified—and chances were, he'd never believe it anyhow. Instead, I said, "I'm not working for anybody. I'm a friend of Jason's."

"You two didn't look like friends to me."

"Whoever did this planted a bomb in my jacket," I insisted. "I'm guessing they waited until they knew I was inside, then used a remote radio trigger. That means they were probably close to the White House, keeping an eye on me. If you don't act now, they'll get away!"

"Remote radio trigger?" the older agent asked suspiciously. "You know an awful lot about how bombs work for someone claiming to be innocent."

"I *am* innocent! The real bad guys are still out there!"

"I'm sure they are," the older agent agreed. "No kid could mastermind an operation like this. Which is why you need to tell us who you're working for. *Now*. If you don't . . . there will be consequences." He said the final word as ominously as he could.

"Consequences?" I repeated. "Like what?"

The agent didn't reply. Instead, he gave me a malicious smile.

The motorcade veered past the Vietnam Veterans Memorial and onto the road that looped around the Lincoln Memorial.

Which meant we were heading out of Washington, DC, and toward Virginia. Most of the U.S. government operated inside the city, but there were several departments located on the other side of the Potomac. The Secret Service worked for the Department of Homeland Security, which was head-quartered in the Pentagon, which I could see across the Potomac River in the distance: an enormous squat building surrounded by acres of parking lots. The CIA also had its headquarters a bit farther away in Virginia, at Langley.

"Where are you taking me?" I asked.

"Where we can get the truth out of you," the older agent replied.

"I'm *telling* you the truth," I pointed out. "You're just not listening to it."

The motorcade passed the Lincoln Memorial, veered onto the Arlington Memorial Bridge—and stopped dead in traffic. A massive road construction project was under way, doing repair work to the bridge. Two construction cranes loomed overhead, maneuvering heavy loads of metal and cement. One side of the bridge was completely shut down to traffic and was instead filled with dozens of trucks and hundreds of workers. Traffic was forced onto the other side of the bridge, which narrowed to one lane in both directions. Even though we had our sirens on, there was no shoulder for the cars ahead of us to pull over on.

"Instead of dragging me all the way to Virginia," I said, "why don't you call Cyrus Hale at the CIA? He's a friend of mine. He'll vouch for me, and we can get this whole thing straightened out."

Once again, the older agent didn't reply. Although this time, he wasn't doing it to make me uneasy. He was distracted by the traffic. "Why'd you go this way?" he asked the driver angrily. "You know this road's a mess."

"I was following *them*," the driver said, pointing at the big black SUV in front of us. "If you've got a problem with the route, talk to those guys."

"There's like a hundred apps that tell you the fastest way from place to place," the older agent griped. "Those guys can't figure out how to use one of them? There's a national security crisis happening and we're stuck in traffic."

I began to grow nervous, and it wasn't merely because I'd been framed for the attempted assassination of the president and arrested by the Secret Service. All that was bad enough, but now we were sitting ducks. We were out over the river, boxed in on both sides by our own SUVs, and SPYDER was on the loose. Given everything that had happened that day—and Erica's concern for my safety that morning—it seemed our current position was a very bad place to be.

I glanced all around us, on the alert for trouble. The roadwork appeared to be progressing normally, with trucks hauling loads and construction workers jackhammering and welding. . . .

Except for one spot. Behind us, on the mainland, by the base of one of the cranes, some of the workers were looking about worriedly, as though something had startled them. I caught a glimpse of someone darting through the construction equipment.

I turned back to the front seat, where the agents were still bickering about the traffic.

"We should've taken the Teddy Roosevelt Bridge," the older one was saying. "This one has been a disaster for months."

"Then why didn't you say something before we got onto it?" the driver asked.

"I was busy intimidating the suspect!" the older one exclaimed, then pointed to the SUV ahead of us. "*They* were supposed to be driving! If they wanted me to do the driving, they can feel free to do the intimidation."

"Uh, guys," I said. "I really think we need to get out of here."

"That makes two of us," the older agent said. He leaned over and pounded on the car horn.

"What's that gonna do?" the driver asked. "We've got all these sirens going already. We're obviously government vehicles. You think now that you've honked, all the other drivers are going to say, 'Oh, *now* I see it's an emergency' and drive off the bridge?"

The older agent simply honked the horn again.

All the other drivers started honking too, pounding on their horns in frustration. The bridge became a cacophony of car horns.

Amid all the clamor, I heard a dull thud right beside me.

I spun around to see a web of cracks spreading across the car window, radiating out from a central divot in the glass.

A year before, I wouldn't have had any idea what could

have caused that. But now that I'd lived through multiple action sequences, I knew all too well.

In quick succession, several more objects thudded into the windows of the car, making a series of webs across the passenger side.

The Secret Service agents instantly forgot all about the traffic.

Someone was shooting at us.

DEATH TRAP

Arlington Memorial Bridge

Washington, DC

February 11

1630 hours

I dropped onto the backseat and curled into the fetal position.

Another line of bullets thunked across the windows, leaving even more webs in the glass. The gunfire then moved on to the SUV ahead of us, riddling the vehicle with golf-ball-size dents.

"Don't worry!" the older agent told me. "This entire car is bulletproof! As long as we stay in here, they won't be able to get us!"

I noticed that, despite his assurances, he was still ducked down below the windows, which made me think that, after a certain number of hits, they might *stop* being bulletproof.

Unfortunately, there wasn't much I could do except stay in the car. I was locked in the back and we were trapped on the road. Many of the innocent drivers ahead of us, who didn't have bulletproof cars, had abandoned their vehicles and leapt into the Potomac. Without drivers, their cars were going to keep sitting there in our way, meaning we were going to stay boxed in and at the mercy of the shooter.

The driver was on the radio, calling for backup. "This is Gamma Team. We are with the package on the Arlington Bridge, stuck in traffic and sustaining heavy fire."

"The Arlington Bridge?" the radio dispatcher replied with disbelief. "That thing's a mess. Why didn't you take the Roosevelt?"

"Because we didn't!" howled the driver. "We need backup right now!"

"Can you tell where the assault is coming from?" the dispatcher asked.

"Not exactly," the driver reported. "Most likely from the construction site."

I chanced a look back through the window, which was now so webbed with cracks, it was like trying to see through a kaleidoscope. The construction workers were all running for cover, but it was impossible to tell where the shots were coming from. There were a thousand places for shooters to hide: stacks of iron beams, pallets of concrete, dozens of construction vehicles.

More bullets rattled the car.

"Why are they shooting at *us*?" the driver exclaimed. "We're not with the president!"

The older agent peered over the front seat at me, a sudden realization in his eyes. "They're *not* shooting at us," he said to me. "They're shooting at *you*! Your associates know you can name them and now they're trying to make sure you don't!"

Which was what I'd deduced myself. Sort of. I wasn't working for SPYDER, but it made sense that they wanted to get rid of me.

If everything had gone the way SPYDER had planned, the president and I both would have been blown to bits—and I'd have looked like the bomber. This fit SPYDER's standard operating procedure: Commit a crime, frame someone else for it, and leave no trace of their own involvement. However, I'd thwarted their plans yet again. The president was still alive and so was I—the only person who knew what SPYDER had actually done and how they had done it. So they had to whack me before I spilled the beans.

Unfortunately, SPYDER knew how to take care of

business. They had manipulated Cyrus into inserting me inside the White House, then tricked me into taking in the bomb. Now they'd picked the perfect spot for an ambush, and chances were, they were well aware I was inside a bulletproof car. Which meant they probably had a plan to deal with it.

I looked out through the front window, to where the other drivers had leapt into the Potomac. It wasn't the safest escape strategy imaginable, but it was the best at hand. "We need to get out of here!" I told the agents. "We're not safe in this car!"

"We're safer in here than we are outside it," the older agent insisted. "I told you, this thing's bulletproof. It can stand up to anything they throw at us."

A mechanical groan echoed across the construction site. I turned back that way to see that one of the big cranes was now in motion. The long arm was swinging our way far more quickly than it should have been, whipping the giant metal hook in our direction.

"Can this car stand up to *that*?" I asked.

"Er . . ." The older agent gulped, worry creasing his face. "Maybe not."

"Then unlock the doors!" I screamed.

The agents did. Except, they only unlocked *their* doors. They might have sworn to protect the president with their lives, but they were apparently perfectly willing to let me die on their watch. They scrambled out of the car and fled down the bridge, leaving me trapped in the backseat.

The cable connecting the giant hook to the crane played out, then stopped short with a sudden resounding twang. As the crane's arm came around, the hook arced through the air on a collision course with the car.

I dropped into the footwell between the seats, curled into a ball, and hoped for a miracle.

The hook slammed into the car. There was a rending of metal and a tinkle of glass. The sedan jolted wildly, then stopped abruptly as it crashed into something. The entire impact took less than a second.

I felt a blast of cold air.

I'd been jostled hard by the impact, but was otherwise all right, save for the sudden chill. Wishing I still had my winter jacket (without the bomb), I unfolded myself to see what had happened.

The roof of the car was no longer there. Instead, there was only slate-gray sky above me.

I cautiously got to my feet.

The crane's hook had sheared the roof right off the sedan, turning it into a convertible, and then thrown the car itself up onto the guardrail. The car's entire front end now jutted off the side of the bridge, the tires dangling over the water.

Meanwhile, the hook—with the car's roof still speared on it—reached the high point of its trajectory over the river and swung back toward me. It was coming in fast, as big and deadly as a wrecking ball.

As if that wasn't bad enough, the sedan suddenly tilted forward and began sliding over the guardrail. It was about to tumble into the river—with me in it.

I judged the pitch of the car, the speed of the hook, and the depth of the water below, then quickly calculated the optimal moment to leap from the car and not get killed.

Then I leapt.

The hook and the car roof whizzed back mere inches above me, then collided with the rest of the sedan as it tumbled off the guardrail. I didn't see the results, as I was currently plummeting toward the water, but I felt it. The gas tank ruptured and the sedan exploded, sending a wave of heat, fire, and auto parts into the air.

I plunged into the river. The water was murky and opaque, darkened with mud and silt and the poop of a million Canada geese, but I went as far down as I could anyhow. Above me, flaming bits of sedan plunked into the river, so hot that they sizzled as they sank past.

The current grabbed me and whisked me downriver. I held my breath and drifted as far as I could before surfacing.

Back on the bridge, things were even more chaotic now

than they had been before. In addition to the panic induced by SPYDER, there was now the flaming wreckage of the car and the crane hook swinging about wildly. People were running every which way, and the Secret Service agents—easily visible since they were the only ones wearing sunglasses—seemed to have forgotten all about me for the moment.

SPYDER probably hadn't, though.

I dove back down into the water again and swam with the current. It was hard going and the water was freezing, but I wanted to stay out of sight as long as I could. The murkiness now worked to my advantage. I didn't have to go far below the surface to vanish from sight.

I couldn't stand the cold for very long, though. In the icy water, I felt like I was turning into a Popsicle. I lasted until a point about an eighth of a mile from the bridge, then swam to the bank behind the cover of a clump of trees. I was still within sight of the bridge, but several other people who'd jumped off it were climbing out of the water there, so I was able to camouflage myself among them. I clambered up the bank and bolted across the riverside road, angling back toward the city. A cold wind knifed through my damp clothes, but I kept running as fast as I could, hoping to leave both the Secret Service and SPYDER behind.

No one shot at me. No one even seemed to notice me.

Or so I hoped.

Thirteen months earlier, Erica Hale had rescued me from SPYDER at virtually the exact same spot where I'd climbed out of the river, then led me to safety in one of the strangest places I could have ever imagined. Now I retraced our steps. I cut across the baseball fields in Potomac Park, crossed Independence Avenue, and ducked into the small fringe of woods that lined the south side of the Reflecting Pool.

Tucked away in the trees, overlooked by tourists and forgotten by locals, stood a small monument to President Chester Alan Arthur. I made sure no one was watching me, then twisted a ring on his stone finger, exactly the way Erica had.

An ancient keypad popped open on the monument. I'd been paying close attention when Erica had entered the code, and thanks to my gift for memorizing numbers, I still knew it by heart. I tapped it into the keypad.

With a grumble, the statue rotated ninety degrees, revealing a staircase hidden beneath it, descending into the earth. I slipped down it and the statue slid back into place over my head.

The stairs led down one floor into an old stone tunnel. I fumbled along the wall for the light switch and flipped it on. A series of antique Edison bulbs flickered to life, illuminating the length of the tunnel, which led all the way back under the Mall to the base of the Washington Monument.

At the other end was a secret hatch that led to the ground floor of the obelisk. The monument itself, Erica had taught me, wasn't actually designed for tourism at all, but had been constructed by one of the earliest U.S. spy agencies as a lookout tower during the Civil War. Unfortunately, while I knew how to access the tunnel, I couldn't get into the monument. I needed a key for that, and Erica and her family were the only ones who had them. Erica had locked the door behind us when we'd left the monument that night, and given the look of things, no one had been back inside the secret tunnel since then. I could still see the imprints of my own shoes from thirteen months before in the dust on the floor.

Not that it would have been a great idea to enter a crowded monument at the moment anyhow. At least a few of the photographers who had snapped pictures of me being arrested after the White House bombing would have certainly uploaded the photos to the Internet. By now I was quite likely the most famous fugitive in America, and a drenched teenager suddenly emerging from a secret passage in the floor of the Washington Monument would probably get a lot of attention from the tourists inside. Someone was bound to recognize me and call the police, or the FBI, or maybe even the army.

Even worse, SPYDER was also looking for me. I was far more concerned about them finding me than I was about law enforcement. Law enforcement would arrest me. SPYDER would kill me.

So for the time being, the tunnel itself was the safest place I could think of. SPYDER hadn't known about it before, so they probably didn't know about it now, and no one in any branch of U.S. security knew about it either. It was dank and gloomy, but it was better than being dead.

It was also cold, though. In my wet clothes, I was shivering as though my body was experiencing its own private earthquake. Thankfully, when I'd been in the tunnel before, I'd left a jacket behind. It was a shimmery silver jacket made out of some kind of space-age heat-retaining material designed by NASA. Erica had given it to me when we'd hid out there before, but she'd made me leave it behind when we'd left. We'd been lying low at the time, and shimmery silver jackets tended to make you stand out in a crowd.

It was still right where I'd left it, folded up and tucked in a wedge of rock.

I peeled off my wet clothes and slipped the jacket on. It sealed my body heat in and warmed me quickly.

Then I dug out my smartphone. It was an official academy model, completely untraceable, so I wouldn't have to worry about SPYDER tracking my calls.

To my dismay, it was dead. Whether it had been killed by the water or the various explosions, I couldn't say. It didn't matter. It was no longer useful. Which meant I couldn't call any of my friends back at spy school for help. (Erica had never seen fit to give me her phone number, but I knew everyone else's by heart.)

The ground above me was now most likely crawling with SPYDER agents, law enforcement agents, and possibly even SPYDER agents pretending to be law enforcement agents. It was going to be a long time before I could risk going back up there again.

I was wanted for trying to kill the president, on the run from SPYDER, and completely on my own, without any way to contact help.

All in all, it had turned out to be a tremendously cruddy day.

Still, moping around wasn't going to solve any problems for me. If I had learned anything from Erica Hale, it was that if I wanted to solve my problems, I had to be proactive.

I started looked for something I could set on fire.

WARNING

Underneath the National Mall
Washington, DC
February 12
0100 hours

The ancient wooden beams that supported
the secret tunnel turned out to be dry and flammable. I used
a rock to chip off a few pieces of several different ones—I
didn't want to weaken any of them to the point where the
tunnel might collapse on my head—and gathered a pile of
kindling. Then I found two pieces of flint among the rubble
and banged them together to get a spark. The academy's
wilderness survival instructor, Woodchuck Wallace, usually
took only about thirty seconds to ignite a fire this way.

It took me forty-five minutes.

I finally managed it, though. By this time, despite my shimmery space-age jacket, I was very close to freezing to death. The jacket didn't cover my legs, which now felt like they were made of ice, and my fingers and toes had numbed to the point that I could barely sense them. I hovered over the flames until I got some feeling back, then wrung out my wet clothes and lay them to dry by the fire.

The rest of my time in the tunnel was the most boring seven hours of my entire life.

Yes, I was on the run from both the U.S. government and an exceptionally evil organization. But that didn't change the fact that sitting in a dark tunnel with nothing to do but stare at a fire is excruciatingly dull. At times I actually missed the earlier part of the day when I'd been actively fleeing for my life. However, I didn't miss it quite enough to want to relive the experience of nearly dying again, so I stayed put and waited.

I spent much of my night trying to work out how SPYDER had managed to take advantage of me in the first place.

To begin with, they had obviously tricked Cyrus into believing an assassination plot was under way and that they had an agent inside the White House. Cyrus had told me he'd picked up chatter to this effect, meaning he'd heard it from various sources, but SPYDER had planted fake chatter before. It simply took a few people plotting on phone lines that they knew the CIA had tapped. It wouldn't have been easy to fool Cyrus, but SPYDER was an extremely patient and devious organization. It was likely they'd spent months, if not years, planning this attack.

Getting the bomb in my jacket would have been trickier. Since the heating was awful at spy school, I had worn my jacket most of the day, even in class, but a talented enemy agent could have slipped a bomb into the lining even while I was wearing it, like a pickpocket working in reverse. The best opportunity for this seemed to be my subway ride down to the White House. The Metro had been extremely crowded; I had passed thousands of people closely in the tunnels and been crammed in with hundreds on the train. I had also been distracted, focused on the task ahead of me—how to handle Jason Stern and root out SPYDER's mole—rather than what was going on around me at the moment. It was a rookie mistake that Erica would be disgusted by. When confronting SPYDER, you always had to be on the alert. I had been so busy thinking about who their inside man might be that I'd dropped my guard, allowing them to turn me into the very inside man I was looking for.

I couldn't guarantee SPYDER had armed me on the train, but I didn't have much else to go on. It would have been helpful to see the remnants of the bomb itself, but they had probably been vaporized along with half of the Oval Office. If any evidence was left, the Secret Service would have it locked up tight by now.

By one in the morning, I couldn't take it anymore. SPYDER or not, I had to move. My clothes were now warm and dry, and I was starving. More importantly, I had to stop worrying about SPYDER catching me and start thinking about how I could help catch SPYDER. The longer they had to regroup after their failed bombing, the more time they had to cover their tracks. Hopefully, Cyrus and Erica were already on their tail, but I needed to get back in contact with them and join the hunt.

I got dressed, stomped out my fire, left the shimmery jacket behind—Erica was right; it was way too noticeable—and returned to the hidden staircase. Then I waited there for five minutes, listening to the world above for any telltale sounds that SPYDER was lying in wait for me. I didn't hear any. I didn't really even know what those telltale sounds might be—except for someone whispering "Has anyone killed Ben yet?"—but I was anxious and paranoid and trying my best not to get killed.

Eventually, I gathered my nerve and entered the code that made the statue swing out, uncovering the staircase. Then I emerged into the thicket of trees beside the Reflecting Pool.

No one was lying in wait for me.

I made my way back toward the heart of Washington.

I did my best to stay in the shadows and avoid being seen. Sometimes being a kid can really work against you, like when you're trying to get around a city at one in the morning. No one looks twice at an adult walking around at one in the morning: There were even a few of them visiting the monuments that late, enjoying having the sites almost to themselves. But people notice a kid on his own, out long after curfew, without a jacket in the dead of winter. Quite often, they call the police, thinking that something bad must have happened—or that you're up to no good. The last thing I needed was the police; they'd bounce me right over to the Secret Service. So I kept my distance from any other humans.

The closest part of the city to where I'd hidden out was the area around the White House. I figured it was actually somewhat safe to head there. The Secret Service probably assumed that the *last* place I'd go was right back where I'd theoretically committed the crime.

The White House was even more cordoned off than usual. The streets and sidewalks all around the building had been shut down. The closest glimpse I could get was from all the way across the Ellipse to the south of the White House. From that distance, I couldn't tell if any investigating was still going on, but it appeared that construction crews had already gone to work trying to cover up the damage. Plastic sheeting had been stretched over the gaping hole to protect what remained of the Oval Office from the elements, as though they were saran-wrapping the world's biggest sandwich. The hole was a dark scar on the building, and I felt terrible for my part in causing it.

There was a hotel only a few blocks east of the White House, across the street from a public fountain. Like any fountain in Washington, tourists had thrown change into it for no good reason. The spouts had been turned off for the night, which allowed me to scoop a few dollars' worth of change out. I then slipped through one of the less-used hotel doors and found an actual working pay phone on the conference level by the bathrooms.

I dialed Zoe's number, which I knew by heart.

Given that it was the middle of the night, I had expected that I'd wake her with my call. To my surprise, she answered before the end of the first ring. "Hello?"

"Hey. It's Ben. What are you doing up?"

"Hoping you'd call! I've been so worried about you. The news was saying that you . . ." The words seemed to catch in Zoe's throat. "That you might have drowned."

"I didn't."

"Yeah, I figured that out. Where are you?"

"Virginia," I lied. There was an extremely good chance the call was being monitored. Of course, there was also an extremely good chance it was being traced as well, meaning I didn't have much time before law enforcement came looking for me. "Zoe, I swear, I'm innocent. . . ."

"You don't have to explain to me. I know you were set up."

"You do? How?"

"Because I *know* you, Ben. I'm your friend! You would never try to kill the president."

"Well, you're probably one of the only people who believes that."

"No kidding. Campus is crawling with agents. CIA, FBI, Secret Service, and who knows what else. Everyone's looking for you."

"That's why I need your help. Can you get to Erica and ask her to get in touch with Cyrus for me?"

"Uh, Ben . . ."

"Tell her I'm still alive and that I can explain exactly what happened."

"Ben . . ."

"Then figure out a way for Cyrus to meet up with me and I'll call you back tomorrow to find out what it is. . . ."

"Ben!" Zoe said sharply. "Cyrus isn't going to help you!"

"Of course he is. He put me on this mission in the first place."

"Well, now he thinks you betrayed him. *He's* the one leading the whole investigation to track you down."

I fell silent, dumbfounded. I tried to think of what to do next, but came up blank. Having the Hale family bail me out had been my entire plan; I didn't have a backup.

"I'm sorry, Ben," Zoe said. "He thinks you're a mole for SPYDER."

"*Me?* But I helped defeat SPYDER! I blew up their head-quarters!"

"Cyrus says that doesn't mean they couldn't have bought you off anyhow. SPYDER has flipped plenty of agents before. And they have a track record of offering you a job. . . ."

"Which I've always turned down!"

"You don't have to tell *me* that. I'm on your side here."

I calmed a bit, taking heart in that. "Who else is?"

"Jawa and Chip, of course."

"And Mike?"

"I guess. I don't know Mike as well as you do, but he's your best friend, right? And there's also Warren. . . ."

"Really? I thought he'd be leading the crusade against me."

"Warren might be snotty with you a lot, but that's because he's jealous of you. He really respects you."

"Oh." I paused before asking the next name, because I was worried I might not like the answer. "How about Erica?"

Zoe paused too, because she knew I wouldn't like the answer. "I don't know which side she's on."

"Really?"

"I've barely seen her. And you're the only one she talks to. I'd like to think that she believes you're innocent, but you know how by-the-book she is. If you think we can trust her, though, I'll go to her."

"You don't have to go to her," said a voice on the other end of the line, slightly distant, as if from somewhere in the room behind Zoe. "I'm right here."

Erica.

Zoe gasped in surprise. I could guess what had happened. Erica had done her standard suddenly-appear-out-of-nowhere trick, having snuck up on Zoe at some point in the conversation. If they were in Zoe's room, Erica could have infiltrated it without any trouble. The locks on our dormitory doors were disturbingly easy to pick, and frankly, Erica could infiltrate almost any place she wanted.

"How long have you been here?" Zoe asked.

"Long enough," Erica replied, which was followed by the sound of her snatching Zoe's phone from her. She then spoke directly to me, so angry I could practically feel it radiating over the phone line. "I trusted you, Ben. And you betrayed me!"

"I didn't do it!" I exclaimed. "I was set up by SPYDER!"

"Don't try to lie your way out of this. I know exactly what happened. They turned you. Just like they've turned everyone else."

Her words were so harsh, they actually caused me pain. I felt like I'd been stabbed in the gut. I cared a great deal for Erica—and I'd thought that she cared for me too, at least a bit, in her own personal way. Hearing that she thought I'd betrayed her didn't merely mean that she hated me. . . . It also meant that she had never really known what kind of person I was to begin with.

"That's not true!" I heard Zoe argue in the background. "Ben would never . . ."

Her words suddenly trailed off. It was possible that Erica had knocked her unconscious, though equally likely that Erica had simply given her a stare so hard that she'd fallen silent in fear.

"They didn't turn me, Erica," I said. "I swear. And now I need your help!"

"Why would I help you? You're even worse than Joshua Hallal."

Now I felt like the knife in my gut had been twisted. Joshua Hallal had been one of the best students at the Academy of Espionage before defecting to SPYDER. He was one of the most ruthless, dangerous, horrible people I'd ever met—and Erica thought he was a better person than me.

This did give me a hint as to why Erica was so angry, though. She'd had a crush on Joshua and been devastated when she learned of his betrayal. Afterward, she had been wary about trusting anyone else, but I had finally convinced her to be my friend—or at least, the closest thing she had to a friend. And now she thought that I'd betrayed her as well.

I glanced at my watch. I had already been on the phone way too long. Federal agents would be swarming the building soon. But I knew I had to try to plead my case to Erica. If she remained against me, I was lost.

"I'm not like Joshua," I told her. "And you know it. If you think about it—about *me*—I hope you'll realize who I really am. . . ."

"You don't have to hope anything for me," Erica interrupted. "*You're* the one who needs to find hope. You're going to need it. Because I'm coming for you, Ben. There's nowhere you can run. There's nowhere you can hide. I'm going to make it my life's mission to hunt you down. I will not rest until I find you. Do you understand?"

The anger in her voice was so frightening, so immediate, I felt as though she were right there in front of me, instead of speaking over the phone.

I'd had some low moments as a spy-in-training, but this was the lowest by far. The Death Valley of emotion. I had lost the faith of the one person I'd trusted to help me. And now she was so upset, she was determined to bring me to justice herself. Even though SPYDER had tried to kill me twice that day, it was hard to imagine they could have done anything worse than this.

It took almost every ounce of strength I had to say, "I understand."

Then I hung up. I'd already taken too great a risk staying on the phone as long as I had. I heard the distant screech of tires on the street outside the hotel, the Secret Service or the CIA or some other group of agents rushing there to arrest me.

I had maybe three seconds, if that, to get the jump on them.

So I ran.

EVASIVE ACTION

The Knickerbocker Hotel

Washington, DC

February 12

0200 hours

I had already planned out an escape route on my way into the hotel. It was one of the first lessons I'd learned at spy school: Never let yourself get boxed in.

There was a staircase close to the phone bank. I raced down it to the lowest floor. This was the hotel's service area, a warren of cement tunnels that led past the kitchen, laundry, and storage rooms. At this time of night, they were almost empty.

I was far enough down that I could no longer hear the

agents who had come for me, but I presumed they had blocked the main exits and gone straight for the phones, hoping to ambush me there. My main advantage was that they probably thought I was only a normal kid. A kid who'd tried to blow up the president . . . but still a kid. My status as a spy-in-training was classified and my mission at the White House had been unauthorized. So they wouldn't expect me to have the skills and know-how to elude a manhunt.

In truth, I wasn't completely sure I had the skills and know-how to elude a manhunt either, but I was going to give it my best shot.

Even though Erica didn't believe me, even though she was coming after me herself, I still had to fight. If I got caught, I was done for. SPYDER had set me up too well. I'd be charged with their crime and locked up for the rest of my life—if they didn't figure out a way to kill me first. But if I could stay free . . . Zoe still had faith in me. And so did some of my friends. Maybe there was a way we could all work together to prove my innocence and nail SPYDER.

Of course, that wouldn't be easy.

I snatched a jet-black waiter's jacket from the hotel laundry and slipped it on. Not to blend in, but to stay warm. My old jacket had been used as a bomb and it was still cold outside. The new jacket was big on me, but in theory, that would provide even better insulation.

One of the service tunnels led to the loading dock, where hotel supplies were delivered in bulk. The two enormous garage doors were open, leading to an alleyway around the corner from the main entrance to the hotel.

The law enforcement agents, thinking I was a normal kid, hadn't bothered to cover this route. They had focused on the public entrances instead.

I raced outside, dashed to the corner—and slowed to a walk. Someone running down a city street in the middle of the night would get more attention than someone walking. I still kept to the shadows, but did my best to behave in a calm and collected manner, as though I had a perfectly rational reason for wandering around the city at two in the morning.

As I rounded the corner, I noticed that there were, indeed, several black Secret Service SUVs parked in the street in front of the hotel, each with an agent at the wheel. The agents were all a good distance away from me, though, and were focused on the main entrance rather than on me. I only allowed myself a quick glance in their direction—staring too long might have looked suspicious, as well as revealed my face—then turned away and continued down the street in the opposite direction from the hotel.

I had no idea if any of the agents noticed me or not. I didn't look back. I crossed the street at the light and casually slipped around the corner of the enormous federal building, disappearing from the agents' line of sight.

Then I started running again.

In the distance behind me, back by the hotel, I heard shouting. I couldn't make out the words, but it had the urgent tone of federal agents who'd realized that the suspected assassin they were hunting had given them the slip. I heard the SUVs' engines start up again, followed by the squeal of tires.

There was a Metro station entrance ahead of me, an escalator angling down into the subway tunnels far below. I almost went that way, but decided not to at the last second. It would have taken me off the street, but it would have been too obvious an escape route. At another time of day, when subway trains were running every few minutes, it might have worked. But now, in the middle of the night, it could be an hour before the next train, and until one came, the station was a dead end. Yes, I could have fled down the tunnels, but then I'd have to worry about oncoming trains and stepping on the third rail, both of which meant instant death. I wasn't a big fan of instant death.

So I did something that *felt* riskier, although I'd been taught that it wasn't (in theory, at least). I kept running along the sidewalk, right out in the open, even though the Secret Service was coming. I hauled down the street as fast as my legs would carry me, darted across Constitution Avenue onto the grounds of the Smithsonian National Museum of American History . . .

Then I dropped to the ground on the lawn and hid in plain sight.

There was plenty of dense landscaping behind me, but people *expected* you to hide in dense landscaping. They didn't expect you to flatten yourself down on a lawn in front of the landscaping, but when the lawn was cast in shadow and the night was dark, it was amazing how well you could blend in. Plus, you could see a lot better when you were out in the open than you could when you were crouched behind a bush.

Two seconds later, tires screeched around the corner by the federal building. One of the Secret Service SUVs came flying down the road, on the hunt for me. I figured that the other vehicles had fanned out in different directions.

The SUV skidded to a stop by the Metro station and discharged two agents, who raced down the escalator into it.

It appeared I'd made the right call not going that way.

The SUV then sped on toward me, but slowed when it approached the museum. By now it was close enough for me to see there was one agent driving and another in the passenger seat. The passenger aimed a klieg light out the window and cast a blindingly bright beam into the landscaping behind me, scrutinizing every last shrub. The beam swept right over my head, lighting up the plants like it was day-time, but didn't dip down to the lawn. In its glare, I could see the face of the agent holding it: Nasser, one of the guys from the White House. He was in an even fouler mood than usual.

"See anything?" the driver asked. I recognized the voice as that of Fry, Nasser's partner.

Nasser squinted in my direction for what felt like another minute, but which was actually only a few seconds. Then he shook his head. "Nothing. This is a goose chase. There's no chance the kid got all the way over here before we could. He must've gone some other direction. Or into the Metro."

"Let's check around the Natural History Museum."

"I'm telling you, he's not over here. We're gonna be wasting our time, poking around in the trees while someone else gets the kudos for finding that little punk."

"And if he really is over here and we let him get away, then we'll get booted from the Service. We're already on thin ice for letting him get past us with that bomb today." Fry pulled a U-turn and drove across the wide street toward the Natural History Museum. Nasser swept the landscaping there with the klieg light as well.

I stayed put on the lawn, watching them hunt for me, trying to figure out what to do next.

This was the first time since hanging up the phone that

I'd had a chance to really process my call with Zoe and Erica.

My first instinct was to cry.

Erica thought I had gone to the dark side. She had declared herself my enemy, and Erica was as formidable as enemies got. She wasn't merely the best spy-in-training at the academy; she was one of the best spies in the CIA, period. She was smarter than me, more capable than me, knew a whole lot more about spying than me, and she could kick my butt in a fight while reading a book at the same time. (I knew this last part for a fact. Erica had actually defeated me in a self-defense class without ever looking up from her copy of *Carpenter's Practical Guide to Knives and Blades*.)

As if that wasn't bad enough, Erica had a grudge against me too. She wasn't merely looking to capture me for glory. Instead, this was personal. Erica had been devastated when she learned that Joshua Hallal had defected to SPYDER. Now SPYDER had manipulated things so that she thought I'd betrayed her trust as well.

The more I thought about it, the more devious SPYDER's plan was. They hadn't merely made an attempt on the president's life: They had also convinced Erica that I was responsible. True, I had thwarted their ultimate plan and saved the president, but serious damage had still been done. My reputation was ruined. Even worse, Erica might never trust a fellow agent again. Despite her insistence that she didn't need other people, I knew she was wrong. A spy who didn't trust *anyone* could never succeed. So SPYDER had framed me and possibly handicapped Erica's promising career in one shot.

Now Erica would be coming for me. She had said so herself, claiming it was her mission to hunt me down. For all I knew, she was already on her way. If the Secret Service could trace my phone call, then so could she. . . .

I suddenly felt cold in a way that had nothing to do with the weather. My hiding in plain sight might have fooled the Secret Service, but it wouldn't fool Erica. Erica had taught me the trick in the first place. In fact, she had taught me every single thing I had been planning to do to keep from getting caught. For all I knew, she was watching me at that very moment.

Erica also knew where the secret tunnel under the Washington Monument was, so I couldn't go back and hide there again. I was lucky she hadn't found me while I was there. . . .

Something about that struck me as odd.

Why *hadn't* Erica come looking for me in the tunnel? If she was so determined to catch me, what was she doing back at school, eavesdropping on Zoe, rather than actively looking for me?

I tried to remember my conversation with her, straining to recall every last word. The more I thought about it, the more it seemed there was something important in what she'd said. Something I hadn't interpreted properly.

"You're the one who needs to find hope," she'd told me. *"You're going to need it. Because I'm coming for you, Ben. There's nowhere you can run. There's nowhere you can hide. I'm going to make it my life's mission to hunt you down. I will not rest until I find you."*

It had all been very scary when she'd said it, which made sense, because Erica had been trying to sound scary. But if I really reflected on her words, she had never said that she was going to capture me. She had merely said that she was coming for me.

So maybe she wasn't really angry at me at all. Maybe she had only been *pretending* to be angry.

If the government could trace the call, they could also eavesdrop on it, and since I was a fugitive, Erica couldn't say anything that would make her sound like she was on my side. The best she could do was leave hints for me.

Then again, I might have had things all wrong. Maybe Erica really *was* against me, and I was merely grasping at straws, desperately trying to convince myself she wasn't.

Along Constitution Avenue, the Secret Service SUV was still creeping along, Nasser and Fry scanning the landscaping outside the Natural History Museum with their klieg light.

You're the one who needs to find hope.

Even though I was supposed to be lying still, I snapped my head up in surprise. I had just understood what Erica had really meant. Or what I thought she'd meant.

For the first time in hours, I felt a smile creep across my face. If I was right, then maybe I wasn't as alone in this ordeal as I'd thought.

I knew what I had to do.

RECONNECTION

The National Mall

Washington, DC

February 12

0300 hours

It was a long wait until morning.

I watched Nasser and Fry continue on along Constitution Avenue, searching fruitlessly for me, until they got fed up and drove away. Then I spent another hour on the lawn, keeping an eye out for any other law enforcement agents. I spotted a few in the distance over the first fifteen minutes, but eventually they all seemed to give up the search. So I got to my feet and skulked back across the National Mall to the secret tunnel. I didn't know where else would be protected enough—or warm enough—for me to hide out. True, Erica could find me in the tunnel, but by this point I was relatively sure she was on my side. And if she wasn't on my side, well . . . I was screwed anyhow.

Once back in the tunnel, I made another fire. This time it only took me thirty-five minutes to get it going. Then I made a pillow out of my stolen hotel jacket, covered myself with the silver jacket, and tried to get some sleep. That didn't work out so well: The floor was stone, I was cold, and my mind was racing, coming up with thousands of scenarios of how things could go wrong. When I actually did nod off, I was plagued by nightmares about SPYDER that startled me awake.

By seven a.m. I had given up. I spent the next two hours pacing around the tunnel before feeling it was finally safe enough to reemerge. I had spent so much time underground that I was starting to feel like a mole. I was almost blinded by the sun after going so long without seeing it.

It was a surprisingly warm day for winter. I didn't even need my stolen hotel jacket, so I left it in the tunnel. There were already lots of people out: tourists visiting the monuments and locals jogging around the Reflecting Pool and the Tidal Basin. Around the Mall, thousands of schoolkids poured out of tour buses. They were from all over the United States, on their annual winter pilgrimage to the nation's capital. It was easy to blend in with them.

I worked my way around the Tidal Basin to a Starbucks, intending to grab a quick bite, but as I was about to enter, I spotted my face on the TV mounted above the counter.

I was on the morning news. The crawl at the bottom of the screen read: HUNT CONTINUES FOR TWEEN SUSPECT IN WHITE HOUSE BOMBING. Even worse, they were displaying the lousy photo from my fake St. Smithen's student ID. So not only had I been outed as the assassin, but it had been done with the least attractive picture of me possible.

Lots of people were watching the TV—and those who weren't were reading the newspaper. The same photo of me was on the front page of the *Washington Post* and the *New York Times*, above the fold. So pretty much everyone in the coffee shop knew who I was and what I looked like. Given that the bombing had occurred close by, all of them seemed on the alert for any sign of trouble. I quickly turned away before anyone spotted me and called the authorities.

I decided to pass on breakfast altogether. Even though I hadn't eaten since lunch the day before, my stomach was now so knotted up that I doubted I could keep anything down.

I wondered what my parents must be thinking. I was pretty sure they knew I would never have done such a horrible thing and suspected that I'd been named by mistake, but whatever the case, they must have been dismayed that I'd been named at all. I desperately wanted to reach out to them to let them know I was all right, but the government surely would be waiting for me to try. Any line of communication into our home was certainly tapped. Any attempt I made to reach my parents—e-mail, phone calls, texts— would be intercepted and traced. It was a risk I couldn't afford to take. Sadly, for the moment I had to let my parents suffer and focus on proving my innocence.

The Smithsonian National Museum of Natural History opened at ten o'clock. By nine thirty, crowds of schoolkids had already amassed on the front steps. I blended back in with them, trying to keep a low profile. Thankfully, that wasn't hard. The kids were all too busy goofing around with one another—and their chaperones were too busy trying to wrangle them all—to pay any attention to me. At ten, I joined the crush as everyone piled around the museum entrance, jostling to get indoors. I let most everyone else go through first, wanting the crowds to build inside before entering myself.

The museum was free, so there was no need to buy a ticket, and while there was security, the guards were far more focused on the adults than the kids. None of them seemed concerned that the most wanted bomber in America might want to spend the day at the Natural History Museum. I passed through the metal detectors with ease and found myself in the great, soaring rotunda. Most of the tourists had gone directly to the famous taxidermied elephant in the middle or, being kids, made a beeline for the dinosaurs. I headed up the stairs to the second floor, then circled the rotunda on the mezzanine level to the gems and minerals collection.

Given that the museum was full of amazing things like dinosaur bones, stuffed whales, and mummies, the gems and minerals weren't most people's top priority. The crowds thinned greatly as I entered the Harry Winston Gallery.

The entrance passed through an exceptionally thick wall, which concealed a sliding metal safe door. The gallery was actually an enormous vault, as the gems on display inside it were among the most valuable in the world. I passed the Hooker Emerald, the Logan Sapphire, the Rosser Reeves Star Ruby . . . and found the Hope Diamond.

You're the one who needs to find hope.

It sat on a pedestal in the center of the gallery, encased in three-inch-thick glass. One of the world's largest cut diamonds, more than forty-five carats in size, it was an ethereal blue. The few tourists who'd chosen to come here first were all gathered around it, gaping at the enormous gemstone in amazement. Everyone spoke in hushed, reverent whispers—if they were even speaking at all. The room was amazingly quiet compared to the clamor of the echoey, crowded rotunda.

Erica wasn't there.

Did I make a mistake? I wondered. Was it possible that I had misinterpreted what she'd said? Maybe she hadn't been giving me a coded message to find the diamond at all. Or had I simply come too early? Erica hadn't specified a time, but I had assumed she'd meant to get there as soon as I could. Was it possible that some misfortune had befallen Erica herself? Had the government caught her, suspecting that she was helping me? Or worse, had SPYDER gotten to her? My heart began to race as panic gripped me.

"Hey," a voice behind me said.

I whirled around, startled, to find Erica standing there. As usual, she had approached without making a sound. It took me a fraction of a second longer than normal to realize it was Erica, though, because she didn't look like Erica.

Erica had a way of doing this without needing masks or hair dye or so much as a fake nose. Instead, she had an incredible talent for altering her entire personality when she needed to, and this, in turn, made her seem to be a completely different person. In real life, Erica was cold and calculating and almost always sheathed in her standard black outfit. Now she looked like an everyday middle school student. She wore trendy clothes, had her hair done up, and was chomping on a wad of gum the size of a walnut. Even more importantly, her whole persona was different, from the way she talked to her posture to the slightly vacant look in her eyes.

I was at once struck by her transformation—*and* the brilliance of her choice of where to reconnect. The Natural History Museum was the one place in the city that was crawling with kids our age in the middle of a school day. The other people in the gallery weren't paying any attention to us at all.

"Amazing rock, huh?" she asked, indicating the diamond. "What do you think it's worth, like a bajillion dollars?"

"Something like that." I did my best to sound like an average teenage boy, but probably didn't. I *wasn't* an average teenage boy, and I couldn't hide my relief that Erica was actually there. I had never been so happy to see anyone in my life. I had to fight back the urge to hug her.

"Let's go see something else," Erica said, like she was already bored of the world's biggest diamond. She turned and headed out of the gallery.

I followed her. Once we were back on the mezzanine around the rotunda, it was loud enough for me to feel comfortable speaking about my current situation. "Thanks for coming."

"Don't thank me yet," Erica said, dropping her ditzy character. "We're still not in the clear."

"I don't think anyone's recognized me yet," I assured her. "And I know you're too good to let anyone tail you."

"I am," she agreed. "But you have a lot of enemies right now, and I can guarantee you some of them were eavesdropping on our phone call last night. I didn't give you the most clever clue about where to meet me. . . ."

"Why not?"

"I was afraid that if I was *too* clever, you wouldn't get it."

"Oh, right."

"Point being, there's a chance that someone else could put two and two together as well." Erica froze by the mezzanine railing, looking down into the rotunda. "In fact, I'd say about a hundred percent chance."

I followed her gaze. Sure enough, four men in suits and sunglasses had just entered the museum. They had government agent written all over them. Every other person in the rotunda was dressed in tourist casual. The men stuck out like penguins in a flock of chickens.

Erica and I both ducked back from the railing right as the agents glanced our way. It seemed like we had been quick enough to avoid them, though I didn't know for sure. At the very least, they were now blocking the main exit.

"Looks like we're not getting out the easy way," Erica said with a sigh. She continued past the stairs and around the mezzanine, sticking close to the wall so that the agents below couldn't see us.

Three started coming up anyhow, heading for the Hope Diamond. One stayed down by the entrance.

"Who do you think they are?" I asked. "Secret Service? CIA? FBI?"

"Could be any one of them. They're all looking for you. You screwed up pretty big yesterday."

"SPYDER tricked me."

"Well, you, me, and SPYDER are pretty much the only people on earth who believe that." Erica led me off the mezzanine and into the hall with the butterfly pavilion. It was an enormous, cocoonlike structure inside of which hundreds of butterflies and moths flitted around an indoor rain forest.

Behind us, on the far side of the rotunda, the three government agents emerged onto the mezzanine. Two entered the gems and minerals exhibit, while the other posted himself at the railing and cased the rotunda.

"Do you think SPYDER sent agents here too?" I asked nervously.

"I don't see why not," Erica replied. "If our government could figure out we're here, then SPYDER certainly could too. And their agents are going to blend in a lot better than ours will."

"I hope you're ready to fight, then."

"Why?"

"Because SPYDER wants me dead. They tried to kill me on the Arlington Bridge yesterday."

Erica gave me a look that indicated I was the world's biggest idiot. "That wasn't SPYDER. That was *me*."

"You?" I gasped. "Why would *you* try to kill me?"

Erica's look hardened, now indicating that I might be the biggest idiot in the entire universe. "I wasn't trying to *kill* you. I had to do *something* to get you free."

"So you opened fire on an entire convoy of Secret Service agents?"

"It wasn't like I had a whole lot of options." Erica led me through the invertebrate zoo, where display cases were filled with an array of the world's biggest, slimiest, and most revolting insects. "I had to act fast. If they'd gotten you to the Pentagon and locked you up there, it would have been almost impossible for me to free you."

"*Almost* impossible?" I echoed.

"Nothing's completely impossible. But some things are awfully close. So I improvised. Lucky for you, I was keeping an eye on you again at the White House yesterday when the bomb went off."

"Really? I didn't see you."

"Because I didn't want you to see me." Erica cut

through a demonstration where a museum employee was removing insects from Tupperware containers and showing them to a crowd of riveted children. "After the explosion, I saw the Secret Service drag you out and figured they were taking you to the Pentagon. So I grabbed my motorcycle and raced over to the construction site."

I thought back to the flash of movement I'd seen among the construction workers, moving toward the crane. I now realized it had been Erica. "So, you swung that hook at the car on purpose?"

"Yeah. I realize that was a bit dicey, but I'd never operated a crane before. It's harder than you'd think."

"A bit dicey? You realize if you'd been off by another inch or two, you would have killed me?"

Erica considered this, then shrugged. "Well, we all make mistakes. I would have asked *you* to do the math, but you were tough to reach at the time."

Behind us, there was a commotion. I glanced back that way, worried the government agents had spotted us, but it was only the museum employee from the demonstration, expressing concern that some of her insects appeared to have escaped. Panic rippled through the group of children watching the presentation, who were all now terrified there might be a rogue tarantula crawling on them.

Erica and I passed out of the invertebrates and into the mummies.

"If you went through all that trouble to engineer my escape," I said, "why didn't you come find me in the secret tunnel?"

"First of all, I wasn't positive you would go there. You might have forgotten where it was, and I never taught you the code."

"I memorized it when I saw you type it in."

"I couldn't guarantee that. And given that I'd just opened fire on a Secret Service motorcade, I couldn't exactly go for a stroll around the Reflecting Pool. I had to make sure *I* didn't end up getting locked up. So I took evasive action."

We entered the dinosaur exhibit, cutting underneath the massive skeleton of a brachiosaur. "And you couldn't get back down there anytime last night?" I asked.

"Grandpa was keeping tabs on me. I had to be careful. I wasn't even supposed to be down at the White House in the first place, remember? If he found out I'd engineered your escape, he would have made sure I was grounded for life. Thankfully, he also thought SPYDER was behind the attack."

"But now he's even more convinced that I'm working for the bad guys."

"Yes. He feels extremely betrayed by you. The whole thing made him look like a patsy. So he's pretty much running the show to bring you down. And he was definitely suspicious that I might help you. I had to put on a major act to prove I was on board with him, right down to that phone call last night."

"You couldn't even tell Zoe that you're helping me?"

"No way. Everyone knows Zoe's loyal to you. The Feds have been questioning her all day. I know you're pals with her and all, but it's not like that girl can keep a secret. Once you threaten to do something horrible to her family, she spills her guts. So I had to keep her in the dark. . . . Plus, I needed to make some additional arrangements for today in case we ran into trouble."

"Like what?" I asked.

Erica didn't answer me. She had frozen next to a life-size model of a triceratops and was staring at two tourists across the room. "You're about to find out," she said. "Trouble dead ahead." She then spun on her heels and ran back the way we'd come.

Apparently, we had been spotted and there was no longer any point in pretending to be normal kids.

The tourists bolted after us. A man and a woman, they blended in amazingly well with the standard Smithsonian visitors. Both wore souvenir T-shirts and jeans and looked as though they had just stepped off a bus from Iowa. Neither seemed particularly threatening as they came after us, but given Erica's reaction, I had no doubt that it would be very bad if they caught us.

"SPYDER?" I asked as we raced back under the brachiosaur.

"Yes." Erica didn't backtrack through the mummies, but hooked a left into the Hall of Bones.

She could run extremely fast. It took everything I had to keep up with her.

To my surprise, the SPYDER agents didn't do as well. They fell behind us as we dashed through the rooms full of animal skeletons. I was just starting to feel proud of myself when we emerged onto the rotunda mezzanine again—and nearly ran right into one of the government agents. He instantly recognized us and yelled to his partners across the rotunda, "Hey! They're here!" Then he took up the chase.

Erica darted right past the stairs that led down to the first floor and charged into the next room. This wasn't a gallery, but a small gift shop. It appeared to be a dead end to me.

"Why didn't we go down the stairs?" I asked Erica, failing to hide the desperation in my voice.

"Because the Feds could have followed us down the stairs," she explained, in a way that indicated our alternative route was going to be much less traditional.

We passed a large bin containing rocks and minerals for sale. They were inexpensive, but pretty: thousands of polished round pebbles in a cavalcade of colors. Erica deftly upended it behind us. The pebbles cascaded across the floor.

The government agent slipped on them, skidded wildly out of control, and careened into a rack of dinosaur toys, which promptly collapsed, burying our pursuer in a pile of plastic velociraptors and pachycephalosaurs.

We arrived at the back of the store. It *was* a dead end—almost. There was no way to *walk* out, but there was an open space in the wall that looked out over the Hall of Ocean Life. The viewpoint was one story above the main floor; a railing spanned the gap to prevent dumb tourists from taking a header into the exhibits below.

The hall was several stories tall, filled with exotic displays ranging from stuffed anglerfish to an actual giant squid encased in a huge vat of formaldehyde. The centerpiece was an enormous model of a humpback whale, which hung from the ceiling, suspended by thin steel wires. An only-slightly-less-enormous skeleton of a bowhead whale sat on a metal framework below us.

"You're not expecting us to jump to that?" I asked, worried.

"I'm not *expecting* anything. We're *doing* it." With that,

Erica sprang over the railing onto the whale skeleton.

She sailed through the air and landed perfectly atop the skull with an agility and finesse I knew I didn't have in the slightest.

I looked around for another way out. The only other exit was blocked by the government agent, who was digging himself out of the dinosaur toys. He had a livid glare in his eye and a plesiosaur jammed in his ear.

The SPYDER agents appeared to have lost us, but the government agent was threatening enough.

I jumped over the railing.

To my surprise, I landed deftly atop the whale skull. Only, the perfect balance thing was completely beyond me. I pitched forward and nearly took a header into the piranha display below. Erica caught me at the last instant and steadied me, but my weight had thrown her off balance too. She now pitched forward herself and had no choice but to leap from the skull and catch onto the lip of the model humpback whale. The cables supporting it strained under the sudden jolt. One snapped free from the ceiling and the whale shifted wildly.

Erica swung from the whale's lip, launched herself into a backflip, and stuck the landing in the middle of the hall.

The tourists gathered there all applauded, impressed. As though they figured the Smithsonian had started hiring circus performers to spice things up.

Erica looked to me expectantly.

So did all the tourists.

Now I had potential death *and* performance anxiety to deal with.

Knowing I couldn't possibly do what Erica had just done, I carefully shimmied down the metal framework that supported the whale skeleton—and still biffed the dismount. I fell backward and landed on my butt atop a large sea turtle.

The tourists groaned, like I had let them down.

Above us, the government agent appeared at the gift-shop viewpoint, realized there was no way he could follow the way we'd gone, and dashed back toward the stairs.

The remaining cables that supported the humpback groaned ominously.

The tourists around Erica were still staring at her expectantly, as if hoping she would perform another stunt.

"Clear the room!" she ordered them all. "Now!"

Despite her young age, the tone of her voice made them all instantly realize this wasn't a show. They did exactly as she'd said, bolting for the exits.

Another whale support cable snapped above us.

"Guess that wasn't part of the plan," I said.

"Of course it was," Erica replied. "We need a block-ade." She pointed across the room, to where the SPYDER tourists had just entered the exhibit hall. Apparently, we hadn't ditched them at all; they had simply circled around down the stairs to ambush us.

They probably would have been successful—if the humpback hadn't torn free from the ceiling and crashed down to earth between us. It shook the entire building, totaled a dozen exhibits, and shattered the case that held the giant squid, releasing it along with a tidal wave of formaldehyde.

"See what I mean?" Erica asked, then yanked me toward the exit from the hall.

Unfortunately, the three other government agents who hadn't been buried by dinosaur toys raced in that way, blocking our escape. Erica snapped the nose off a model swordfish and hurled it like a javelin, spearing one of the agents to the wall through the sleeve of his sports coat. Then she tossed me a small Tupperware container and said, "Spider."

"You think they're with SPYDER?" I asked, confused.

"No," she said in her standard you're-an-idiot tone. "*Spider*. Like arachnid. Use it." She then grabbed one of the giant squid tentacles, lashed it out like a whip, and took the second government agent down at the knees.

She was too busy to handle the third, though. I looked into the Tupperware container she'd given me and finally realized what she meant. There was a gigantic, hairy spider in it. Apparently, Erica had pilfered it from the insect show as we'd gone by.

The third government agent was quickly closing in on me. I popped the lid off the Tupperware and flung the spider at him. It landed right on his face. The agent screamed in terror, backpedaled away as though he could actually run from something that had latched onto his head, then slipped on the squid and tumbled into what was left of the formaldehyde bath.

In the ensuing chaos, Erica and I fled. We charged out of the exhibit hall, but instead of heading for the exit, Erica made a sudden turn through a door marked STAFF ONLY. She then led me down two flights of stairs and through a door marked STORAGE.

We emerged into an enormous underground cavern. It turned out, all the amazing things on display in the museum above us were only a tiny fraction of the Smithsonian collection, much of which was mothballed around us. We moved quickly through miles of shelves containing everything from stuffed lemurs to mammoth tusks. There were thousands of insects mounted under glass, millions of meteorites, billions of bird feathers, trillions of trilobites. It seemed to go on forever, a labyrinth of artifacts from around the world.

Erica appeared to know exactly where she was going,

as though she had not only been down here before, but had also rehearsed the route and committed it to memory. Which, knowing Erica, was a distinct possibility. After only a minute, an exit door appeared ahead of us, at the end of an aisle full of dinosaur bones.

Before we could get there, though, the SPYDER tourists stepped into our path.

They apparently knew the museum as well as Erica. Both had their guns drawn.

"Nice try," the woman taunted. "But this is the end of the line for both of you."

Erica froze. For once it looked like we were facing something she hadn't anticipated.

At which point, someone dressed in black attacked the SPYDER agents from behind. Our savior whacked the woman on the head with what appeared to be a tyrannosaur femur, instantly knocking her out cold.

The male SPYDER tourist wheeled around, but before he could get a shot off, his attacker whipped the bone around like a ninja staff, thwacked him in the chin, and laid him out like a bearskin rug.

The entire battle had lasted five seconds.

Our savior then set the bone down carefully and turned to face us, finally allowing us a good look at her.

It was a woman. A lithe, athletic woman. Although I

had never seen her before, there was something incredibly familiar about her. It was partly her looks—and partly the bizarre calm she exuded, despite having just rendered two highly trained enemy agents unconscious with a prehistoric weapon. She took a packet of wet wipes from her pocket and dabbed a bit of blood off the tyrannosaur bone, then spoke to Erica in a clipped British accent. "Hello, darling. I see you've gotten yourself into a spot of trouble per usual."

Erica smiled. "Hi, Mom," she said.

FOREIGN RELATIONS

Smithsonian National Museum of Natural History

Washington, DC

February 12

1100 hours

"It's very nice to meet you, Mrs. Hale," I told Erica's mother as we hurried through the Smithsonian employee parking garage.

"Please, call me Catherine." When she wasn't beating enemy agents senseless, Erica's mother was the least spylike person I could possibly imagine. Instead, she came across as the world's most chipper and enthusiastic soccer mom. As far as I could tell, it wasn't an act. She was gracious, kind, charming—and unlike Erica's father, she appeared to be extremely competent. Her lilting British accent was so delightful, she made Mary Poppins sound like a troll. "And it's a pleasure to meet you as well, Benjamin. Erica has told me ever so much about you."

I glanced at Erica, surprised by this. It was hard to tell in the dark garage, but it seemed as though her face might have had a tinge of embarrassment. "It was for the mission," she informed me. "I told you I had to make additional arrangements? That was Mom. I couldn't very well bring her in without briefing her about you."

"Oh, that's right," Catherine said, in a way that merely seemed to be humoring Erica. "All our conversations about you were purely for work, Ben."

We arrived at her car, a well-used, completely nondescript minivan that she'd somehow managed to procure an official Smithsonian parking pass for.

I started to ask one of the dozens of questions I had about Catherine, but she put a finger to her lips and cautioned, "I know there's much to discuss, but at the moment we really ought to focus on our escape. I'm afraid I need both of you to keep mum for a bit." Catherine clicked her key fob. The minivan side door slid open, and the rear seats tilted back, revealing a hidden compartment in the floor of the vehicle. "I'll also need you to get in there."

The compartment wasn't very big. It would be a very tight, cramped fit for Erica and me.

Erica frowned. "No way. Ben's the one who's wanted."

"*Both* of you are wanted now," Catherine informed her. "You aided a known felon in broad daylight and you destroyed the entire Smithsonian gallery of ocean life." She sighed. "I did so love that whale. I hope it isn't too badly damaged. Now, no more chitchat. In you go."

Erica disgruntledly climbed into the compartment and then I got in with her. The only way to fit was to lie on our sides, face-to-face. Except for the part about being fugitives from justice, I found myself quite excited about being in such close quarters with Erica. Despite all our exertion, she smelled fantastic, as usual: her customary heady aroma of lilacs and gunpowder, with only the tiniest hint of formaldehyde mixed in.

Meanwhile, Erica looked like she'd rather be locked in a medieval torture device.

"Now, no kissing in there, you two," Catherine teased. "Our safety is at risk."

"Mother!" Erica gasped, horrified. She flushed red as Catherine shut the compartment, casting us into darkness.

I had never seen Erica like this before. Being around her mother was bringing out a part of her she'd always managed to keep hidden: the normal teenage girl.

There was a heavy *clunk* above our heads as Catherine slid the rear seats back over us.

We kept silent as she drove out of the employee parking garage and headed into the city streets. It was hard to hear anything over the sound of the minivan's engine and the road passing beneath us, but Catherine updated us as she drove along. "Oh my, they've set up quite an impressive dragnet for the two of you. Looks like everyone's coming to the party: FBI, CIA, SWAT . . . I say, you Americans certainly love your acronyms, don't you? They've evacuated the museum and barricades are being erected everywhere. I'm about to hit a checkpoint, so stay silent, children."

The minivan stopped and we heard Catherine lowering her window, followed by the gruff voice of a federal agent. "Sorry, ma'am, but we have to search all cars exiting this area. And I'll need to see some identification."

"Certainly," Catherine agreed graciously. "Here you go, sir. Is all this commotion about those hooligans who caused the ruckus in the museum?"

"That's classified." There was a pause, during which the agent was probably scrutinizing Catherine's driver's license. Then he said, "Can I ask what your business is here?"

"I work for the British embassy as a liaison to the Smithsonian. Helping organize exhibits of British artists, arranging loans of paintings, that sort of thing. I just delivered a rather fascinating item from the British Museum, one of Darwin's original notebooks. . . ."

"Mmm-hmm," the agent said, like he couldn't care less. "Could you open the rear doors of your vehicle for me?"

"Happy to oblige." There was the sound of the automatic door sliding open, and then we could feel the presence of the agent inside the van, snooping around for us. He didn't take long. He simply checked behind the seats and in the back, never expecting that someone as sweet and disarming as Catherine would have a secret hatch for harboring fugitives built into her vehicle.

"All right," the agent said, sliding the door shut again. "You're clear. Sorry for the inconvenience."

"No inconvenience at all. I hope you catch whomever you're looking for. Ta-ta." Catherine rolled up her window and drove away.

"I'm afraid you'll have to stay down there a bit longer," she informed us. "I know it's cramped, but this whole area is crawling with federal agents. It looks like the D-day invasion out here and I'm afraid that if I pull over to let you up, it might raise some suspicion. I do think it's safe to talk, though."

"So you're a spy?" I asked before I could stop myself. I was so desperate to learn more about Catherine, the question practically jumped off my tongue.

"Why, yes," Catherine replied. "I work for MI6. British

Intelligence. Although I must caution you, that is extremely privileged information. Very few people have been allowed knowledge of my true identity. Including Erica's father."

I gasped in surprise. "Your own husband doesn't know you're a spy?"

"*Ex*-husband," Catherine said quickly. "We parted ways several years ago."

"Sorry," I said. "I didn't realize. Erica never said anything. . . ."

"Yes, Erica tends to be rather tight-lipped about her family. I suppose that's my fault, in a sense. There have always been so many things to keep secret."

"Still," I said. "I can't believe Alexander doesn't know."

"Really?" Erica asked from the darkness. "You've met Alexander. I'm surprised he knows *he's* a spy."

"Now, now," Catherine chided. "Your father may have a few faults . . ."

"A few?" Erica echoed testily.

". . . but he's not nearly as awful as you make him out to be either."

"Why are you defending him?" Erica asked. "He was a lousy father and an even worse husband."

Catherine suddenly slammed on the brakes. I had a feeling she was trying to stop this bit of the conversation as well as the minivan. "All right. I think the coast is clear now. You little moles can come out of your hole."

I heard the seats sliding back above us and then the hatch clicked open. Erica scrambled out as fast as she could, like she'd been suffocating inside.

I pried myself out a bit slower, my muscles already cramped from being in the confined space.

We had made it a few blocks from the Smithsonian and were now parked on the street near the International Spy Museum.

Erica helped me replace the hatch and slide the seats back, then called shotgun and climbed into the front passenger seat.

I let her have it. In Erica's family, sitting in the shotgun seat occasionally meant you had to use an actual shotgun.

I buckled myself into the back and Catherine pulled into traffic again. As usual, it was bumper-to-bumper in the middle of the city.

"I expect you're famished, Benjamin," Catherine said to me. "So I brought you some homemade blueberry muffins." She passed a foil-wrapped paper plate back to me.

The muffins smelled incredible. Now that the danger was over and my stomach had calmed, I was so hungry, I probably would have eaten the dead squid from the museum. I tore off the foil and quickly inhaled a muffin.

It tasted even better than it smelled. Even if I hadn't been ravenous, it would have been the single best muffin I'd ever eaten.

"You never made *me* homemade muffins," Erica said, failing to hide the bitterness in her voice.

"I *tried*," Catherine countered. "Back when you were a very little girl. But you argued that carbs were bad for you. Along with ice cream, bangers, saturated fats, and pretty much everything else in the world that's tasty. You always claimed your body was a temple." She met my gaze in the rearview mirror and gave me a conspiratorial grin. "On her third birthday, she actually requested trail mix instead of a cake."

"I did not," Erica said.

"Oh yes you did. And then when we tried to play pin the tail on the donkey, you insisted on using your Chinese throwing stars. After that, we couldn't have any more parties."

"Mother." Erica groaned again. "Please stop sharing."

"Benjamin!" Catherine said suddenly. "I almost forgot. I also made you some tea." She handed back an old-fashioned tartan-plaid thermos bottle with a cap that doubled as a cup. "I know it's very stereotypical for a British person to make tea, but the fact is, it's chock-full of antioxidants and has far less sugar than that Gatorade that Alexander is always swilling."

"Thanks," I said, pouring myself a cup. "By the way, these muffins are delicious."

"That's very sweet of you to say," Catherine replied. "My secret is, I use just a hint of lavender."

"Would you like one?" I asked Erica.

Erica wavered a moment, seeming torn between accepting something made by her mother and consuming carbohydrates. Finally, she said, "I guess."

I handed one to her, then devoured another.

Several police cars shot past us, sirens wailing, heading toward the Smithsonian, joining the manhunt for us.

"So did you meet Alexander through work?" I asked Catherine, my mouth full of muffin.

"Yes," she replied. "In a sense. When I was quite a bit younger, MI6 became aware that the CIA was withholding information from us. Information they should have been sharing. So I was sent over here to find alternative ways to gather it. Alexander was one of my targets. I wasn't supposed to fall for him, but as I'm sure you know, he makes quite a good first impression."

"He does," I agreed, recalling the first time I'd met Alexander. I had been extremely impressed by him. It might have taken me much longer to figure out what a lousy spy he was if Erica hadn't tipped me off.

Catherine sighed. "He was so handsome and charming. He just swept me off my feet."

"Ick," Erica said, under her breath.

"Of course, I could never tell him that I'd been sent here to gouge him for information," Catherine went on. "Revealing the truth would have ruined the bond of trust that is integral to any marriage. So I kept everything secret. And then, as the years went on, I began to realize that Alexander had concealed some things from me."

"Like the fact that he sucked eggs as a spy?" Erica asked.

"Well . . . yes."

"So how long have *you* known about your mother?" I asked Erica.

"I've always known," Erica replied.

"I never hid it from her," Catherine told me. "It was very difficult to live a secret life around my husband. I simply couldn't do it to my daughter."

"And Cyrus?" I asked. "Does he know?"

Catherine considered this for a while before responding, "I don't believe so. Cyrus might be greatly invested in Erica, but he's awfully blinkered where women are concerned. He comes from a time when women weren't supposed to be spies. Which made it quite easy for those of us women who *were* spies to run circles around the men."

"But, then, if Grandpa *did* know, he might never have let on," Erica pointed out.

"I suppose not," Catherine agreed.

It occurred to me that having a family in the spy business

was far more complicated than having a family in the grocery business. The biggest intrigue we ever had in my family was when Mom got upset with Dad for coming home smelling like baloney.

We arrived at Dupont Circle again. Sometimes, it seemed like there was no way to get from one part of Washington to another *without* going through Dupont, which was probably why the intersection was almost always a nightmare. Today, however, the traffic was surprisingly mild. There were still plenty of cars, but we were actually moving forward.

"As much as I'd love to discuss our family and all its foibles," Catherine said, "I'm afraid we ought to put the kibosh on this conversation."

"You mean, there are other things to discuss?" I asked.

"Yes," Catherine said. "Plus, this is all highly classified. We've taken you into great confidence here. I've only done it because Erica swears you're trustworthy. But I'm afraid I still must warn you, you can't share any of this with another living soul. If you do . . ."

"You'll have to kill me," I finished. I'd heard this refrain from Erica plenty of times before.

Catherine was taken aback. "Kill you? Goodness, no. That's a bit drastic, isn't it? I wouldn't kill you, dear. I'd only maim you a little."

"Oh," I said, unsure if that was actually better.

"But you're right," Catherine pressed on. "There is another, far more serious issue we must discuss: You've gotten yourself into quite a pickle, Benjamin. And we need to figure out how to, er . . . unpickle you. Now, Erica claims you believe that SPYDER is behind all this trouble, is that correct?"

I glanced at Erica, unsure what to say. We had always been told that SPYDER's existence was highly classified and that we weren't supposed to discuss it with anyone.

"It's all right," Erica told me. "We won't get in trouble for sharing agency secrets. Mom already knew about SPYDER way before this."

"As you may recall, one of our MI6 spies-in-training, Claire Hutchins, was there when you thwarted SPYDER's attempt to blow up Camp David while the prime minister was visiting it last summer," Catherine explained. "She filled us in on everything she'd learned. By the way, Benjamin, the prime minister is very thankful to you for saving his life. MI6 has been authorized to extend you every courtesy we can in return for that."

"Thanks," I said. "Well, then, yes, I'm quite sure SPYDER was behind framing me. I think they planted the chatter to get Cyrus to place me inside the White House, got White House security used to seeing me, and then slipped a bomb into my jacket on the subway yesterday afternoon and made me a Bombay Boomerang."

"And the Secret Service didn't detect the bomb on you?" Catherine asked.

"They did," I said. "But the bomb dogs had gotten all excited the day before when they smelled my jacket, and there was nothing in it. So the second day, when the dogs went nuts, the agents figured it was a false alarm."

"The dogs got all excited about you the first day?" Catherine asked suspiciously. She and Erica shared a look.

"SPYDER must have planted something on you then, too," Erica told me. "Something to provoke the dogs. Like a tiny bit of meat. Or a trace of explosive so small that the sensors couldn't detect it, even though the dogs could. They *wanted* the dogs to make a big deal about you, so when it happened again the second day, the agents would think it was another false alarm."

I shrank back in my seat, disturbed by how easily SPYDER had manipulated me—and the Secret Service. "I took the subway to the White House the first day too. Someone must have slipped the bait into my jacket then."

"Not necessarily," Erica said. "They could have planted it quite a bit earlier. Even a few days ahead of time. Those dogs would have still smelled it."

Catherine nodded agreement. "Nice deductive work,

children. From what I know about SPYDER, that sounds like the sort of devious plot they'd attempt. Unfortunately, most people—including those in our own agencies—haven't even heard of SPYDER, and therefore, this will sound exceedingly far-fetched to them. I don't suppose you have any evidence to back up your speculation, Benjamin?"

"Er . . . no," I admitted.

"Then you'll have to get some," Catherine said. "It's the only way to clear your name. And if you can't prove your innocence, you'll have to flee the country."

"Flee the country?" I repeated.

"Why, yes. Even with Erica helping you, there's no way you'll be able to stay ahead of the entire American intelligence force for long. However, should you choose to, I could arrange for you to be spirited away to one of Britain's many territories and establish a new identity for you."

"Like where?" I asked.

"It'd be up to you. The British Empire still controls some very lovely islands in the Caribbean: Bermuda, Anguilla, Turks and Caicos, Virgin Gorda. We could set you up as an orphan on one and perhaps get you a nice internship with one of the many scuba diving operations. It would be a rather nice life—although you wouldn't ever get to see your family or friends again, which I suspect might put a damper on things."

I had never been to a Caribbean island—or any beach

beyond the Atlantic Coast for that matter—which made this more intriguing than being relocated to many other places. Afghanistan, for example. But I certainly didn't want to spend the rest of my life as a fugitive without ever being able to see my parents, my friends . . . or Erica. I looked to Erica and thought I caught the slightest glimpse of emotion in her eyes, indicating that she wasn't thrilled with this prospect either.

"I don't want to go on the run," I said. "I want to prove my innocence."

"That will be dangerous," Catherine cautioned.

"I don't care."

"There's also a chance you'll fail and end up in jail here for the rest of your life. A tropical island would be *much* nicer."

I hesitated for a moment, considering the wisdom of that.

"Ben's not going to jail," Erica said confidently. "We're going to find the evidence to save him."

Catherine looked to her, concerned. "*You?* I don't think so. You've already risked far too much for Benjamin. Now, I'm sure that, with your grandfather's help, we can arrange a cover story claiming that you were actually trying to capture Benjamin at the museum today, rather than abetting his escape, but it will take every bit of clout Cyrus has to get you back into the good graces of the CIA. If you put your neck on the line for Ben now and fail, your entire future will be in jeopardy."

I expected Erica might pause to think that over, the same way I had. But she didn't waver in her conviction for a moment. "I don't care. Ben was framed by SPYDER and I'm not going to let them get away with it."

Catherine appeared to have conflicting emotions about this. She seemed simultaneously proud of her daughter and worried about her. However, she couldn't respond right away, as we had finally arrived at the British embassy.

There were actually two embassy buildings. There was the original: a large, beautiful, stately brick manor that looked as though it had been plucked right out of the Cotswolds and deposited in the middle of Washington. And there was the new embassy, which had been built in recent years to handle a much bigger staff. This one was boxy and dull and looked like a post office. (As one of our closest allies, Britain had one of the biggest diplomatic corps of any country—as well as one of the choicest embassy properties in the city.)

Catherine pulled up to the gate and put on a good show for the guard posted there, sweet as could be. "Morning, Tristam!"

"Good morning, Mrs. H," Tristam replied cheerfully, then glanced through the window at Erica and me.

Thankfully, he didn't seem to recognize us. But then, the chance that one of Britain's diplomatic employees might be harboring two fugitives was probably a stretch for anyone. "No school for the kids today?"

"No," Catherine said with a motherly sigh. "It's yet another one of those American holiday weekends. Presidents' Day, I think. They've got a whole slew of days off and I have nowhere to send them. You've met Erica before, of course. And this is her friend Mortimer."

"Hey, Tristam," Erica said with a wave, slipping back into ditz mode for a second.

"My, my," Tristam said. "Erica, you get bigger every day. And it's a pleasure to meet you, Mortimer." He nodded graciously to me. "Well, come on through." He waved us through the gates.

As we rolled onto the property, Catherine resumed our conversation. "Erica, I know you consider Benjamin a friend, but I would be negligent as a mother if I didn't point out the severe risks associated with helping him. SPYDER is as cunning and savage an organization as MI6 or the CIA has ever encountered. They have certainly planned for the possibility of Benjamin trying to prove his innocence and taken steps to prevent that from happening. Going up against them will be arduous, demanding, and potentially deadly. Plus, they've covered their tracks so well, we've never been able to develop a single lead to them. I wish I could be more helpful, but I don't have the foggiest idea where you could even start tracking them down."

"I do," Erica said. "We need to talk to Ashley Sparks."

Catherine slammed on the brakes as she pulled into her parking space. Then she wheeled on Erica, astonished. "Ashley Sparks?" she repeated, worried.

"You know about her?" I asked.

"Erica has kept me up to date on all your missions," Catherine explained. "As well as all the miscreants you have encountered on them." She returned her attention to Erica. "I don't like this at all."

I shared Catherine's concern. Ashley Sparks had been a student at SPYDER's evil spy school, a former gymnast who'd turned to crime after barely missing the cut for the U.S. Olympic team. She had originally come across as kind and friendly—if a bit misguided—but had ultimately proved to be fully committed to SPYDER and extremely dangerous. She was the only person I knew of who had ever come close to defeating Erica in a fight.

While Nefarious Jones, a fellow evil spy school student, had turned his back on SPYDER and helped thwart their plans, Ashley had been unrepentant. Both were now serving time for their crimes, although Nefarious had been given a far shorter sentence in return for his help. Since Ashley and

Nefarious were minors, the government couldn't send them to a federal penitentiary. And yet both had been deemed too important to send to a standard juvenile detention facility. (Especially after the CIA's previous attempt to send a SPYDER agent to a standard juvenile detention facility had resulted in disaster.) So a new version of juvenile detention had been created solely for them, a place where they could still be educated while being kept under maximum security.

"Ashley Sparks is incarcerated at the Academy of Espionage," Catherine said.

"I know," Erica replied. "I'm the one who told *you* that."

"And you want to talk to her?"

"I think she might know something."

"You're currently on the run from your government, and you want to go to the one place where everyone knows exactly who you are?" Catherine asked.

"Yes."

"You want to break into a highly secure CIA facility to seek help from a known felon who absolutely despises you?"

"Yes."

"And your plan is to get some crucial information about SPYDER out of that very felon, even though the entire CIA hasn't been able to get her to reveal a single thing in the past six months?"

"I know how to get her to talk," Erica said confidently.

Catherine sighed heavily, then looked to the sky, as if imploring the heavens. "How on earth did you ever get to be such a stubborn, presumptuous, bullheaded firebrand?"

"I learned it from my mother," Erica answered.

A tiny smile creased Catherine's lips. "Yes, I suppose you did."

"So what's the plan?" I asked.

INFILTRATION

The British Embassy
Washington, DC
February 13
0200 hours

The location of the relatively new juvenile deten-tion center at the academy was supposed to be a secret, but of course Erica knew exactly where it was. Erica knew the academy grounds better than anyone—including most of the professors—and trying to keep a secret from her was like trying to hide candy from a kindergartner. It turned out, the holding area had been built inside the Cheney Center for the Acquisition of Information, down on a secret subterranean level of the campus.

Erica figured that the best time to infiltrate the academy would be in the middle of the night, when everyone was asleep, and her mother reluctantly agreed. So I spent most of the rest of the day recuperating at the old British embassy.

I had to keep a low profile, though. Despite Catherine's assurances that MI6 and the British government owed me thanks, that didn't mean they wanted her harboring me at the embassy. In fact, Catherine had gone rogue by rescuing me, and she warned me that if anyone realized who I was, they'd probably alert the CIA immediately. Luckily, the old British embassy was really only a showpiece: a place to hold fancy events like state dinners and charity balls, while the *real* diplomatic work was done at the new, modern embassy. There were plenty of nearly forgotten rooms in the aging building. Catherine found me a small bedroom up on the third floor, which looked as though it might not have been used since the Thatcher administration.

Despite its apparent neglect, it was warm and cozy with extremely stereotypical British furnishings like paintings of the countryside, ceramic bulldogs, and a bust of Winston Churchill. After my recent adventures and my nearly sleepless night, I was exhausted, so I collapsed onto the bed and promptly fell asleep until well after nightfall.

When I woke, I was famished. Thankfully, Catherine had realized this would be the case; she had already made me a meal and left it on the dresser. There were several peanut butter and jelly sandwiches (no crust), two thermoses (one with chicken soup and one with tea), a package of English "crisps" (which turned out to be potato chips), and some unidentifiable puddinglike substance that I figured must be a British food I'd never heard of. Normally, I might have avoided it, but I was hungry enough to eat dingo kidneys, so I gulped it down with everything else.

There was a TV in the room, so ancient that it actually had an antenna attached to it, though it was also connected to cable. I flipped between 24-hour news channels as I ate.

Unsurprisingly, the news was all about me.

Even though it was well over a day since my "attack" on the White House, the ongoing manhunt for me was still the top story. This late at night, the news channels were mostly rerunning the same reports they'd had on all day. While there was a general consensus that I was now America's public enemy number one, there was considerable debate about who I was working for. Each channel had a coterie of experts discussing this, and every last one of them had a different conclusion, all of which were wrong. Within fifteen minutes, I was accused of being connected to six different extremist terrorist groups, twelve hostile foreign governments, and three crackpot conspiracy theories, one of which involved the CIA, the FBI, the NSA, *and* NASA. Even the "experts" who suspected I was acting alone couldn't agree on why. My attempted assassination was blamed on everything from video games to Facebook to a misguided crush on the president's daughter.

Nobody mentioned SPYDER. But then, it was doubtful any of them knew about SPYDER at all.

Not a single person suggested the possibility that I might have been innocent and merely used by someone trying to assassinate the president. The closest anyone got to that was a severely deranged U.S. representative who suspected that I was a Soviet sleeper agent. The congressman then went on to suggest that most children who had been adopted from other countries were probably sleeper agents as well, and that the process of international adoption ought to be immediately terminated.

I terminated that interview instead, switching to a different channel, where I found Jason Stern mouthing off about me. It wasn't an official interview; instead, Jason had been posting about me on social media—probably without his family's permission—and the news was wantonly parroting everything he said.

Unsurprisingly, Jason was being awful to me—and very supportive of himself.

"My father would have been dead if it wasn't for me," Jason had proclaimed on his blog. "I suspected Ben Ripley was a possible assassin all along. The kid was real weird. So when he came over, I was on guard. When I heard his jacket ticking, I risked my own life to rip it off him. Sucks that it blew up the Oval Office, though. And that the Secret Service let him escape. Losers."

On Twitter, he had been much more succinct: "Stopped #AssassinBenRipley from killing my father today. You're welcome America."

Since Jason wasn't actually giving interviews, no one could ask him why he'd invited me over for a playdate if he suspected I was an assassin all along. Somehow, none of the news commentators thought to point this out either.

For about the thousandth time that day, I found myself thinking about my parents and wishing there was some way to contact them.

I flipped off the TV in disgust and wolfed down the rest of my food.

I had just finished it when there was a knock at the door. "Benjamin?" Catherine asked. "Are you awake?"

"Yes. Come on in."

Catherine stepped in, carrying the sort of box that clothes from a fancy store came in. Only, there was no store name on the box. It was completely black. "Oh, good. You've eaten," Catherine said. "Did you enjoy the trifle?"

"Er . . . yes," I said, deducing that that's what the pudding-like substance has been.

"Wonderful. I hate to disturb you, but Erica feels the time for your covert mission is nigh."

"I figured as much."

"Although, before you go, I thought you might want to wear something a bit more . . . appropriate." Catherine handed me the box.

I opened it and gasped with surprise at what lay inside. It was a sleek black outfit, like the ones Erica always wore, except tailored for a boy. It even had its own utility belt. "Wow," I said.

"Do you like it?"

"I *love* it. I've always wanted one of these."

Catherine beamed. "It's from the same top secret tailor where I get Erica her clothes. Unfortunately, the utility belts don't come fully loaded and I didn't have time to procure much for you. All I could get on short notice was pepper spray, cyanide capsules, and some chewing gum. Try not to get them all mixed up."

"Thanks," I said, and then, even though I barely knew Catherine, I gave her a hug. After being accused of treason and insulted in the press, I was feeling awfully emotional, and she gave off such a maternal vibe, I couldn't help it.

Catherine hugged me back, comforting me. "There, there, now. Everything will be all right."

"I don't know," I said. "It's all pretty messed up."

"Yes, but you have my daughter on your side."

"And the entire U.S. intelligence agency on the other."

"Perhaps. But who do you trust more?"

I didn't have to think about that too long. "Erica."

"Exactly."

I pulled away from Catherine, feeling better. Not a whole lot better, but at least a little bit. "Do you have any idea how my parents are handling all of this?"

"Ah. I suspected you might want to know that. I've done my best to keep tabs on them while you were asleep and . . . well, it's probably no surprise that this has been very difficult for them. The best I could do to allay their grief was to send them an extremely secure e-mail claiming to be from the Secret Service, in which I stated that the U.S. government was well aware that you were actually not the assassin but merely happened to be at the White House at the time—and that the media has gotten the story all wrong."

"Thanks."

"I then went on to say that various crime-fighting agencies have found your mistaken accusation to be advantageous in the pursuit of the true assassins, so unfortunately, we have to request that your parents keep mum about your innocence until the government announces it publicly—although steps are being taken to rectify the situation as quickly as possible."

"Do you know if that made them feel any better?"

"Sadly, I don't. We can only hope. Of course, it will all be a load of poppycock unless you and Erica can actually rectify the situation. So, why don't you try on that outfit and we'll hit the road?" Catherine gave me a reassuring smile, then slipped out of the room to give me privacy.

I put the suit on. It was extremely snug, but besides that, it felt great. When I checked myself out in the bedroom mirror, I looked rather suave and primed for action. I performed a few test karate chops and jujitsu kicks, then modeled some debonair poses. "The name's Ripley," I purred smoothly. "Benjamin Ripley."

It was at this point that I noticed Erica standing in the doorway.

"What on earth are you doing?" she asked.

"Nothing!" I said quickly. "Just testing out my suit."

"Save it for the bad guys. We have to go."

When I looked back at the mirror again, I no longer looked that suave. Instead, I was bright red from embarrassment. In my black suit, my head looked like a maraschino cherry atop a chocolate sundae. I wadded my old clothes into a ball and quickly followed Erica out the door.

By that time, most of the embassy employees had gone home. In the dark, the guard on duty didn't even notice Erica and me hunkered down in the back of the minivan when Catherine drove us out.

The embassy wasn't far from spy school. Catherine drove us to a residential street a block from the academy's rear wall, where we all synchronized our watches. "I'll pick you both up right here in ninety minutes," Catherine said, as though she were a normal mother dropping us off at a movie. "If you're not back by then, I'll have to assume something's gone wrong and come looking for you. . . ."

"Nothing will go wrong," Erica said confidently. Like it was a fact, rather than a guess. "I know this place inside and out." With that, she hopped out of the minivan and started down the street.

"Good luck!" Catherine called, then blew her a kiss good-bye.

"Thanks for everything," I said, then followed Erica.

In our dark suits, we blended into the shadows perfectly as we made our way to the academy wall.

"You're aware that what we're doing here is insane, right?" I asked. "I'm wanted by every branch of law enforcement in the country, and now we're breaking into a CIA facility."

"It's the last thing they'd ever expect us to do," Erica replied.

"Unless they're expecting us to do the last thing they'd ever expect us to do, in which case, this is exactly what they'd expect us to do."

"Shhh," Erica warned. "We need to be quiet. And your logic is making my head hurt."

The wall was an imposing stone barricade, topped with electrified barbed wire and monitored by dozens of security cameras, but Erica felt we ought to go over it anyhow. Even though there was a secret tunnel under the wall that almost no one but us knew about.

"Why don't we use that?" I asked.

"Because my grandfather knows I know about it," Erica replied. "So he probably has security keeping an eye on it."

"You think he's expecting you to come back here?"

"It's a possibility, though security can't keep tabs on the entire wall. It's more than a mile long. And to be honest, the security here isn't exactly the most competent staff at the CIA. In fact, it's pretty much the dregs."

I knew that from experience. SPYDER had once kidnapped me from inside the academy's own safe room. Still, Erica and I didn't take our infiltration lightly; if Cyrus thought we were coming, he would have beefed up surveillance as much as he could.

Only about a fifth of the spy school property was the actual school. The remainder was a good-size pocket of forest, virtually untouched since the founding of Washington. It was mostly used for practicing war games and to provide a buffer to hide the academy from the rest of the city.

Erica knew exactly where the best spot to get over the wall was, as though she'd surveyed the entire length of it many times during her time at school. She scrambled up a grand old oak tree on a corner across from the campus, as quickly as a panther would.

It took me a bit more time to scale it, but eventually I joined her on a thick branch high above the ground.

Erica used a small crossbow to fire a thin steel wire into another oak on campus, then secured the wire to our tree and quickly rigged a zip-line harness to it. I had used a zip-line with Erica enough times to know exactly what to do without asking questions. We clipped ourselves to the harness, skimmed over the wall, and climbed down the other tree.

Close by was an ancient toolshed that served as an access point to the school's hidden network of underground tunnels. I had used this one before as well. We entered the shed and shifted the deceptively nondescript trowel on the wall that triggered the secret elevator. The floor instantly lowered, taking us down into the first subterranean level of the school.

The academy's tunnels were very different from the one I'd spent the previous night in. They were newer—although not *that* new, being mostly relics of the Cold War—with smooth cement walls and fluorescent lights. They contained everything from bomb shelters to food storage for the cafeteria to the school morgue. (Our meals were so awful, students often wondered if the cooks had gotten the food storage and the morgue confused.) The whole thing was a sprawling labyrinth; every tunnel looked exactly the same, and the designers had purposefully omitted any signs in order to make it even more confusing. It was gloomy, dank, and unsettling. Whenever I was down there, I half expected to run into a minotaur. Left on my own, I might have wandered about in circles for hours, but Erica knew the place by memory.

Although the campus above us was closely monitored with security cameras, the subterranean levels weren't. There wasn't enough money in the school budget for that, and the designers had figured that anyone who knew about the tunnels was probably on our side. This allowed Erica and me to move quickly, without fear of having our presence recorded.

Erica led the way through a mind-boggling series of lefts and rights—pausing every now and then to let guards wander through distant intersections—until we found ourselves outside a door mundanely marked C414. There was a coded keypad entry for security, but Erica knew the code. The door clicked open, allowing us into the Cheney Center.

I'd been here before as well, on the receiving end of the CIA's information-acquisition practices. The center was actually designed to be calming, rather than frightening, as current CIA research showed that this was the better way to coerce people into spilling their guts. There was a reception area that seemed more suitable to a spa, with comfortable chairs, bamboo screens, and a burbling Zen fountain. New age music played softly from hidden speakers.

There was also a heavily armed guard, lying unconscious on the sisal carpet. A chloroformed rag lay crumpled beside him.

Uh-oh, I thought.

At which point, someone leapt out from behind one of the bamboo screens and attacked us.

NEGOTIATION

Cheney Center for the Acquisition of Information

CIA Academy of Espionage

February 13

0300 hours

Our attacker was clad in black from head to toe, armed with another chloroformed rag, and had the element of surprise. However, he made one key mistake:

He attacked Erica instead of me.

According to Professor Georgia Simon, my self-defense instructor, I had the fighting skills of "a wet piece of tissue paper." If I had been attacked first, I probably would have been unconscious before I'd even realized what was happening.

Erica, on the other hand, could kick Professor Simon's butt. Our attacker didn't stand a chance against her. She sensed his assault, whirled to face him, grabbed his arms, and calmly flipped him into the Zen fountain. Then she whipped out her dart gun and aimed it at him.

"Wait!" I exclaimed.

I had recognized our attacker's groan of pain.

Erica's finger twitched on the trigger of her gun but didn't depress it. "Give me one good reason," she said.

"It's Mike," I told her.

"Ben?" Our attacker struggled to his feet, slightly dazed and sopping wet, then pulled off his mask, revealing that he was, in fact, Mike Brezinski. "What are you doing here?"

"What are *you* doing here?" Erica demanded.

"I asked you first," Mike said.

"I'm the one with the gun," Erica reminded him.

"Good point," Mike conceded. "I was trying to help you."

"By attacking us?" I asked.

"That was an accident," Mike explained. "I thought you were with SPYDER. I didn't realize it was you until I was in mid-attack. I mean, the entire CIA is looking for you. Why on earth would you infiltrate here?"

"It's the last thing anyone would expect," I said.

"Oh." Mike nodded understanding. "Gotcha."

Erica kept the gun trained on him, as though she still

wasn't sure whether to believe him. "Did you knock that guard unconscious?"

"Um . . . yes," Mike admitted, sounding a bit embarrassed. "I didn't *want* to, but he wouldn't listen to reason. He was going to call the administration on us."

"Us?" Erica and I asked at once.

"Me and Zoe," Mike said. "She's already inside, talking to the prisoners."

I turned to Erica. "Looks like they had the same idea that we did."

"Was your idea to come down here and ask them what SPYDER was up to?" Mike asked.

"More or less," I said.

"Then, yeah, we had the same idea," Mike agreed. "Cool! Great minds think alike."

Erica still didn't lower her gun.

Mike looked to me. "Zoe said you called her last night and claimed SPYDER had framed you for the attack on the president. Unfortunately, no one else at the CIA seems to believe that—except for your friends."

"Who are . . . ?" I asked.

"Me, Zoe, Warren, Chip, and Jawa. We spent the whole day trying to convince people you were innocent, but no one would listen. In fact, the principal claims he suspected you were a mole for SPYDER all along."

"Of course he does." I groaned.

"So we figured we had to get some more evidence ourselves," Mike went on. "But this was the only place we could think of to look for it."

"Why'd you wait until now?" Erica asked.

"Probably the same reason you did," Mike said. "Everyone else is asleep right now. The CIA warned us not to do anything to help Ben, so we had to pretend like we understood and wait until everyone let their guard down. Except that guy." He pointed to the unconscious guard on the floor.

"If you and Zoe are here," I said, "where are Warren, Chip, and Jawa?"

"On patrol in the halls outside, making sure no one catches us by surprise."

"Like we did?" I asked.

"Yes," Mike replied. "Apparently, their patrolling techniques could use some work."

"They're probably keeping an eye on the more common entrances from campus," Erica pointed out. "The one we came through isn't well known." Finally convinced that Mike was on our side, she lowered her dart gun and slipped it back into her holster. "This has cost us enough time. Let's find out what we came here for."

A door opened from the reception room into the rest

of the complex. Erica led us through it. We passed down a nicely decorated hallway with more new age music playing, past a series of rooms where people were "coerced" into coughing up information.

Now that Erica wasn't aiming a gun at him, Mike had the time to look over my new outfit. "Nice suit," he told me.

"Thanks," I said. "I just got it."

"Did it come with the utility belt?"

"Yeah. But you have to load it yourself."

"Do you have anything cool in yours?"

"Not unless you think gum is cool."

"Would you two mind canning the chitchat?" Erica asked. "This is a covert mission, not a slumber party."

"Sorry," Mike and I said.

We arrived at a thick metal door that looked as though it had recently been installed. The computerized keypad lock had been shorted out and the door was propped open with a wad of paper. Zoe's handiwork.

We entered the recently remodeled incarceration area. The walls between a few information-extraction rooms had been knocked down to create a larger, significantly less comfortable space, which was divided into three sections: two jail cells, positioned side by side, and a longer, thinner corridor that allowed people like us to visit the prisoners. It felt like being at a very old zoo where bars were still on the cages.

The cells were sparsely decorated. Each had an army surplus cot for sleeping and a cheap desk for dining and homework. The toilets were metal and sat right out in the open, next to the cots. (Although there was a wall between the cells to provide a tiny bit of privacy.) The only amenity was an extremely large television and gaming console in the cell to the left, which Nefarious Jones had been given as a reward for good behavior.

Despite the late hour, Nefarious was playing video games.

This came as no surprise. Back at evil spy school, Nefarious had done almost nothing except play video games. It occurred to me that being incarcerated with a gaming console probably wasn't much of a punishment for him; in fact, it might have even felt like an improvement over his previous life. He had already spent so much time sitting on his cot staring at the TV screen that he'd created a large divot in the mattress under his rear end. He was playing *Target: Annihilation*, the exact same game Jason Stern had been playing, although he was significantly better at it. Jason had been struggling with level three. Nefarious was on level 638.

"Hey, Nefarious," I said. "How's it going?"

"Fine," he said, then went right back to his game.

This qualified as a decent bit of conversation for

Nefarious. I had gotten an entire word out of him, as opposed to his usual "Mneh." I figured it meant he actually liked me.

I got a considerably stronger reaction from the other two people in the room.

Zoe, who was standing in front of Ashley Sparks's cell, squealed with delight, then raced over and threw her arms around me. "Ben! I can't believe you're here! I was so worried about you! I'm so happy you're not in jail!"

"Me too," I said.

Zoe noticed Erica and crowed, "And you! You were only pretending to be upset with Ben, weren't you? Oh, I could hug you, too!"

"Don't," Erica warned. As if, maybe, Zoe had threatened to punch her.

Zoe backed off. "I only said I *could* hug you, that's all."

"Well, well, well," said a voice from the second cell. It was chirpy and yet oddly malicious at the same time. "Looks like all the jidiots are finally here."

Mike looked at me, confused. "Jidiots?"

"Ashley always does this thing where she combines two words to make a new one," I explained. "Jerks plus idiots equals 'jidiots.'"

"Oh," Mike said, then realized he should take offense at this. "Hey! We're not either one of those things!"

"You're with these other jidiots," Ashley taunted. "So you're a jidiot by association."

I moved down the corridor so I could get a better look at her. She was using the bars of her cell as makeshift gymnastic equipment, hanging by her hands from them several feet above the floor, her legs spread in a midair split. Instead of her usual sparkly pink leotard, she was in drab prison garb, but she still had a bit of her traditional glitter in her hair. While Nefarious had grown paunchy during the time since I'd last seen him, Ashley had actually become even more fit in jail—which was really saying something. She had been in excellent shape at evil spy school. Now her muscles bulged so big, they strained the legs and sleeves of her uniform.

However, the contemptuous glare she'd last had for Erica and me was still on her face. Her prison time hadn't softened it at all.

"I've been trying to talk to them for ten minutes," Zoe whispered to Erica, Mike, and me. "They both claim to not know anything about SPYDER's current plans. I buy it from Nefarious, but I think Ashley's hiding something."

"Why's that?" I asked.

"Nefarious coughed up everything he knew about SPYDER weeks ago," Zoe explained. "That's how he got the TV and the game console—and why his sentence has been shortened. He's almost done his time. So why keep anything else secret? But Ashley . . . well, she's giving off this cocky vibe. Like she knows more than she's letting on and is thrilled that we don't know it."

"I can hear you," Ashley taunted. "But I can't help you. Looks like you're in serious treopardy, Ben."

"See what I mean?" asked Zoe.

"Treopardy?" Mike echoed. "What's that, trouble plus jeopardy?"

"Sounds right," I agreed.

Mike grinned. "I think I'm getting the hang of this."

Erica approached Ashley's cell, then shimmied up the bars until she was staring Ashley in the face. "I think you know plenty about what SPYDER is up to," she said.

"Well, I don't." Ashley tucked her legs and sprang backward off the bars, doing a flip before sticking the landing, a move that would have made most gymnastics fans gasp in awe. "I've been cooped up in this stupid jail ever since September. How could I possibly know what SPYDER has been plotting since then?"

"Because SPYDER isn't reckless," Erica replied. "They plot everything out well ahead of time with extreme care and caution. This assassination attempt would have taken months of planning, if not more. You were at evil spy school for more than a year before Ben arrived. Therefore, it's extremely likely you heard something about this." With that, Erica performed the exact same backward spring off the bars that Ashley had—only she did *two* flips before sticking the landing.

Ashley gaped in surprise, then caught herself and tried to act like she wasn't impressed. "Why would they have told me anything? I was only a student."

"I didn't suggest that anyone *told* you anything," Erica clarified. "I'm saying you might have *heard* something. You're a smart girl. You certainly kept your eyes and ears open. There's a good chance you picked up on a plot or two."

"If I did—and I'm not saying that happened—why on earth would I tell *you* about it? You're the one who put me in this horrible place." Ashley shifted her angry gaze to me. "And you! You stabbed me in the back! You let me think you were on my side! You promised to go to Disney World with me!"

"I never actually promised that," I said.

"You still betrayed me! You're a quaitor!"

"Quisling plus traitor?" Mike asked.

"Duh," Ashley sneered.

Erica returned to the bars of Ashley's cell. "You are going to tell me exactly what I want to know about SPYDER. And here's why: because I can bust you out of here if you do."

"What?" Ashley said, completely caught by surprise.

"What?" Zoe asked, even more surprised than Ashley.

"What?!" I asked, even more surprised than either one of them. "We never discussed that!"

"Because I figured you'd say no," Erica told me.

"Of course I'm going to say no!" I exclaimed. "It's bad enough that I'm wanted for trying to assassinate the president! Now you want to add breaking a major criminal out of jail to that?"

"If we don't break her out, then we don't get the evidence to clear your name," Erica explained.

"So to prove my innocence from one federal crime, I have to commit another?" I asked.

"Yes. The irony is incredible." Erica removed a formal document from her pocket and unfolded it for Ashley to read. "This is a notarized affidavit from an emissary of MI6. In return for your help, they are willing to spirit you out of this country and help you establish your own gymnastics training academy in any of the British territories."

"Any of them?" Ashley asked, so intrigued that she'd forgotten all about being spiteful. "Including Turks and Caicos?"

"Including Turks and Caicos," Erica said.

"Wow." Ashley's angry grimace disappeared and was replaced by the excited smile I'd seen for most of my time at spy school. "I've always wanted to go to Turks and Caicos.

And having my own gymnastics training academy would be swawesome."

"Sweaty plus awesome?" Mike asked.

"*Sweet* plus awesome," Zoe corrected.

"Oh." Mike looked disappointed that he'd gotten one wrong.

"You could bring your family with you," Erica told Ashley. "But we'd have to give you all new identities, and you'd never be able to return to the United States."

"Big deal," Ashley said. "This country stinks. First, the dimwit judge at our Olympic trials docked me a point by mistake. And then, when I tried to move on from that, the government threw me in jail."

"You *did* try to destroy a large part of New York City," I reminded her.

Ashley waved this off, unconcerned, as though I'd merely accused her of being a litterbug. She studied the affidavit carefully, then nodded approval and turned to Erica. "Okay, let's do this. I'm good to go right now."

"So are we," Erica said.

"We are?" I asked. "Don't you think we should talk this through a bit more?"

"No," Erica said flatly. "We've already gone through the trouble of breaking in and the guard is still unconscious. We won't get a better chance to spring Ashley and we're running out of time. If you want to clear your name, we need to know what she knows—and this is the only way we're going to get it."

I turned to Mike and Zoe, hoping they might serve as voices of reason and back me up, but neither of them did. In fact, Mike was thrilled about the whole thing. "We're springing a prisoner from maximum security!" he exclaimed. "This is so cool!"

"It's a felony," I pointed out to him.

"To save *you*," he said. "Man, this school is amazing! The most exciting thing we ever got to do at our old school was dissect a frog. And mine had some kind of frog fungus."

Meanwhile, Zoe wasn't arguing my side either. Instead, she asked Erica, "Do you think we should maybe spring Nefarious too?"

"Why?" Erica asked. "He doesn't know any crucial information."

"I know, but it doesn't seem fair to leave him here and free Ashley. He actually helped thwart SPYDER's plans, while she tried to kill us."

"Don't worry about me," Nefarious said, without even looking up from his game. "I'm good here."

"Really?" Zoe asked.

"Really," Nefarious answered. "I get to play games all day and have all the food I can eat. What more is there?"

"Uh . . . freedom?" Zoe suggested. "Fresh air? Not having your toilet be six inches from your bed?"

"Mneh," Nefarious grunted. "I like having the toilet right here. That way I can keep gaming while I do my business."

"See what I have to deal with in here?" Ashley asked. "It's hisgusting."

"Horrible plus disgusting?" Mike asked.

"Bingo," Ashley told him. "So please, guys, let's get out of here. Now."

"I'll decide when we spring you," Erica said. "And we're not taking you anywhere until you tell us what SPYDER's plotting."

"Ha!" Ashley barked. "I'm not a boron. If I tell you what I know first, then you'll just leave me here. I'm not saying anything until I'm safe and sound in Turks and Caicos."

"That's unacceptable," Erica countered. "It will take weeks to get you set up there, and we need that information right now. So cough it up."

"No way." Ashley crossed her arms over her chest defiantly.

"Then you're staying right here. For the next twenty years." Erica started for the door. "C'mon, guys. Let's find someone else who'll talk."

Mike, Zoe, and I dropped in behind her—although I didn't really want to. For all my concern about springing

Ashley, I didn't have any idea who else we could go to for information. I was pretty sure Erica didn't either. I could only assume she was bluffing, hoping to get Ashley to crack. . . .

Which was exactly what happened. "Wait!" Ashley cried. "You don't have to get me out of the country! All you have to do is spring me. Once we're off the spy school property, safe and sound, I'll tell you everything I know!"

Erica turned back to her. "Is it enough to clear Ben's name?"

"It's enough to take down SPYDER once and for all. Those schmerks deserve it after making me take the fall for them."

"Schmoes plus jerks?" Mike asked.

"Schmucks plus jerks," Ashley informed him. "But close enough."

"All right," Erica agreed. "We've got a deal." She went to the electronic keypad for the cell door and entered the combination. The cell door clicked open.

"How'd you know that code?" Zoe asked.

"The principal keeps all the top secret codes for campus written down in a folder in his office so he won't forget them," Erica explained. "It's labeled 'Top Secret Codes.'" She removed the dart gun from her holster and aimed it at Ashley. "Try anything funny and I'll knock you out, drag you back in here, and make sure they add sixty years to your sentence."

Ashley raised her hands in surrender. "I won't try anything, I swear. Let me just get my stuff." She grabbed some hair glitter, pink nail polish, and a few scrunchies, shoved them in her pockets, and said, "Let's go."

I led the way out of the Cheney Center, wanting to get off campus as quickly as possible. Mike and Zoe followed me, and Ashley followed them. Erica came last, keeping her eye—and her gun—on Ashley.

"Bye, Nefarious!" Zoe called.

"Mneh," Nefarious replied. He was so engrossed in his game, he barely even seemed aware we were leaving.

We passed down the hall of information-extraction rooms, through the reception area, then back out into the labyrinth of tunnels under the school.

Where we ran into Warren Reeves. Literally.

He was dressed in a gray outfit that blended perfectly into the cement tunnels. I didn't even see him until I slammed into him and knocked him right on his butt.

"Ouch!" he whined.

"Hey, Warren!" Zoe said excitedly. "Ben came for Ashley, the same way we did! Now we're springing her so she'll turn traitor on SPYDER!"

"No you're not," Warren replied with surprising confidence.

An entire squad of campus security agents stepped into the hallway behind him, their weapons pointed at us.

"You're all under arrest," Warren said.

ESCAPE

CIA Academy of Espionage

Subterranean level B

February 13

0400 hours

I was caught completely by surprise, not so much because we had been ambushed, but because it was Warren who had engineered it. While many of my fellow classmates at spy school were incredibly capable, Warren wasn't. It was hard for him to so much as fill up a glass of water without screwing it up. Erica seemed to be equally surprised by Warren's sudden competence, while Mike merely seemed disappointed that our adventure had come to an end so quickly. Meanwhile, Zoe and Ashley were both livid.

"How dare you?" Zoe shouted at Warren, betrayal in her eyes. "You're only here right now because I *told* you we were here!"

"You told him?" I repeated. "When?"

"I sent him a text when you showed up by the jail cells," Zoe said through gritted teeth. "He was supposed to tell Jawa and Chip that you were here. But instead he's turned us in." She glared at Warren hatefully. "I thought you were my friend!"

"I *tried* to be," Warren said petulantly. "But you've always sided with Ben. On everything. Even now that he's turned out to be a covert assassin, you're *still* siding with him instead of me! Well, now you're going down with him too."

The guards surrounded us. While some kept us at gunpoint, the others advanced forward to handcuff us.

"You jidiot," Ashley hissed at Warren under her breath. "You're not supposed to do this *now*."

Warren appeared far more disturbed by this than he had by anything Zoe had said. He reared back from Ashley and looked around skittishly to see if anyone else had heard her.

And just like that, SPYDER's plot suddenly became clear to me.

However, there was no time to share my revelation.

Five of the guards shoved me, Erica, Mike, Zoe, and Ashley up against the wall, face-first, then wrenched our hands behind our backs to cuff us. Erica was directly beside me. I started to tell her what I'd realized, but she cut me off, having something even more important to share. "In three seconds, hit the deck."

Before I could even ask what she meant, a metal pellet the size of a half-dollar dropped from her utility belt. The moment it hit the cement floor, a cloud of smoke exploded from it and enveloped us.

I did exactly as she'd ordered, yanking my hands free from the startled guard behind me and dropping to the floor myself.

From the side of me where Erica was came the distinct sound of another guard getting punched someplace very painful. Then I had the sense of something like a leg whipping quickly through the space over my head, followed by the sound of the guard who'd been behind me getting kicked hard somewhere even more painful.

If I hadn't hit the deck as Erica had ordered, she would have just sent me to the hospital.

From my other side, where Ashley had been, I heard the sounds of yet another guard being pummeled.

Meanwhile, the guards with the guns were somewhere farther away in the cloud. "Stand down!" one of them yelled, though he sounded far more worried than authoritative. "If you don't, we will have to . . . Aaugh!" His scream of surprise turned to one of pain, then abruptly cut off, as though he'd suddenly been rendered unconscious.

I remained where I was, curled in a ball on the concrete floor. I knew it wasn't very chivalrous of me to let Erica and Ashley handle all the fighting, but then, a big part of being a good spy was playing to your strengths. I was good at solving problems, doing complex calculations, and working out what SPYDER was up to, but I was pathetic at fighting—while Erica and Ashley were astoundingly good at it. If I tried to help, I'd only get in the way and would most likely end up unconscious, which wasn't going to do anyone any good.

In addition to the various thumps, punches, and yelps of pain around me, I could also hear Warren growing more and more panicked. "Erica?" he asked worriedly. "What are you doing? Erica . . . ?" Then I heard him fleeing through the cloud of smoke. Or trying to flee. There was a distinct thud, followed by a yelp, as he blindly ran into a wall.

An alarm went off. Warren or one of the guards must have triggered it. A shrill whooping echoed through the tunnels—and most likely, the entire campus above us as well.

The smoke began to dissipate after only a few seconds, but that was all Erica and Ashley had needed. I found myself lying on the floor surrounded by the bodies of guards who were either unconscious or in too much pain to stand. Erica emerged from the cloud, grabbed me by the shoulder, and hoisted me to my feet.

Another guard sailed out of the smoke nearby, crashed into the wall, and collapsed into a whimpering lump. I expected Ashley to follow him from the cloud—but to my surprise, it was Zoe who appeared, revealing herself as the one who'd taken the guy out. She noticed the shock on my face and said, "I've been practicing."

Mike and Ashley emerged behind her. Ashley had an ear-to-ear grin, as though she'd been enjoying herself. Mike was agog with amazement. He leaned close to me and whispered, "The girls here are *so* much cooler than the ones back in regular middle school."

As the final wisps of smoke melted away, I cased the tunnel. All the guards were still there, crumpled on the floor in various pained states, but Warren had vanished. The cement corridor was too long for him to have run out of, so he'd obviously put his camouflage skills to work, blending in somewhere around us.

"Anyone see Warren?" I asked.

"Forget him," Erica said. "We have to move. More guards are coming."

"We can't leave him," I told her. "He's . . ."

But Erica didn't give me the time to explain. Instead, she grabbed me by the arm and dragged me down the hall.

"More guards are coming *now*," she clarified.

Sure enough, the sound of more guards approaching echoed from the end of the corridor. *A lot* more guards.

Ashley, Mike, and Zoe followed us as we fled. In the distance behind us, I heard the guards yell, "Stop or we'll shoot!"

We didn't stop. So they shot. Erica led us around a corner right as the sound of gunfire erupted. Hundreds of rubber bullets zinged past where we'd just been. They wouldn't have killed us, but they would have hurt us badly enough to slow even Erica down.

We ended up in another long corridor. I thought it might have led back toward the far end of campus, where Erica and I had first entered the complex, but I couldn't really tell. Another set of guards was coming down it in the distance, blocking that route of escape.

"Freeze!" they yelled.

"Nuts," Erica said, then suddenly yanked me through a door to my left. Mike, Zoe, and Ashley plunged through it after us.

A staircase spiraled upward. It wasn't a very well-used stairwell, like some of the other entrances to the tunnel complex. Instead, it was old and dusty and looked like everyone but Erica had forgotten it even existed.

"Zoe, can you call Chip or Jawa?" I panted as we raced

up the stairs. "Tell them to be on the lookout for Warren."

"Why are you so concerned about Warren all of a sudden?" Zoe asked. "The weasel tried to have us arrested!"

"He's working for SPYDER," I said.

Below me on the stairs, I heard the sound of Zoe stumbling in surprise. "Warren?" she gasped. "No way."

Ashley burst into laughter. "You didn't know? That little schmerk really snowed you good!"

I glanced upward at Erica to see what her reaction was, but couldn't deduce anything. If she was surprised, she didn't show it.

The top of the staircase dead-ended at a cement wall with a bolting mechanism embedded in it. Erica flipped the bolt and the wall suddenly became a door, swinging open into the boys' locker room in the school gymnasium. There were ten lockers on the opposite side of it, one of which was my own. I had been using it for a year without having the slightest idea there was a hidden door behind it.

Unfortunately, the gym was in the dead center of campus, meaning we had a long way to go to get to safety.

The campus guards entered the stairwell below us and began pounding up it. We swung the secret door closed behind us, wedged a bench against it to jam it shut, and fled the gym.

As I'd suspected, the alarms were ringing all over campus.

The lights in all the school buildings had come on, indicating that everyone was now awake. We could hear students and faculty forming ranks near the dormitory, grabbing weapons inside the armory, and closing in on us from almost every direction. Flashlight beams sliced through the darkness outside, searching for us.

We ran the only way we could: south, toward the wooded section of campus.

Our route took us straight through the obstacle course.

We couldn't circumvent it, the way Mike had done the morning before. It was too big, and our pursuers seemed to be closing in around it. Our only hope was to make it through the course as fast as possible.

We didn't bother crawling through the mud. It had frozen solid anyhow. The paint guns were still set up to blast us if we triggered them, but at the moment we had far more pressing problems. So we ran, skidding and sliding on the frozen muck, while paintballs whizzed past us—and occasionally pegged us as well. My brand-new, awesomely sleek black outfit was quickly splattered blue and red.

"You're sure about Warren?" Zoe asked me. She had a wounded look in her big brown eyes.

"Yes." I winced as a paintball clipped my shoulder. "He's the one who planted the bomb on me. I thought some SPYDER agent had done it on the subway, but I didn't wear my jacket when we ran this course yesterday; I had my gym clothes on instead. My jacket was in my locker. Warren had plenty of time to plant the bomb after he washed out and got sent back to start over."

"But plenty of other people had the opportunity to plant a bomb then too," Zoe protested. "How are you so sure it was Warren?"

"For starters, he was with us in the library right before I got activated the other day." I ducked as a flurry of paint-balls whistled over my head. "That's when he put something on my jacket to attract the dogs at the White House. Erica said it might have been meat—or a trace of bomb residue. That way, when he put an actual bomb in my jacket the next day, the Secret Service thought the dogs were making a mistake."

"Still," Zoe said, "there were other people in the library too. . . ."

"But Warren's the only one in cahoots with Ashley," I said. Then I turned to Ashley herself. "How long has he been on your side? Since I was in evil spy school?"

"No," she replied, seeming to enjoy how much this was upsetting Zoe. "But we already had him pegged as a strong candidate to recruit back then. So our guys went to work on him right after you blew up our headquarters. . . . Oof!" She gasped as a paintball nailed her in the thigh.

Zoe flinched as another paintball clipped her in the elbow, then asked me, "How'd you know?"

"Because of Ashley's reaction when Warren surprised us just now. She obviously knew the plan already. Warren must have gotten word to her somehow. But he showed up too early. I'm guessing he was supposed to wait until *after* Ashley was free to capture us."

"You think?" Ashley asked sarcastically. "That jidiot nearly got me arrested all over again."

We reached the far side of the mud patch where the climbing wall stood. Erica scaled it without breaking stride, while Ashley vaulted to the top with the agility of, well . . . a professional gymnast. Mike wasn't much slower, but Zoe and I still struggled getting over it.

"Warren's job wasn't to merely plant the bomb on me," I grunted, straining to climb the wall. "He was also going to take the credit for capturing me—and you—and everyone else. SPYDER suspected I might try to return to talk to Ashley, so they must have alerted him to be on the lookout for me. . . ."

"They *did*," Zoe said suddenly. "Warren was the one who suggested we stake out the jail. And he insisted I notify him if you showed up. I thought he was just looking out for you."

"No," I said. "He was looking out for SPYDER."

A flashlight beam caught me as I reached the top of the wall.

"There they are!" Professor Simon shouted.

Zoe and I dropped over the wall. A second later, a hailstorm of rubber bullets rattled against the other side. It sounded like every student and faculty member had unloaded upon us at once.

Ahead of us, Erica, Ashley, and Mike were already scrambling across the balance beam over the pit of water—which was now a pit of ice. Luckily, the grease that had covered the beam in the daytime had frozen as well, so running across it was significantly easier now. It wasn't *easy*—as we watched, Mike almost lost his balance and tumbled off the beam— but when people were coming to arrest and/or shoot you, it was always nice when the straightest route to retreat through wasn't as slippery as a bucket of eel guts.

Zoe and I ran after the others. "Think about it," I said. "Warren sets me up as the assassin. Then he catches me and turns me over to the CIA. He commits the crime *and* solves the case, which makes him look less like the assassin that he actually is—and more like the hero, which he isn't."

"But that doesn't work if you can prove what he did."

"That's why SPYDER wants to take care of me before I get the chance."

"You mean . . . kill you?"

"They already tried to blow me up with the president. I don't think they like me very much."

"I just can't believe Warren planted the bomb on you." Zoe looked queasy as we reached the far end of the beam and followed the others down the winding wooded path; the idea that Warren had turned traitor seemed to be taking a toll on her. "I can't believe he set us up like this. Why would he turn against us?"

I didn't answer—because I didn't really know the answer. All I could think of was, *Warren has always been a pinhead.* But before I could say it, Mike piped up.

"Warren didn't turn against *us*," he said. "He turned against Ben."

"I don't understand," Zoe said.

"You don't?" Ashley chided. "I thought you guys were supposed to be a bunch of geniuses here!"

"Er . . . ," Mike said, sounding uncomfortable, "Warren has a crush on you, Zoe."

"He does?" Zoe asked, aghast.

"And . . . ," Mike went on, sounding even more uncomfortable, "Zoe has a crush on *you*, Ben."

"What?" I asked, stunned. I had just been thinking that Zoe was rather unobservant for never picking up on the fact that Warren liked her—and I'd apparently done the exact same thing. I turned to Zoe, who quickly averted her eyes in embarrassment, which confirmed that Mike was right—and nearly caused Zoe to run straight into a tree.

Now that Zoe's crush was out in the open, a flood of memories came rushing back that I probably should have picked up on earlier: the time when Zoe had asked me to help her study for her History of Espionage exam when she turned out to know the subject better than I did; the time when she'd asked me to kill a spider in her room even though she could clobber a man twice her size; the time on Operation Snow Bunny when I'd made an offhanded comment that I would go to Disney World with her even though I wasn't really into her and she'd suddenly become very annoyed at me.

I wondered if I hadn't picked up on it because I'd been too focused on Erica, or if I simply wasn't used to girls paying attention to me. For most of my life, not a single girl had shown interest in me, and now it turned out that, not only had I missed the signals from my closest friend at spy school, but I had missed signals so obvious that they'd driven Warren to frame me for a presidential assassination.

"You guys didn't know any of this stuff?" Ashley taunted. "Man, for a bunch of spies-in-training, your social skills *stink.*"

"So this whole attack on the president . . . ," Zoe said, still trying to get her mind around it all. "It was all about getting even with Ben?"

Ashley laughed mockingly. "You jidiots actually thought

it was about killing the president? You don't understand how SPYDER works at all, do you?"

"I'm beginning to," I said. Every time I'd gone up against SPYDER, they had used misdirection, leading me—and the rest of the CIA—to believe they were plotting one thing when they were actually plotting something else. It seemed insane that they had targeted the president merely to frame me for his assassination (although his death might have been a nice side benefit for them), and yet it also fit the pattern of how SPYDER worked. They had a bone to pick with me for thwarting them so many times. However, if they killed me directly, the CIA would immediately suspect them: Who else but SPYDER wanted me dead? So SPYDER had come up with an indirect way to kill me—and ruin my reputation as well. Even though the plot hadn't worked as well as SPYDER had intended, they were still manipulating things to their advantage. Now my only allies at spy school—Erica, Zoe, and Mike—were also on the run from the CIA, while the one person who *really* worked for SPYDER—Warren—would look like the hero for catching us, leaving him free to cause further chaos and mayhem in the future.

It was all quite confounding, clever, and devious. Classic SPYDER. And yet I still had the sense that there was more to their plan. It felt like I had missed something important, something I couldn't quite put my finger on. . . .

"Oh, crud," Mike said suddenly.

His words snapped me back to the problem at hand: We were still on the run with the entire spy school closing in on us. Our ragtag band had emerged from the narrow wooded path to find ourselves facing the final obstacle on the course:

"Freaking pendulums," Zoe muttered.

A strong wind was blowing, swinging the massive pendulums back and forth over the balance beam. To make matters worse, they were almost impossible to see in the darkness.

Erica didn't hesitate. She ran right onto the beam and deftly dodged the hurtling logs. Ashley followed directly behind her.

"You go next," Mike told me, glancing back toward the woods. The flashlight beams of the CIA flickered in the trees, growing brighter as they came closer. "You're the one they want."

I didn't argue. It would have only wasted time. I gathered my nerve—and made sure my shoes were tied this time. (They were.) Then I charged onto the beam, trying to focus on the pendulums around me, rather than the people pursuing us. I had the sense of something enormous flying in toward me, hesitated, and felt a pendulum swing past an inch away. Then I moved on a few more feet and did it again. And again.

I was getting the hang of this. Though I warned myself to not get cocky, to concentrate and stay alert. . . .

There was a startled cry from ahead of me.

Erica.

To my surprise, she had lost her balance. She wobbled precariously on the balance beam.

And then a pendulum clobbered her. She sailed off the beam and thudded onto the ice below.

I was so astonished, I forgot all about my own surroundings.

Which was why I didn't notice the pendulum coming at *me* until it was too late.

It seemed to appear out of nowhere. I had the sickening sensation of tumbling through the air, and then I thwacked onto the ice and skidded across it like a hockey puck. I came to a stop, gasping and winded, right next to Erica. She was already scrambling to her feet.

"What happened?" I asked.

"Ashley shoved me!" Erica pointed to the gymnast and shouted, "Stop her!"

Unfortunately, Ashley had already made it to solid ground at the end of the balance beam, with a big lead on Zoe and Mike, who still had several pendulums to get past. Ashley gave us a devious smile, her perfect white teeth gleaming in the darkness. "So long, doosers!" she shouted, and raced into the darkness.

"Dorks plus losers?" Mike asked.

"Give it a rest," Zoe told him, then screamed as a pendulum smacked her off the beam.

Erica tried to go after Ashley, but she couldn't get any purchase on the ice. Instead of going in a straight line, she skidded around wildly on the surface.

She was still doing better than me, though. I was struggling to merely get to my feet. I almost stood, then slipped and face-planted right back on the ice.

Four dozen flashlight beams lit us all up at once, coming from every direction. The beams were blinding. We couldn't see who was aiming them at us, only that they had us surrounded.

"Put your hands up, traitors!" someone shouted.

Erica did exactly as ordered. There was no way she could fight back against so many people from inside the pit.

I raised my hands too. So did Zoe and Mike.

I heard the sound of a weapon being fired, followed by a small grunt from Erica.

"Erica?" I called out. "Are you okay?"

"No!" she shouted back. "Some dipstick just shot me with a sedation darrrrpppplthhhmmm." She promptly sagged on the ice, unconscious.

We had been captured for good this time, by our own agency.

While Ashley Sparks, the very person we'd risked our safety to find, had escaped.

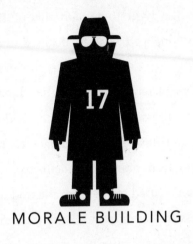

MORALE BUILDING

CIA Academy of Espionage
Hammond Quadrangle
February 13
0500 hours

Mike, Zoe, and I were handcuffed and marched
across campus. Erica was carried, seeing as she was unconscious. Greg Hauser, who was one of the biggest kids at school,
slung her over his shoulder like a sack of potatoes. Professor
Simon insisted on handcuffing her anyhow, in case she was
merely pretending to be drugged to get everyone to drop their
guard. Erica didn't seem to be pretending, though. She was
snoring softly and dreaming about arresting people; I could tell
this because she was issuing the Miranda warning in her sleep.

"You have the right to remain silent," she murmured drowsily. "Anything you say can be used against you in a court of law."

Now that we weren't blinded by their lights, I got a better look at our captors. I knew every one of them.

They were all fellow students and faculty. There were fifty of them, ranging from first-year students to Coach Macauley. As they had been roused to action in the middle of the night, most had dressed haphazardly. Some had thrown combat boots and Kevlar vests on over pajamas, while others had mismatched outfits of hastily gathered clothing. Nate Mackey's shirt was on backward and his fly was gaping open. Coach apparently hadn't been able to find his Kevlar vest, so he'd looted a baseball catcher's chest protector and mask from the gymnasium. The only thing anyone had in common was the hateful glare they fixed on us. They probably were under orders to not speak to me, but most couldn't keep themselves from hissing things like "Traitor," or "You're a disgrace."

"Ben isn't a traitor!" Zoe informed them defiantly. "He's been set up by SPYDER! And now you're doing SPYDER's dirty work for them by capturing us!"

That didn't convince anyone. It only provoked everyone to start hissing mean things at Zoe, too.

I didn't see Chip Schacter or Jawa O'Shea anywhere among them and wondered where they could be. I could only hope they were lurking in the shadows somewhere nearby, ready to take everyone else by surprise and rescue us.

"You have the right to an attorney," Erica said dreamily. "And to have her present while you are being questioned."

Meanwhile, Mike seemed completely unfazed by our situation. He was walking beside me with his head held high and a broad smile.

"Sorry I got you into this," I said.

"You didn't get me into anything," he replied cheerfully. "*I* chose to be here. I'm sure you'll figure out how to get us out of it, though."

I was at once impressed and disturbed by his confidence. "Uh, Mike . . . We're in a huge amount of trouble here. There *is* no way out of it."

"Well, there won't be if you're going to have a negative attitude like that."

"I'm not being negative. I'm being realistic."

"No you're not. Why are you being such a downer about all this?"

I looked around at the several dozen people holding us prisoner, wondering if Mike was no longer occupying the same reality that I was. "Because there's nothing to be optimistic about!"

"Of course there is. SPYDER tried to kill you."

I considered that a moment, then asked, "Did you by

any chance get hit in the head really hard out on the obstacle course? I'm worried you have brain damage."

"Nope. My brain is working perfectly."

"Really? Exactly how is SPYDER trying to kill me a good thing?"

"Think about it. SPYDER tried to kill *you*. Not Cyrus. Or Erica. Or anyone else. Only you. Why?"

"Um . . . because they don't like me?"

"Yes!" Mike exclaimed. "But it's not because of your personality or anything like that."

"It's because you're a threat to them," Zoe piped up, seeing where Mike was going with this. She suddenly sounded as excited as he did.

"Exactly!" Mike agreed. "*You're* the one who always figures out their plans, Ben. *You're* the one who thwarts them all the time. SPYDER, the most evil organization on the entire planet, wants you dead because they're *scared* of you. Honestly, you shouldn't be worried about all this. You should be flattered."

I thought that over. Mike's logic was more twisted than my small intestine, and yet it made a bizarre kind of sense. Which actually made me feel a tiny bit better. Not a whole lot better, but even that little bit helped.

"If you cannot afford an attorney," Erica said quietly, "one will be appointed for you."

"You guys are all full of crap," Hauser growled. "You're *working* for SPYDER. You're not fooling any of us."

"No offense, Hauser," Mike said, "but you're routinely outwitted by your own breakfast cereal. It doesn't matter what *you* believe. It matters what the truth is. And the truth is, if anyone can figure out what SPYDER is really up to right now, it's Ben."

"We already know what SPYDER is up to," I said. "They framed me for killing the president to make me look like a criminal. But no one's going to believe it without any evidence. . . ." I trailed off, wondering about this. I suddenly had the same feeling that I'd had on the obstacle course, right before confronting the pendulum. The sense that I'd missed something important.

"What's wrong?" Zoe asked.

"I think Mike's right," I said. "There's more to all this. SPYDER might be plotting something much bigger than merely framing me."

"Like assassinating the president?" Hauser asked. "'Cause that's pretty big."

"No," I said. "It's something else entirely."

"What?" Mike asked.

I frowned. "I don't have the slightest idea."

"But you know it's *something*, right?" Zoe asked. "And like Mike said, you *always* figure their plots out. So all you have to do is figure out this one, and then the CIA will realize what's really going on here and let us go."

I sighed, my confidence deflating once again. I wasn't so sure the CIA would cop to its mistake that easily—and I was even less sure that I could figure out what SPYDER was plotting. I had almost no information to work from. All I had was a hunch. And even if I wanted to investigate SPYDER further, I couldn't really do it as a prisoner.

The procession of captors led us into the Nathan Hale Building.

I glanced around the gothic foyer, looking desperately for Chip and Jawa. If they were planning to rescue us, they were running out of time. I paid particular attention to the shadowy nooks and crevices, hoping to see them lurking there.

They weren't.

Meanwhile, Erica was still snoring away on Hauser's shoulder.

To the side of the library, two secure steel doors stood open.

I had never seen them open before—although I had known of the room behind them. In fact, I had once prevented SPYDER from blowing it up, along with the heads of every intelligence division in the United States. But I had never been inside it. It turned out to be a large lecture hall, used only on rare occasions when big groups of important people had to gather at the academy.

"Do you understand your rights?" Erica asked sleepily.

A stage stretched across the far end of the lecture hall, where speakers could stand at a podium and address the crowd. However, the podium had been removed, and now there was a table with seven people sitting at it. I couldn't tell who any of the people were, as blindingly bright lights had been arrayed behind them, leaving them mere silhouettes.

Hundreds of seats faced the stage, but for now only the front row was being used. Two people sat there with their hands cuffed behind their backs.

My heart sank when I saw who it was.

Chip and Jawa.

TRIBUNAL

CIA Academy of Espionage

Angleton Meeting Room

Nathan Hale Building

February 13

0530 hours

"Hey," Chip said, looking embarrassed.

"What are you guys doing here?" Zoe asked them.

"We tried to hold off all these bozos outside the dormitory," Chip said, nodding toward our captors. "So you could have a little extra time to get away."

"It obviously didn't work," Jawa said miserably.

"Sorry," Chip apologized.

"Thanks for trying," I told them. Although it was

dispiriting to see them there, I was also flattered by their loyalty to me.

"Sit down!" a voice boomed from the center of the table. I recognized it instantly: Cyrus Hale. His voice echoed throughout the cavernous room, like the Wizard of Oz speaking to Dorothy.

Mike, Zoe, and I sat in the front row. Hauser looked to the stage nervously, unsure what to do with Erica. "Er . . . should I just leave her on the floor? Or do you want me to try to put her in a chair like she's sitting?"

"What happened to her?" Cyrus demanded, sounding concerned.

"I shot . . . er . . . I mean, *someone* shot her with a sedation dart," Hauser stammered.

"You sedated my granddaughter?" Cyrus shouted.

"She's very dangerous when she's awake!" Hauser said defensively.

"Aw, thanks," Erica said dreamily, then looked to the stage and waved at Cyrus with her cuffed hands. "Hi, Grandpa."

"Crikey, she's doped to the gills," Cyrus said, then ordered, "Just set her on the floor and clear out. That goes for everyone who isn't a prisoner here!"

Hauser placed Erica on the floor by our feet and scurried toward the exit as quickly as he could. It was strange to see someone his size scurry, but he managed it. So did everyone else in the hunting party, including the faculty. They all seemed relieved to get far away from Cyrus when he was angry.

"Don't worry," Mike whispered to Chip and Jawa while everyone else was evacuating the room. "Ben's going to get us all out of this."

"How?" Jawa asked.

"I don't know," Mike replied. "Ask Ben."

Jawa looked to me. "How?" he repeated.

"I don't know either," I admitted.

Jawa sighed morosely. "This is terrible. I'm going to be kicked out of school. I've spent the last two years slaving away for a perfect grade point average and now I've completely squandered it."

"Silence!" Cyrus yelled.

We all fell silent and straightened up in our seats. Except Erica, who had nodded off to sleep again on the floor, and Mike, who remained casually slumped in his chair, like this was no big deal.

Cyrus banged a gavel on the table. "Benjamin Ripley, you stand before this tribunal accused of collaborating with SPYDER to assassinate the president of the United States of America, while the rest of you are accused of criminally abetting him."

"What?" gasped the silhouette seated next to Cyrus. I recognized that voice as well: Alexander Hale. "Erica too?"

Cyrus sighed heavily. Then he turned to Alexander and said, "She helped Ben escape our agents at the museum yesterday. Not only did she aid a known criminal, but she also destroyed a prized model of a humpback whale in the process."

"I know," Alexander said. "But she's your *grand-daughter*."

"Being a blood relative of mine doesn't entitle her to preferential treatment," Cyrus said coldly.

"She's also a blood relative of *mine*," Alexander protested. "I don't want her going to jail."

"Neither do I," Cyrus said. "But she broke the law, so she must suffer the consequences."

"But . . . ," Alexander began.

"That's enough!" Cyrus snapped.

Alexander's silhouette shrank in what looked like embarrassment.

Cyrus returned his attention to us. Even though I couldn't see his eyes, I got the distinct sense they were boring into me. "Agent Ripley, how long have you been working for SPYDER?"

"I've never worked for SPYDER," I replied.

"Ha!" barked another person on the panel. Given the

sharp tone and the silhouette of what looked like a dead badger perched on his head, I knew it was the principal. "You're not fooling anyone, Ripley! I've known you were a bad egg since the moment I first laid eyes on you! You've been working for SPYDER the whole time you've been at this academy, haven't you?"

"I *thwarted* SPYDER right after I came to this academy," I pointed out, "when I kept them from blowing up this very conference room and everyone in it. Why would I have done that if I was working for SPYDER?"

"Er . . . ," the principal said dully, "ah . . . um . . . It was obviously a fiendish plot to convince us that you weren't a mole for them."

"So . . . ," I said, "your theory is that SPYDER exposed Murray Hill as a mole—when you didn't even know about him—in order to convince you that *I* wasn't a mole—when you didn't suspect me at all?"

"Yes!" the principal declared, then seemed to think better of this. "Uh, well . . . possibly. SPYDER is extremely devious. It's impossible to fathom what they're ever thinking."

"It's impossible to fathom what *you're* ever thinking," Cyrus muttered. "Or if you're even thinking at all."

"I think plenty!" the principal said defensively. "My mind is a constant whirlwind of thinkery!"

Cyrus groaned, then spoke to the other people on the panel. "Careful analysis shows that Ripley was not a mole upon his recruitment to this institution but was most likely turned by SPYDER during his undercover mission at their evil spy school."

"The mission that you initiated without authorization, Agent Hale?" one of the other silhouettes asked. It was a woman with a stern voice I didn't recognize.

"Yes," Cyrus answered, without a trace of shame. "I felt it was an appropriate decision at the time, and I still believe I was right. However, I will also fully accept responsibility for placing Agent Ripley in a situation where he could be brainwashed."

"I wasn't brainwashed!" I argued. "In fact, I thwarted SPYDER on that mission too. I blew up their base!"

"We consider it likely that the base may have blown up due to missile malfunction," Cyrus informed the panel.

"It didn't!" I exclaimed. "It blew up because I defeated SPYDER, and their missile system was designed to blow up their own base in order to destroy any evidence. All these guys were there to see it—except Mike." I tried to point to my friends, then remembered that my hands were cuffed.

"That's right!" Zoe said supportively. "We saw Ben engineer the whole thwarting!"

"I'm aware of your version of the story," Cyrus said to

me. "However, I find it extremely suspicious that the people who can corroborate that tale are the very ones now on trial for treason with you. The only exception would be Warren Reeves, who not only engineered your capture, but who also reports that the story of your thwarting of SPYDER at their evil spy school did not play out as you claim."

"Warren's the one working for SPYDER!" I said. "Not me!"

"Warren didn't blow up the White House," Cyrus reminded me. "Nor did he spring Ashley Sparks from jail. *You* did."

I frowned, realizing this was a hard point to argue. All I could come up with was, "You've worked with Warren before. You weren't very impressed by his abilities then. Do you really think he could have engineered our capture all by himself?"

"Just because someone is often incompetent doesn't mean they're *completely* incompetent," Cyrus said. "My own son is evidence of that."

"Hey!" Alexander yelped, offended.

"Meanwhile," Cyrus went on, "your competence is no argument against your being corruptible." I started to interrupt, but he cut me off. "There is nothing to be gained by continuing to lie to us, Benjamin. However, there is much to gain by admitting the truth. If you tell us everything you know about SPYDER, we will be lenient with your punishment."

"That's a laugh," Chip said under his breath. "He means he'll only send you to jail for fifty years instead of life."

"I can hear you, Mr. Schacter," Cyrus said. "May I remind you that telling the truth is in your interests here as well?"

"We're *all* telling the truth," I argued. "Warren Reeves is the only one who's lied to you. What makes more sense: that all of us are moles for SPYDER—including your own granddaughter—or that only one person at this school is?"

Cyrus hesitated briefly before answering. When he spoke again, his voice was tinged with regret. "Sadly, SPYDER has turned several students at this school before you, as well as many respected agents at the CIA. So yes, I do think it's possible that all six of you might be working for them—and I am even willing to condemn Erica if the evidence points to her."

"This is *Erica*," I reiterated. "The best spy-in-training at this academy . . ."

"And before her, Joshua Hallal was the best spy-in-training at this academy," Cyrus reminded me. "As you are well aware, SPYDER turned him, too."

"That doesn't speak very highly of this academy," the stern woman said.

"SPYDER is unlike any organization you have ever encountered," Cyrus told her. "But I assure you, we will find out who is working for them and root out that evil once and for all. Starting right . . ."

Cyrus trailed off suddenly, listening to a faint sound in the room.

My friends and I all listened too, trying to pinpoint it. I heard a series of squeals and squelches, with tinny music in the background.

"What is that?" Jawa asked.

"Flapjack Frenzy," Zoe answered.

Cyrus suddenly wheeled on the principal. "Are you playing a game on your phone?"

The principal's head snapped up so quickly, his toupee almost flew off. "No!" he said, although it was obviously a lie. He desperately fumbled with his phone, trying to turn the sound off.

"You are!" Cyrus roared. "You're playing a game in the midst of a tribunal!"

"I was only checking my e-mail," the principal said weakly. "And the game came on by mistake."

"You shouldn't be checking your e-mail in the middle of a tribunal either!" Cyrus snapped. "Give me your phone right now."

"No," the principal said. "It's *mine*."

"Alexander, take his phone," Cyrus ordered.

Alexander snatched the phone from the principal and handed it to his father, who promptly smashed it with his gavel.

"Hey!" the principal yelped. "I had critical information on that!"

"I'll bet." Cyrus rubbed his temples with his fingers, like he was fighting off a major headache. "Sorry for the interruption," he told the other members of the tribunal. "Where were we . . . ?"

"You were going to root out SPYDER once and for all," the stern woman said. "Starting now."

"Right." Cyrus swiveled back toward me. "I am running out of patience, Benjamin. If you do not freely own up to what you know about SPYDER, we will be forced to use less friendly methods to find out what you know."

"Oh no," Jawa whispered to me. "He means torture."

"I'm telling you what I know!" I exclaimed. "But you're not listening to any of it!"

"Because I'm not an idiot!" Cyrus exploded. "So stop playing me for one! *You* were the one who walked a bomb into the White House! We have dozens of witnesses!"

"I was tricked into doing it," I said. "The same way SPYDER tricked you into authorizing the entire operation in the first place."

"What's that?" the stern woman asked.

"SPYDER planted chatter about the potential assassination to fool Agent Hale," I explained. "They used channels they knew he was monitoring and made him *think* there was a mole in the White House so that he'd send *me* in to investigate. Then SPYDER had Warren Reeves plant a bomb on me. . . ."

"There is no evidence to support that," Cyrus stated, sounding a bit defensive.

"If I was actually trying to kill the president," I argued, "why would I throw the bomb *away* from him? If I hadn't tossed it into the Oval Office, he'd be dead right now."

"You *didn't* do any such thing," said another voice from the panel. It was a thin, reedy voice I didn't recognize.

"I did so," I replied.

"That's not what my agents say," the reedy voice countered. "They claim that *they* were the ones who threw the bomb into the Oval Office."

This caught me by surprise. I was trying to figure out what was going on when Jawa stepped in.

"Are you the director of the Secret Service?" he asked.

"Yes," the reedy voice answered.

"Your agents are lying to you," Jawa told him. "Probably to make up for the fact that their negligence allowed the bomb into the West Wing in the first place."

"Yes!" Zoe agreed. "They were probably embarrassed about screwing up so badly, so now they're lying to you to make themselves sound better."

"My agents would never behave so unprofessionally," the reedy voice insisted.

"They allowed the bomb to enter the premises," the stern woman argued. "That wasn't very professional."

"Now, wait a minute!" the Secret Service director cried. "I'm not the one on trial here!"

"Well, maybe you should be," Mike said.

"What?" the Secret Service director gasped.

"Cyrus just said he suspects SPYDER has turned lots of people at the CIA," Mike explained. "Why couldn't they have turned agents at the Secret Service, too? Including *you*. Maybe you and all your agents were in on the plot and let the bomb get through on purpose."

All the heads on the panel turned toward the director of the Secret Service suspiciously.

"That is an erroneous accusation!" the director howled. "My agents are incorruptible!"

"That's exactly what I would expect someone who'd been corrupted by SPYDER to say," Mike said.

"Yeah!" Chip chimed in. "Maybe *you're* the one who planted the bomb on Ben!"

"That's preposterous!" the Secret Service director spluttered.

"It's not any more preposterous than suggesting Ben is working for SPYDER," Mike argued. "If being tricked into bringing a bomb into the White House is enough to condemn Ben, then why isn't it enough to condemn you? Or Cyrus Hale?"

"Me?" Cyrus asked, caught by surprise.

"Yes, you," Mike said. "You authorized this mission in the first place. And you authorized the mission where you sent Ben to evil spy school and claim he was flipped. Maybe *you're* the one working for SPYDER, and they ordered you to do all that in order to frame Ben."

"Hey," Alexander Hale said thoughtfully. "That's a very good point."

"You're actually buying this?" Cyrus exclaimed. "I'm your father! You can't possibly think I might be working for SPYDER!"

"You accused my daughter of working for SPYDER," Alexander replied testily. "So apparently being a Hale doesn't free you from suspicion."

"Maybe *you're* working for SPYDER!" the principal shouted, pointing at Alexander accusingly.

"Well, maybe *you* are," Alexander said, pointing back at the principal.

The panel erupted into chaos, everyone shouting at

once, pointing fingers at one another, accusing each other and defending themselves.

Mike sat back in his chair, grinning from ear to ear, enjoying what he'd wrought.

"That's enough!" Cyrus exploded. He pounded his gavel on the table so hard that the head cracked off and clattered to the floor by my feet. "This tribunal hasn't been called to condemn any of us! It has been called to condemn them!" He pointed at my fellow students and me. "They're turning us all against one another on purpose!"

"I'm simply pointing out that the logic you've used against us can easily be used against all of you," Mike said.

"Shut your trap, you impudent scamp!" Cyrus yelled at him. "There is no concrete evidence to condemn any of us on this panel, whereas there is ample evidence against all of you, particularly Agent Ripley! Thanks to his actions, the Oval Office was blown up and the president of the United States was nearly killed, along with half a dozen other high-ranking government officials!"

I snapped upright in my seat, struck by a thought. Cyrus rambled on, accusing me of several other crimes, but I didn't hear any of it. Something that Ashley Sparks had said right before she escaped came back to me.

You actually thought it was about killing the president?

You don't understand how SPYDER works at all, do you?

"Which other government officials?" I asked.

Cyrus paused in the midst of his litany of accusations. "Excuse me?"

"Which other government officials were nearly killed?" I asked.

Zoe now sat up next to me, as intrigued as I was. "I know that look," she told me. "You're onto SPYDER's plot, aren't you?"

"Maybe," I said.

Now Mike, Jawa, and Chip sat up, intrigued as well.

The stern woman consulted some papers in front of her. "The secretary of defense was nearly killed," she read. "Also the secretaries of the army, the navy, and the air force, along with many of their aides and assistants. And, as we all know, the chairman of the Joint Chiefs of Staff had to be hospitalized due to severe smoke inhalation."

"He did?" I asked. Apparently, the news channels had been too distracted by the story of the manhunt for me to give that story much coverage.

"Yes," the stern woman answered. "In fact, he had to resign from his position only a few hours ago due to health concerns." She looked to the other people on the panel. "That hasn't been made public yet."

"Oh no," I said, worried.

"You did it, didn't you?" Mike asked me. "You've figured out SPYDER's plot!"

"I think so," I said. "It was never about killing the president at all. It was about the chairman."

"Hold on a second," Cyrus said. "Are you honestly suggesting that SPYDER tried to kill the president of the United States merely to distract us from the fact that they were really trying to kill the chairman of the Joint Chiefs of Staff?"

"Yes," I replied. "Or at least, to get him to step down."

The tribunal erupted into chaos once again.

"Silence!" Cyrus ordered all of them. He tried to bang his gavel on the table, but since he'd broken it, all he could do was bang the handle, which didn't work so well.

"This is how SPYDER works," I explained. "They're never doing what we *think* they're doing. They're always using misdirection, trying to throw us off. Think about it: If they simply assassinated the chairman of the Joint Chiefs, then we'd *know* that was their plan. But if they take out the president, who'd ever think they were really going for the chairman, even though he has just as much power over our military as the president does?"

"Even more power, in certain areas," Jawa put in.

"Way to go, Ben!" Mike crowed. "I knew you could figure this one out!"

"He always does," Zoe said proudly.

The people on the panel didn't seem quite as convinced. They looked from one to another for a bit, then finally seemed to settle on all looking at Cyrus expectantly. Cyrus kept staring right out at me. He stayed riveted on me for a few long, uncomfortable seconds.

Then he asked, "Do you have any proof that this was SPYDER's plot?"

"Um . . . ," I said. "Well . . . this is based on my general knowledge of how SPYDER operates."

"So, you have no actual proof at all," Cyrus said.

"Er . . . I guess not."

"No one knows SPYDER better than Ben!" Zoe argued supportively. "He's figured out more of their plots than anyone else!"

"Did I ask for your opinion on this, Miss Zibbell?" Cyrus asked.

"No, but . . ."

"Then keep quiet." Cyrus turned to the rest of the panel. "There's only one thing Agent Ripley has said here that makes any sense at all, which is that SPYDER is constantly using misdirection. That's all this cockamamie theory is: yet another attempt to distract us from the truth. And the truth is that the young people seated before us have all been corrupted by SPYDER. Instead of admitting that, however, they're using smoke and mirrors to confound us."

"That's right!" the principal exclaimed, pointing at me. "You've been confounding me ever since you arrived at this school!"

The people on the panel murmured assent, apparently convinced by Cyrus.

"I'm not trying to confound anyone," I objected. "And if SPYDER really has managed to oust the chairman of the Joint Chiefs, that's a big problem."

"The big problem here," Cyrus said, "is that despite multiple opportunities to admit your guilt and give us information on SPYDER, none of you have done it. Therefore, it is obvious that more aggressive steps need to be taken to get you to admit the truth."

"More aggressive steps?" Chip asked, sounding worried. "You're going to torture us?"

Cyrus didn't answer the question. Instead, he spoke to the stern woman. "Normally, I would say the CIA could handle this, but I still fear my agency is compromised by SPYDER. Since SPYDER is a threat to national security, rooting them out also falls under the jurisdiction of the military. Perhaps we could use your facilities to extract the information we need?"

"Certainly," the stern woman answered. "They're ready whenever you want them."

"Then let's get started right away," Cyrus said. "Time is of the essence. I move that we transfer the prisoners immediately."

"To the military facility?" Alexander asked, aghast. "You can't be serious, Dad! You know what happens there!"

"It won't *have* to happen if they tell us what we need to know," Cyrus replied. "All agreed?"

"Agreed," the stern woman said.

"Agreed!" the principal exclaimed, as though he was excited by the idea of having terrible things done to me.

"Agreed," said the director of the Secret Service, as though he was relieved no one was accusing him of being a SPYDER agent anymore.

"Agreed," said the two other silhouettes at the table. It was the first time either of them had said anything.

"Very good." Cyrus banged what was left of his gavel on the table. "This tribunal is concluded."

The doors to the room opened and a dozen military police stormed in, heading directly for me and my friends.

"You're making a mistake!" Jawa yelled. "A huge mistake!"

"That's right!" Chip echoed. "While you guys are dorking around with us, you're playing right into SPYDER's hands!"

No one on the panel responded to us, though. Alexander was the only one even looking our way. The rest were now all talking among themselves, congratulating one another on a job well done, probably trying to avoid thinking about what they had condemned us to.

The military police surrounded us. One hoisted Erica onto his shoulder while the rest dragged us to our feet.

Mike no longer looked relaxed. Instead, he was flummoxed by everything that was happening. "But you *solved* this," he said to me. "Can't they see that? Why are they treating us like the bad guys?"

"You'd be surprised how stupid an intelligence agency can be," Zoe told him.

The military police marched us back out of the lecture hall. On the stage, the people who had sat on the tribunal were ignoring us. I wanted to shout to them that they were making a mistake, but it didn't seem as though it would do any good. Every attempt I'd made to convince them of my innocence had failed.

SPYDER had once again manipulated everyone brilliantly. They had pulled off a major crime and made me and my friends look like the bad guys. Despite my lack of evidence, I was now positive that SPYDER had targeted the chairman of the Joint Chiefs—only I couldn't prove it and, in truth, I had no idea why SPYDER had done it.

Not that it would do me any good to figure out what they were up to. I was in no position to stop them. My own agency had decided that I—and everyone I trusted—was a criminal.

SPYDER had won.

INSPIRATION

Covert transportation

En route through Washington, DC

February 13

0700 hours

My friends and I were all bundled into the back of a paddy wagon, strapped into jump seats along the walls, and locked inside. Chip, Jawa, and Zoe sat on one side; Mike, Erica, and I were on the other. There were no windows. The only light came from a single bulb in the ceiling, so feeble that I could barely see Mike beside me.

Erica slumped against my shoulder, remaining stubbornly asleep.

Many people were speaking outside, but their voices

were all muffled through the thick, bulletproof walls of the truck. I tried to eavesdrop, but couldn't understand anything. Plus, someone inside the truck was crying. At first I thought it might have been Zoe, but then realized it was Jawa. "My own agency thinks I'm a criminal," he sobbed softly. "My parents are going to kill me."

I finally picked up a sliver of conversation. Cyrus Hale said he would provide protection during our transfer, then climbed into the passenger side of the paddy wagon. Someone else got into the driver's side, after which the engine started.

That made it even harder to hear, although I thought I detected a few other engines starting, indicating there was a convoy of vehicles escorting us.

The paddy wagon lurched forward and headed out into the city.

The sudden motion jolted all of us. Erica's head jounced against my shoulder roughly, startling her awake. She was still drowsy, though, her eyelids drooped at half-mast. "Hey," she murmured. "This looks bad."

"It is," I agreed. "Cyrus just arrested us all for collaborating with SPYDER."

"Grandpa?" Erica asked. In her drugged state, more emotion crept into her voice than she normally would have allowed. She sounded startled and worried. "He arrested *me*?"

"Because you tried to help me," I explained. "And you freed Ashley."

Erica glanced around the interior of the paddy wagon, then frowned. "She got away?"

"The CIA was too busy nabbing us instead," Zoe said bitterly, then added, "Morons."

The paddy wagon hooked a sharp right turn. I knew that meant we had pulled out of the main gate of the academy and were heading into the city.

Erica shook her head violently, trying to clear the cobwebs from her mind. When she looked back at me again, she seemed much more lucid. "Where are they taking us?"

"Some military facility where they're going to torture confessions out of us," I answered. "I don't know where it is."

Erica blinked in surprise. "Military?"

"Your grandfather handed us over to them," I explained. "He said he didn't trust the CIA to handle the job."

"He doesn't usually trust the military, either. Who'd he hand us over to?"

"Some woman. We never saw her face."

"Did you hear her? Could you imitate her voice?"

"Um . . . maybe." I tried my best to imitate the stern woman and said, "You kids are in big trouble."

"Ben," Chip said, "I don't want to hit you while you're down, but you stink at imitating people. That didn't sound anything like that woman."

"Oh?" Zoe challenged. "And you can do better?"

"Definitely," Chip said. And then, to all of our amazement, he repeated the same words I had, sounding so much like the stern woman that for a moment I thought she was in the paddy wagon with us. "You kids are in big trouble."

"Holy cow!" Mike exclaimed. "That was you? How'd you get so good at that?"

"It just comes naturally to me," Chip said. "It's one of my many awesome talents."

"Actually, Chip secretly takes an acting class three nights a week," Erica announced.

There were several gasps from the other side of the truck: Jawa and Zoe expressing disbelief; Chip expressing surprise that he'd been found out.

"You told me you were going to a martial arts class!" Jawa said.

"I *am*," Chip insisted.

"No you're not," Erica said. "In fact, before Chip was recruited to spy school, he was at an arts academy, where he specialized in acting, singing, tap dance, and playing the oboe. I have to admit, he's quite good. His acting instructor wants him to play the lead in their upcoming production of *Guys and Dolls*."

Chip was so astonished now, he didn't even try to hide it. "How did you . . . ?"

"I'm studying to be a spy," Erica said. "It's my job to know things. By the way, that woman you imitated is Felicia DuVray, assistant director of information acquisition for the U.S. Army. She's as tough as they come. Three minutes in the room with her and you'll be telling her everything you've ever done wrong in your entire life."

"Which lead are you up for?" Zoe asked Chip. "Nicely-Nicely or Nathan Detroit?"

"I don't know," Chip admitted. "I didn't even know I was being considered for the lead."

"Nathan Detroit," Erica told him.

"Really?" Chip asked excitedly. "Cool!"

"As thrilling as that may be," Erica went on, "we need to focus on the task at hand. Letting DuVray take a crack at us won't be fun and it's going to waste valuable time. We have to figure out what SPYDER is up to right away."

"Oh, Ben's already done that," Mike said.

"He has?" Erica asked. "Then why are we still in this paddy wagon?"

"They didn't believe him," Jawa replied.

"SPYDER wasn't going after the president," I explained.

"They were really targeting the chairman of the Joint Chiefs of Staff, who was in the West Wing at the exact same time."

"So they merely tried to make it *look* like a presidential assassination to distract from the real objective," Erica said, putting everything together quickly. "Of course. Typical SPYDER. But why go after the chairman?"

"I haven't worked that part out yet," I admitted. "But I figure it has something to do with SPYDER's general mission to cause chaos and mayhem."

"If that's all they were up to, they could have caused plenty by simply taking out the president," Erica said. "There has to be something more to this, Ben. Think back to the explosion. Use your memory training. Is there anything else you can recall?"

I did my best to think back, but the events leading up to the explosion were a jumbled blur. "Not really. Everything happened so fast. . . ."

"I need you to try," Erica said. "It's important. I know it's difficult, but you can do it. I believe in you."

"Erica?" Zoe asked. "Did you actually just say that? You sounded like a greeting card."

"It's this stupid sedative I got hit with," Erica said with a sigh. "It's dampening my usual tendency to play down my emotions, making me far more honest than I normally feel comfortable with. It's really annoying."

Zoe giggled. "So, if I asked you if you considered us friends . . ."

"I'd say yes," Erica replied, then cursed under her breath. "Ugh! Stupid honesty. I hate it!"

Meanwhile, I was struggling to recall the moments before the explosion. I closed my eyes and tried to re-create the scene in my mind, imagining the West Wing exactly as it was.

I had been passing through with Kimmy Dimsdale and Jason Stern. Then Vladimir Gorsky and all the military officers had exited the Situation Room. There was the secretary of the army, the navy, and the air force, the secretary of defense, and the chairman of the Joint Chiefs himself, an older man with a steel-gray crew cut and a chest full of medals.

"Do you consider *me* a friend?" Jawa asked Erica.

"Yes," Erica conceded, in a tone that made it sound as though her honesty was actually causing her pain.

Gorsky had responded with surprise upon seeing me, which had startled the chairman and the other officers with him. And then the president had emerged from the Oval Office, tailed by several Secret Service agents.

"What about me?" Chip asked Erica. "Do you like me as a friend?"

"Not really," Erica said honestly. "I've always felt you were kind of a jerk."

An image suddenly came to me, a freeze-frame from moments before the bomb went off. Gorsky and the other military officers were all staring at me, Gorsky appearing surprised I was there, the others wondering why he was reacting to me in that way. . . .

Except one.

One of the high-ranking officers had his back to me as he was hurrying into the Situation Room. I couldn't remember his face—it was possible I'd never seen it—but he was definitely in a rush. Like he was trying to get away from me as quickly as possible.

My eyes snapped open again. I had an insight. A very scary insight.

I said, "If Cyrus is right, and SPYDER really does have operatives deep inside all branches of the government, what's the chance that they have a high-ranking agent in the defense department?"

"Anything is possible where SPYDER is concerned," Erica told me. "How high?"

"Vice chairman of the Joint Chiefs of Staff," I said.

A hush fell over the paddy wagon as we all considered that. We swerved through another turn. The vehicle was moving surprisingly fast for Washington, DC; we must have been out before morning rush hour had begun.

"It makes sense," Jawa said. "The chairman and vice

chairman of the Joint Chiefs are positions assigned by the president. If you're vice chairman, you're not guaranteed to become chairman . . ."

"Unless the chairman dies or steps down," Zoe concluded. "Who's the vice chairman?"

"Elmore Finch," Erica answered. "He's had a sterling service record, but that doesn't mean he couldn't have been a SPYDER operative all along. Which means SPYDER might now have control over the highest-ranking military officer in the entire U.S. armed forces. . . ." She trailed off, as though struck by a frightening thought. "Oh no."

"What?" I asked.

"The chairman of the Joint Chiefs controls the launch overrides for our entire nuclear missile system," Erica said.

"You mean he can start a nuclear attack?" Mike asked, astonished. "I thought only the president could do that."

"No," Erica corrected. "The president can authorize a launch, but that still has to be confirmed by the military. The ultimate authority lies with the chairman."

"Um . . . ," Jawa said nervously. "That's not the way the military *claims* it works. They're not supposed to have that sort of control over the nuclear arsenal."

"I know," Erica agreed. "But they do. The military doesn't want everyone to know the truth because, well . . . it's a pretty stupid system. But the military has always felt *they* should be able to make the ultimate call on this, not the president. I don't think it ever occurred to them that maybe, someday, a sleeper agent from an international consortium dedicated to causing chaos and mayhem would actually become the chairman of the Joint Chiefs and gain the ability to launch a nuclear strike anywhere, anytime he wanted to. Which seems to have happened."

"So how does the system work?" I asked worriedly. "Does Elmore Finch just get handed some sort of launch button?"

"It's not quite that simple," Erica said. "There *is* a portable control system kept in a secure briefcase, but there are several layers of security to authenticate the identity of the chairman before he can initiate an attack. Thumbprint readers. Retinal scans. Voice-recognition software. All that has to be set up before the portable system can be used, and the only place that can be done is in a secure room at the . . ." She trailed off once again, only this time it wasn't in fear. This time she seemed pleased. In fact, she actually started laughing.

"Is the idea of thermonuclear war funny to you?" Mike asked. "Because I've always found it pretty terrifying, myself."

"The secure room is at the Pentagon," Erica said.

"I still don't see the humor in this," Mike told her.

"The military's information-extraction facilities are *also* at the Pentagon," Erica explained. "That's why Grandpa handed us over to the military! He isn't suspicious of us anymore! He's getting us through Pentagon security!" She broke into gleeful laughter again.

This was unsettling. Erica rarely laughed, and she was almost never gleeful. Hearing her do it seemed as bizarre as a cat barking.

"Erica," Zoe said cautiously, "I know you missed the whole tribunal, seeing as you were unconscious and everything, but your grandfather didn't seem like he was on our side at all."

"Well, he couldn't admit that, could he?" Erica asked. "He knows SPYDER has people everywhere. He already suspects the CIA is corrupted, and he probably suspects the same thing about the military—rightly so, I might add, given Ben's current revelations. Plus, if you aren't familiar with SPYDER, the idea that they'd assassinate the president simply to hide the fact that they were *really* trying to kill the chairman of the Joint Chiefs in order to install their own mole as the head of the entire military would probably seem a bit far-fetched. You'd be accusing the second-highest-ranking person in the military complex of being corrupt—*and* plotting to kill his superior. There's no guarantee Cyrus could convince anyone else he was right, and if he suspected that's what SPYDER was up to, he would have known he didn't have time to waste. So he had to pretend he was still on their side."

"Just like you did when you spoke to Ben on my phone the other night," Zoe said.

"Yes," Erica said. "We Hales can be very devious. It's our thing. But Grandpa had one other reason for playing along. Have any of you ever been to the Pentagon?"

"My family took a tour once," Jawa said.

"How long did it take you to get through security?" Erica asked.

"An hour," Jawa replied.

"Exactly," Erica said. "And that's after Pentagon security has already run a dozen background checks on you, because you normally have to apply for access months ahead of time. In addition, most people can only visit the official public levels, not the top secret levels down below. Now, imagine that my grandfather wants to get all of us inside the Pentagon quickly. If he has to go through the proper chain of command, it'll take hours to get approval, and it'll probably tip off SPYDER that we're onto them. But if he turns us over to the military . . ."

"They walk us right through the door themselves," Chip finished. "You have to hand it to that old coot. He's as sneaky as they come."

I wasn't convinced as quickly as Chip, but as I mulled over Erica's argument, it began to make sense. I was pretty sure Cyrus hadn't been on our side throughout the tribunal;

it seemed he'd truly suspected we were working for SPYDER for at least the first half of it. But once I had explained what I thought SPYDER's plan was, things had changed. Cyrus had remained suspicious and crusty on the outside, but he'd suddenly been in quite a hurry to end the proceedings and hand us over to the military.

Beside me, Mike wasn't completely convinced himself. "Are you *positive* that's what your grandfather is up to?" he asked Erica. "Because if you're wrong, we're all about to have a really terrible morning."

"I'm ninety percent positive," Erica said. "First of all, if SPYDER has gone through all this trouble to elevate Elmore Finch, then they probably want him to take control of the portable launch system as soon as possible. Which would be first thing this morning. Second, given the pattern of turns we've been making, this paddy wagon is definitely heading for the Pentagon."

"You've been keeping track of every turn this vehicle has made?" Jawa asked, astonished.

"Yes," Erica said. "As well as timing how long we've spent on every road to assess how far we've gone on them and then comparing all that to the complete map of the city that I've memorized. Haven't all of you been doing that too?"

"Er . . . yes," Chip lied. "That's exactly what we've been doing. And you're right. We're heading for the Pentagon."

We all quickly agreed with him, pretending to be equally as talented as Erica.

The paddy wagon suddenly slowed to a stop. From the front, we could hear the driver talking to someone outside the vehicle.

"We're at the security checkpoint for the Pentagon's eastern gate," Erica said. "Since we're prisoners and they're taking us to an information-acquisition complex that isn't even supposed to exist, seeing as it violates the Geneva Conventions, they're bringing us in through the secure zone, rather than any of the official entrances."

"There's one more thing," I said. "Even if we are getting inside past security, we're *still* prisoners." I jangled my handcuffs. "What are we supposed to do about that?"

"I'm guessing Grandpa has a plan," Erica told me.

All we could do after that was hope she was right.

PERSONAL ISSUES

The Pentagon

Arlington, Virginia

February 13

0745 hours

The paddy wagon passed through two more security checkpoints, then pulled a U-turn and backed up to the Pentagon.

"The Pentagon is the largest office building on the planet," Erica informed all of us. "It covers more than twenty-eight acres. There are more than seventeen miles of hallways and twenty-six thousand employees. I don't know where Elmore Finch will be in all that, but we're going to do our best to find him. Be on the alert for anything out of the ordinary. Keep your eyes and ears open. Oh, and remember, we're not supposed to know Grandpa is on our side, so treat him with utter contempt."

The engine shut off. We heard the rear doors being unlocked. Four heavily armed soldiers opened them. They were all wearing green army camouflage outfits, which was a little strange, given that we were a dozen miles from the closest forest.

We had backed into a covered loading area. It was quite dim, and yet after the darkness of the paddy wagon, the sudden light was still blinding. I had to blink a bit before I could make out the faces of the soldiers.

They were all quite shocked to see us. "They're just kids!" one exclaimed. He seemed like the leader, and he was built like an oak tree. The name stitched into his camouflage was MARTINEZ.

"Don't let that fool you, soldier," Cyrus Hale warned. We couldn't see him, as he was still somewhere off to the side of the paddy wagon. "They are extremely dangerous. Do not drop your guard for a second."

"Get out of the vehicle," Martinez ordered us.

We obeyed, filing out onto the loading dock.

I quickly assessed our surroundings. The rest of the convoy that had accompanied us—three black SUVs, of course—had parked around the paddy wagon. Several other soldiers climbed out of them along with a stern-looking woman I assumed was Felicia DuVray. She wore a military uniform so starched it looked bulletproof. Everything about Felicia seemed starched as well: her dour expression, her crisp movements, her snow-white hair, which was pulled back into a bun so tightly, it looked as though it might be painful.

I spotted Alexander Hale. He looked miserable. Obviously, Cyrus hadn't let him in on his secret plan to sneak us into the Pentagon.

If that was really Cyrus's secret plan at all. There was still a chance that Erica was completely wrong and that we were all on our way to having the worst morning of our lives.

Beyond the soldiers, the glare of daylight made it hard to see much outside the loading area, but I could make out the security checkpoints we'd come through and several square acres of Pentagon parking lot.

"Eyes forward, kid!" Martinez informed me. "Keep moving!"

I fell in line with my fellow students.

The soldiers lined us up two by two, as though we were boarding Noah's ark: Erica and me in the front, Mike and Zoe behind us, Chip and Jawa at the rear. Then they herded us toward a secure door flanked by two more soldiers.

Cyrus emerged from around the paddy wagon and

approached Erica. "I'm glad to see you're all right," he said. "I trust your friends filled you in on what transpired while you were asleep?"

Erica spat in his face.

"I'll take that as a yes," Cyrus said sourly.

"Erica!" Alexander gasped, mortified this had occurred in front of so many people. "We do not spit on our grandfathers in this family!"

"That's all right. I deserved it." Cyrus wiped the phlegm off his cheek with a handkerchief, then put a hand on Erica's arm. "Sweetheart, this isn't personal. . . ."

Erica recoiled from him. "Don't touch me. You don't get to condemn me to this and still act like my grandfather."

"You brought this on yourself," Cyrus told her coldly. "I can't get you out of it. But you can. Just give us the information we need. Do it now, before we're forced to take more extreme measures."

Felicia DuVray smiled at this, like it excited her.

Erica didn't deign to answer Cyrus. She spun away from him and marched onward.

The soldiers led us through the secure door and into the Pentagon.

Even though Erica had warned me how big it was, I was still taken aback.

The outer hallway, which looped the entire building,

stretched a mind-boggling distance in both directions. Even at the early hour, it was filled with hundreds of people, as crowded as an airline concourse. Most of them wore military uniforms, but there were quite a few civilians as well. I noticed a group of older men in military tracksuits who appeared to be simply cruising the halls for exercise, the same way civilians might walk laps around the shopping mall. There were also a few souped-up golf-cart-like vehicles zipping about, shuttling around people who were too important, too hurried, or too lazy to walk through the miles of hallways.

A lot of people were carrying Starbucks coffee cups. Or takeout bags from McDonald's.

"Is there a Starbucks and a McDonald's in the building?" I asked Erica.

"Yes," she replied, in an all-business tone that indicated she had already put the exchange with Cyrus behind her. "In fact, there are four Starbucks. As well as two dozen other places to eat, a tailor, six gift shops, five post office branches, a florist, a barbershop, two pharmacies, and a hospital. It takes so long to get in and out of here, it saves time to have all these businesses inside the building."

"So it's like a self-contained city in here," Zoe said.

"Doesn't look like it's too hard to be a barber here," Mike observed. "Everyone has the exact same haircut."

This was true. Every man we passed had a military crew cut. So did a lot of the women.

"None of them looks like a potential SPYDER operative," Chip said.

"A good SPYDER operative wouldn't look like a potential SPYDER operative," Jawa pointed out.

"Well, then, since none of them looks like a potential SPYDER operative, I guess they *all* look like potential SPYDER operatives," Chip replied.

It was the same problem I'd had at the White House: Anyone SPYDER had corrupted would blend in perfectly. It would be impossible to pick them out with a mere glance.

We turned into another hallway. This one angled toward the middle of the Pentagon, slicing through five rings of offices, then dead-ended an eighth of a mile away at a bank of windows that revealed a central courtyard. The courtyard had a large lawn, several trees, and what looked like a nice outdoor café. In front of the windows was a glass case holding two dozen swords.

"Are those swords for emergency attacks?" Chip asked.

"No," Erica said disdainfully. "That's a museum case. There are thousands of military artifacts on display in the Pentagon. Those appear to be part of a presentation on Revolutionary War armaments."

I could barely even make out the swords from our

distance, let alone tell what war they were from, but I had no doubt that Erica was right.

The soldiers led all of us into a stairwell. We descended two floors to yet another secure door. This one had an ID card scanner. The soldiers all looked to Felicia DuVray expectantly; apparently, none of them ranked highly enough to access this area.

Felicia swiped her ID through the scanner with surgical precision. The door clicked open, and our procession passed through.

The basement level was laid out the same way as the ground floor, only due to the elevated security, there was almost no one else down there. Now the enormous size of the building made everything feel eerier somehow—as though, if the military wanted to, they could lock us up down there and no one would ever be able to find us again. Our footsteps echoed ominously throughout the empty halls.

There were a hundred things I should have been concentrating on, but at the moment only one was at the forefront of my mind—and it had nothing to do with SPYDER. Thanks to the sedative she'd been darted with, Erica was in a rare mental state. For once in her life, she'd actually answer me honestly. However, it would probably wear off soon, and there was a question I was desperate to ask her. It was a completely unprofessional question, but I had been dying to know the answer for weeks.

So I leaned in close to her as we walked and whispered, "Erica, do you like me?"

She gave me a wary glance. "You're taking advantage of my weakened mental condition."

"Yes, and you're avoiding the question. Do you like me?"

"You mean as a friend?"

"No. I mean as more than that."

"You mean the way you like me?"

"Er . . . yes."

Erica pursed her lips tightly. It seemed like she was fighting the urge to respond to me truthfully. Finally, she said, "It's complicated."

This was disappointing. I had been hoping for something more along the lines of "Yes. I love you with the white-hot passion of a thousand suns."

"Oh," I said sadly, and then, before I could stop myself, asked, "Why? Do you like Mike instead?"

"Mike?" Erica asked, confused, then nodded back to where Mike was following just out of earshot behind us. "That Mike?"

"Yes."

"Why would I like *him*?"

It wasn't a particularly nice thing for someone to say

about my best friend, and yet it filled my heart with joy. "Well, because he's *Mike*. He's cool and fun and you actually complimented him the other day. . . ."

"That doesn't mean I like him."

"Well, how should I know that? You never compliment anybody."

"That's not true. I gave you a compliment only two months ago."

"Most people do it a little more often than that."

"Really?"

"Yes!" We rounded a corner into an even eerier hallway. About a hundred yards ahead of us, two more soldiers stood guard by a nondescript white door. It seemed this was where we were heading, which meant I was running out of time to get an answer from Erica. "If it's not Mike, what's so complicated about us?"

"Everything. Our *lives* are complicated, Ben." Erica's tone caught me by surprise. There was a sadness in her voice that I'd never heard before. "If we went to a normal school, it'd be weird enough with me being two years older than you. But we *don't* go to a normal school. There's nothing normal about our lives at all. We live in a dangerous world, and serious relationships make it even more dangerous. . . ."

"Not necessarily. You can't get by in this business without friends."

"You're not asking to be friends. You're asking for much more. And that kind of emotion is dangerous. It affects our ability to make decisions. It gives our enemies leverage over us. It creates an enormous risk."

"So, you're planning to go your whole life without ever connecting with someone?"

"I connected with someone once before. And look how that worked out."

"Erica, I'm not Joshua Hallal."

"I know. But . . ." Erica turned to me for the first time since we'd started this conversation. She looked torn between opening up and fighting to keep closed. To my surprise, emotion won out. "The other thing is, Ben . . . *I'm* complicated. Think about the family I've grown up in. My father's a liar. My mother kept her job a secret from *him*. And look how my grandfather's using me right now. That's what this job does to relationships. It screws everything up. But I'm always going to be a spy, no matter what. So something has to give."

"Maybe not. We could try it."

The soldiers in front of us snickered. Despite my attempts to whisper, they had probably heard everything we'd said.

Erica realized this as well. Her eyes narrowed at them angrily. And yet she still answered me. "I'm not ready for a relationship, Ben. And I don't think you are either. Sorry. I know that's not what you want to hear, but you wanted the truth, so you're getting it. Plus, there's a fifty percent chance we're not going to make it out of here alive. . . ."

"What?" I gasped.

"Admittedly, that's a rough estimate, but we're in pretty dire straits right now."

"Fifty percent?" I repeated, still stuck on those odds.

"You did want honesty, didn't you?"

"Um . . . maybe not that much honesty."

"The fact is, we have to find Elmore Finch right away, so we'll need to do something drastic to get away from all these soldiers."

The soldiers in front of us glanced back our way, their steps faltering slightly. They'd obviously overheard this, but they didn't know whether to take it seriously or not.

"She's joking," I said.

"No I'm not," Erica told them. "If you don't release us right now, I'll be forced to knock you all unconscious."

The soldiers laughed harder. "Yeah, right," Martinez scoffed.

"I'd really prefer not to do it," Erica said. "I don't like the idea of hurting a soldier who serves this country. So why don't you all just hand over your guns and walk away quietly? I know it sounds humiliating, but when we bust SPYDER, you'll end up looking like heroes."

We reached the protected door and came to a stop. Martinez stared down at Erica. "You're going to hurt us?" he asked, amused.

"If I have to," Erica replied casually.

"With your hands cuffed behind your back?"

"Oh," Erica said. "Remember back on the loading dock, when my grandfather came over to me and I got all upset and spat in his face?"

"Yes."

"That was all an act. He was really slipping me the key to the handcuffs."

The soldiers' eyes widened in surprise. Before they could even raise their guns, Cyrus launched himself into action. The soldiers had been distracted by Erica, so he quickly got the jump on them. Moving with the agility and speed of his granddaughter, he sent four men reeling within seconds.

Then Erica joined the fray. Like she'd said, her wrists were no longer cuffed behind her back. The whole time she'd been talking to me, she had been furtively unlocking them with the key Cyrus had given her. In the confined space of the hallway, it was as though a wildcat had been let loose in a chicken coop. She was a flurry of motion, punching, kicking, and pounding anything unfortunate enough to get in her way.

Chip, Jawa, and Zoe did their part as well. They still had their wrists cuffed, but each was formidable enough with only their legs, taking out the soldiers with powerful karate kicks—as well as the occasional knee to the crotch.

Even Mike got into the act. When Felicia DuVray realized the tide had turned against her team and tried to flee, Mike tripped her.

Felicia sprawled onto the floor. Alexander Hale quickly grabbed a gun that one of the soldiers had dropped and pointed it at her. "You were actually prepared to torture my daughter," he snarled.

"It was your father's idea!" Felicia whined, not sounding so stern anymore.

"He was leading you on," Alexander spat. "And you were only too happy to help him."

Meanwhile, I did my standard "get low and stay out of the way" tactic, crouching by the wall and making sure no one punched or shot me by accident. It wasn't exactly manly, but it didn't mess anything up, either.

As it was, my team had things covered. In less than thirty seconds, the soldiers were all piled on the floor, unconscious, and my friends were all looking very pleased with themselves.

Cyrus didn't bother to even say so much as "good job." Instead, he told us, "We need to move," then looked to

Alexander. "Get all these guys cuffed so they can't sound the alarm if they wake up."

"With what?" Alexander asked.

"These," Erica said, tossing him the cuffs she'd been wearing, then unlocking mine as well. She and Cyrus quickly freed Mike, Zoe, Chip, and Jawa. We piled the cuffs at Alexander's feet, then helped ourselves to the weapons of the unconscious soldiers.

Alexander knelt to cuff Felicia DuVray.

"You're making a huge mistake," she hissed. "You'll never get out of here. This building is crawling with soldiers. And when you get caught, I'm going to make sure they bring you right back down here to me, so I can make you pay for what you've—"

"Alexander, shut her up," Cyrus ordered.

"Gladly," Alexander replied. He yanked a sock off an unconscious soldier and stuffed it into Felicia's mouth.

"The room where Finch will come to activate the portable nuclear launch unit is this way," Cyrus said, then took off down the hall as fast as he could go—which was surprisingly fast.

The rest of us did our best to keep up with him. We raced through the endless maze of basement corridors.

"So, you believed Ben about SPYDER's plans after all?" Chip asked Cyrus.

"You wouldn't be down here if I didn't," Cyrus replied.

"But you actually thought we were working for SPYDER up until then," Erica pointed out.

"What of it?" Cyrus asked curtly.

"An apology might be nice," Zoe suggested. "Like, 'Sorry I thought all of you were betraying your country. I realize SPYDER tricked me into it. My bad.'"

"The room is right up here," Cyrus said, completely avoiding the conversation.

We rounded a corner into another hallway.

Ahead of us was the room in question.

It didn't look particularly important. It merely had a nondescript door with a random number on it. But then, in my experience, important rooms *rarely* looked important. They were often designed to be overlooked.

As we approached, the door opened. Elmore Finch, the brand-new chairman of the Joint Chiefs of Staff, stepped into the hall. He was squat and bald, with a gray goatee. Six armed soldiers flanked him, along with an aide who carried a thin steel briefcase.

Up until that very moment, I hadn't been completely sure that Finch was a covert SPYDER agent. But a few things immediately convinced me that I had guessed correctly and that the thin steel briefcase was, in fact, the portable launch system for our nuclear arsenal.

First, Finch was very startled to see us. He apparently recognized Cyrus and realized he had just been caught with his hand in the nuclear cookie jar.

Second, he ordered the soldiers to open fire on us.

And third, the aide holding the briefcase was my nemesis, Murray Hill.

PURSUIT

The Pentagon

Arlington, Virginia

February 13

0815 hours

I almost didn't recognize Murray. He had really
cleaned himself up so he could infiltrate the Pentagon.
Normally, Murray was slovenly and unkempt, his clothes
covered in food stains, his hair looking as if he had forgotten to wash it for the past few months. Now he wore
a military uniform, had a crew cut, and stood ramrod
straight. He had even grown a thin mustache, making him
look much older than his actual fifteen years. However,
he completely failed to hide his astonished reaction to my

presence. "Ripley!" he gasped. "Not again!"

Then he turned and ran away while the soldiers started shooting at us.

I was pretty sure the soldiers weren't in league with SPYDER. They were simply normal soldiers who believed that Elmore Finch was the legitimate new chairman of the Joint Chiefs of Staff, rather than a highly placed stooge for an evil organization, and thus they obeyed his orders.

We didn't fire back at them. We didn't want to kill any innocent men. Instead, we scrambled for cover, racing around the corner while bullets tore up the hall behind us.

"Get them!" Elmore Finch roared, and then we heard the clomping of combat boots charging after us.

"You know another way through down here?" Jawa asked Cyrus.

"Of course," Cyrus replied. He shot a pipe as we ran past it. A burst of steam vented through the hole, clouding the hallway behind us and hiding us from the pursuing soldiers.

Alexander Hale rounded a corner ahead, running to catch up to all of us. "Hey, guys!" he exclaimed. "I cuffed everyone and was hoping I could join you. . . ." It suddenly dawned on him that us running back his way probably wasn't a good sign. "Oh dear. Have things gone bad?"

"Extremely," Cyrus told him, then led us around another corner and into a stairwell.

"What's the plan?" Mike asked as we sprinted upward, taking the stairs two at a time.

"We do whatever it takes to get that briefcase," Cyrus said. "As long as Finch has it, nothing can stop him from launching a nuclear strike wherever and whenever he wants. If he gets out of here with it, the entire planet will be at SPYDER's mercy."

"He's now the chairman of the Joint Chiefs and we're in the Pentagon," Erica pointed out. "There are twenty-six thousand employees here who'll shoot us if he tells them to."

"Yeah, that's a problem," Cyrus admitted.

We burst out a door onto the main floor and found ourselves in the innermost ring of the Pentagon, the one with the windows onto the central courtyard. Two of the souped-up golf carts I'd seen before idled close by, right outside a Starbucks, waiting for several high-ranking military officers to get mocha lattes. An aide sat at the wheel of each cart . . . until Cyrus and Erica grabbed them by the collars and tossed them to the floor.

"We need to commandeer these," Cyrus informed them, taking the wheel of one cart. "National security." Chip, Jawa, and Zoe leapt into the cart behind him, while Alexander, Mike, and I got into the one driven by Erica.

Cyrus and Erica each pounded the gas pedal and we took off. The vehicles were designed to go much faster than regular golf carts, so we moved with surprising speed, especially considering that we were *inside* a building. We sluiced through the crowds of Pentagon employees and swerved around the museum displays—which, as Erica had deduced, were all about the Revolutionary War.

"If I recall correctly, the closest stairwell to where we left those criminals is right up here," Cyrus announced. "Aha!"

Sure enough, Elmore Finch and Murray Hill had just exited the stairs. Their own souped-up golf cart idled close by. Only two soldiers now accompanied them; the other four were probably still searching for us in the basement. Both SPYDER operatives were acting as if nothing unusual was going on, trying not to attract attention. Murray kept the silver briefcase clutched to his chest, but to most people, it would have looked like an average, everyday briefcase rather than something that could be used to end all life on earth.

This time we got the drop on them. They expected us to still be down in the basement, rather than barreling toward them. Chip, Jawa, and Zoe sprang from Cyrus's cart, pouncing upon the military men before they could do anything. They all tumbled to the floor in a tangle of arms and legs.

Murray Hill did what he always did in situations like this: He fled. Elmore Finch did exactly the same thing. They leapt into their nearby cart, Finch taking the wheel while Murray protected the briefcase, and sped away.

Our high-speed drive through the Pentagon became a high-speed chase. Now, instead of two carts careening wildly through the building, there were three. Pentagon employees scattered out of our paths as we raced around the inner hallway.

"Hand over the briefcase!" Cyrus yelled.

"These people are terrorists!" Elmore Finch yelled to the crowd. "Somebody shoot them!"

Thankfully, even though we were in the military headquarters for the United States, no one in the immediate vicinity was carrying weapons. However, some exceptionally fit soldiers chased after us on foot.

Cyrus pulled up on one side of Finch and Murray's golf cart while Erica pulled up on the other, boxing them in.

"I've got this!" Alexander yelled, and sprang from our cart onto theirs.

Or at least, he tried to. He timed his jump wrong, missed the cart completely, and ended up bowling over three women exiting yet another Starbucks.

Murray whipped out a gun.

Before I even knew what I was doing, I had leapt at him myself.

Normally, I wasn't one for leaping at people with guns. Experience had taught me that it usually made far more sense to leap *away* from them. But during my time at spy school, I had apparently developed some new instincts. Plus, we were running out of spies-in-training—and if there was any enemy agent I stood a chance of beating in a fight, it was Murray Hill.

I slammed into him and caught his gun hand before he could fire. Mike jumped into the cart as well, grabbing Elmore Finch. And then a few things happened very quickly.

I wasn't sure exactly *why* they happened, as I was busy fighting Murray when everything went wrong.

Maybe Erica or Cyrus attempted to run Elmore Finch into the wall, or maybe someone swerved to avoid an innocent pedestrian. Whatever the case, the carts all slammed into one another and spun out of control. Finch, being in the middle, had the least room to maneuver. Another museum display loomed in our path, and there was no way to avoid it. Instead, we plowed right through it, smashing the glass and destroying everything inside. The display featured three mannequins in traditional Revolutionary War dress: a British regular, a member of the Continental army, and a gassy-looking George Washington, which we hit head-on. The soldiers and their armaments all went skidding across the hallway, while the father of our country immediately burst apart upon impact, pieces of him flying far and wide. His disembodied head ricocheted off the wall and decked a three-star general.

The cart I was in spun sideways and toppled. It wasn't as dangerous as a car wreck would have been, but we still went flying. Murray and I tumbled across the linoleum floor for twenty yards. We both lost our grip on the gun, which discharged as it bounced away, blasting a hole in the ceiling, severing a power line, and shorting out the lights. Several hundred people who had been too far away to notice the cart chase heard the gunshot and, being military, either dropped into defensive postures or took cover. Murray lost his grip on the briefcase as well; it slid much farther than we did, eventually clonking into another display case.

The severed power line dropped through the hole in the ceiling, sparking wildly and writhing like an angry snake. It blocked the hallway, cutting Murray and me off from everyone else.

Meanwhile, Mike somehow managed to hang on to our cart even as it fell over, so he ended up landing atop Elmore Finch. Cyrus and Erica crashed their own carts into the wall. Before they could run to Mike's aid, the angry soldiers who'd set after them on foot arrived. Cyrus and Erica had no choice but to fight them off hand-to-hand, leaving Mike to handle Elmore Finch by himself.

I was banged up from the wreck and hurting in twelve different places, but I scrambled to my feet anyhow, determined to get to the nuclear briefcase before Murray could.

Normally, Murray had the reflexes of a koala bear, so I figured I could beat him. Unfortunately, Murray was already between me and the briefcase—and he had a bayonet.

It had been in the museum case we had destroyed, part of the British regular's uniform. It was more than two hundred years old, but it still looked sharp enough to cause serious harm. Murray waved it menacingly, keeping me at bay. "Back off, Ben!" he warned.

"You're not going to get away with this," I told him.

"Yeah, yeah, yeah," he said dismissively, backing toward the briefcase. "Let me guess: You figured out our devious plans once again and now think you're going to thwart us. Well, you've thwarted our plans enough. Frankly, I'm getting a little tired of it. It's not happening this time." There was a menace in his voice that I'd never heard before. He might have been scary if his mustache hadn't come off in the wreck. It turned out to be a fake, and it now dangled from his chin like the world's lamest soul patch.

"Don't you want to hear how I figured it out?" I asked, edging closer. Murray had always shown interest in that topic when we'd faced off before.

"You mean the old 'distract-Murray-with-my-brilliance-so-I-can-get-the-jump-on-him' routine? No thanks." Murray jabbed his bayonet at me. "Come any closer and I'll gut you like a fish."

"I thought you didn't like killing people."

"I've changed my mind where you're concerned! You're a menace, Ben! You've defused my bombs, you've rerouted my missiles, and you totally messed things up with me and my girlfriend."

"You're not seeing Jenny Lake anymore? What happened?"

"You pointed out that I'd lied to her!"

"Maybe you shouldn't have lied in the first place."

"Maybe you should keep your nose out of other people's business for once!" Murray slashed at me with the bayonet, forcing me to leap back. "Would it kill you to not thwart just one of my plans?"

"Er . . . possibly," I said. "Given that they usually involve killing people. You're going to use that briefcase to start a nuclear war!"

"Wrong!" Murray exclaimed. "We're going to use it to get countries to pay us *not* to start nuclear wars. There's a difference."

"You're going to blackmail the entire planet?" I asked.

"Exactly. Now, if a country doesn't think their own citizens' survival is worth a few million dollars, well . . . that's *their* problem." Murray had almost reached the briefcase now, but there was no way I could get past the bayonet.

Something gleamed on the floor to my right. An honest-to-God sword. Since Murray had a weapon, I figured I needed one too. So I dashed over and grabbed it. To my astonishment, there was a plaque on it indicating it had belonged to George Washington himself.

Meanwhile, Murray grabbed the briefcase. He tried to make a run for it, but I was faster, cutting off his escape and waving the blade.

Murray held up his bayonet defiantly. "Back off, Ben. Don't make me hurt you."

"Drop the briefcase," I said.

"Fine. Be that way." Murray lunged at me with his bayonet. I parried it with Washington's sword.

Back by the wrecked golf carts, Elmore Finch was screaming at everyone to take us out. Or, he was trying to scream. Mike had gotten the upper hand and was smushing him face-first into the floor, so everything he said sounded like gibberish.

Erica and Cyrus were still fighting the soldiers. While Erica and Cyrus were amazing fighters, the soldiers were no slouches—and more were coming. Every time Erica or Cyrus knocked one out, another arrived.

Meanwhile, Murray and I were having a good old-fashioned swashbuckling sword fight. Neither of us was particularly adept at swordplay, but that made us evenly matched. Our blades clanged off each other as we struggled for the upper hand.

Pentagon employees began to gather around us, though all of them seemed extremely confused by what was going on. In their defense, even I found the whole thing confounding, and I was part of it.

"I thought you weren't working for SPYDER anymore," I said, deflecting an attack. "I thought you hated them after they left you behind to die in New Jersey."

"I don't know what you're talking about," Murray said for the benefit of the crowd. "I'm just a normal, regular military aide." As he came in closer, however, he whispered, "What can I say? They offered me a great deal and apologized."

"You mean you sold out," I said.

"Yes. Honestly, the potential earnings are incredible. You should have joined us when you had the chance." Murray made a sudden stab that nearly shish-kebabed my spleen.

I dodged it at the last second, then whipped my sword around. Murray had no choice but to use the briefcase to defend himself.

Washington's sword was still awfully sharp after all those years. It sheared right through the briefcase handle, letting the case tumble free again.

"Dang it, Ben!" Murray yelled in frustration. "That case is expensive!" He made a grab for it, but I was faster. I kicked the briefcase away before he could reach it, sending it sliding across the floor toward the writhing electrical wire.

The wire whipped into the metal briefcase, sending a powerful electrical surge through it, frying the circuits and instantly destroying the deathly machinery inside.

Or, that's what I had *hoped* would happen.

Instead, when the briefcase was only a few feet from the electrical wire that *would* have fried its circuits, Elmore Finch stepped into its path.

He was no longer fighting Mike. He hadn't won the battle fairly, though. Instead, several soldiers had subdued Mike, while a dozen more had subdued Erica and Cyrus. Behind them, Alexander, Chip, Jawa, and Zoe had also been overwhelmed. There were simply too many soldiers to fight.

A dozen more soldiers now surrounded me. These guys had guns, and they were all pointed in my direction.

"Drop that sword," one ordered.

Swords don't do very well against guns. So I dropped mine.

"Arrest him!" Elmore Finch ordered. "That's the boy who tried to kill the president!"

The soldiers all closed in on me.

I thought about arguing, once again, that they were making a mistake and that I'd been set up by SPYDER.

Only, that hadn't been working very well for me.

However, it suddenly occurred to me that there might be a different way to handle things. The Mike Brezinski way.

Mike had solved his bomb-defusing exam by realizing that sometimes there was an advantage to simply letting the bomb go off.

So I figured maybe I shouldn't fight being arrested anymore. Maybe I should just let it happen and use it to my advantage.

"Okay," I said to the soldiers. "You got me. But I didn't do it alone. I'm only a kid. I don't know how to build a bomb."

The soldiers paused. This seemed to make sense to them. "Who helped you?" asked one.

"Him!" I said, pointing directly at Elmore Finch. "He wanted me to kill the chairman so *he* could take over the Joint Chiefs!"

There was a gasp from the crowd of Pentagon employees around me. Most of them seemed shocked that I had dared make such an accusation—although a few looked as though they might have believed me.

"That's insanity!" Finch shouted. "I did no such thing!"

"Actually, he did," said Cyrus, who'd quickly caught on to my plan. "I'm Agent Cyrus Hale with the CIA. My son, Alexander, and I apprehended Mr. Ripley this morning and, along with Felicia DuVray, the assistant director of information acquisition for the army, brought him here for questioning. Ripley cracked and revealed copious information, including the fact that Finch here masterminded the entire attack so he could get his hands on that briefcase."

"He's lying!" Finch exclaimed. "Agent Hale attacked *me* so that *he* could get this briefcase!"

"If I wanted to steal that briefcase from you, why would I do it *inside* the Pentagon?" Cyrus asked calmly. "You're surrounded by soldiers who work for you. It'd be a million times easier to steal it somewhere else."

A murmur of agreement rippled through the crowd. Cyrus's argument made sense.

"I don't know how your depraved mind works!" Finch argued, then tried to shift the attention to me. "I'm not the criminal here! That kid is! He's telling lies about me!"

"I tried to keep our secret, Mr. Finch," I said. "But they gave me some sort of truth serum and forced the answer out of me. I'm sorry." I caught sight of Murray Hill trying to sidle away and pointed at him. "That guy was in on it too, by the way."

Several guns swung toward Murray, who dropped his bayonet and tried to act innocent. "Me?" he asked.

"He came here with Finch to steal the briefcase this morning," Cyrus said. "His name's Murray Hill. Fingerprint him and run his file if you don't believe me. I know he looks young, but he's a known juvenile offender with a long list of infractions."

The soldiers all looked back and forth between me, Murray, Cyrus, and Finch, trying to make sense of what they should do.

"Why are any of you listening to this?" Finch screamed. "I'm the chairman of the Joint Chiefs and I'm giving you a direct order! Arrest these men now!"

"Fine with me," Cyrus said, offering his hands to the soldiers. "But I'd recommend hauling your boss in as well. Believe me, you guys don't want that briefcase leaving this building in the wrong hands. Unless you're a big fan of nuclear war."

"Sounds like a good plan to me." The three-star general who'd been clocked by Washington's mannequin head arrived on the scene. He was back on his feet and looked like he was already wishing this day was over. "Soldiers, take everyone involved in this whole insane fracas into custody right now. And lock them up tight until we get to the bottom of this."

The soldiers swarmed around me, Cyrus, Alexander, Erica, Mike, Chip, Jawa, and Zoe—but also Murray Hill and Elmore Finch. Once again, we were handcuffed. None of my friends objected. Meanwhile, Elmore Finch protested wildly, threatening every last soldier with a court-martial. Murray Hill just glowered at me. "I'm getting tired of this thwarting, Ben," he growled. "*Really* tired of it."

One soldier looked over my friends curiously and asked the question most everyone else in the Pentagon had been thinking: "What's the deal with all the kids here?"

"It's 'Take Your Child to Work Day' at the CIA," Mike said.

"It got a little out of hand," Erica explained.

I locked eyes with her as the soldiers cuffed us. She gave me a smile, seeming pleased with how things had worked out.

Next to her, Mike mouthed the words, *Nice thinking, pal.*

I grinned back. Yes, I was being arrested for the attempted assassination of the president and probably a dozen other crimes, but I was relatively sure Cyrus could provide enough evidence to get me off the hook. Plus, SPYDER's plans had been foiled. And, frankly, I was looking forward to a little time in a nice, quiet jail cell.

It had been a rough couple of days and I really needed a nap.

COMMENDATION

Rose Garden

The White House

February 16

1200 hours

I had a lovely time in solitary confinement.

The bed was decent and it was incredibly quiet. I slept the entire time I was there—twelve hours—and when I finally awoke, everything had been sorted out.

We had each been allowed one phone call upon our arrest, and Cyrus had used his to contact the president. He told Stern everything that had happened, and Stern had promptly ordered the Pentagon to let Cyrus go. Cyrus then went to work amassing the evidence he needed to prove our story, which turned out to be easier than expected: Murray Hill lasted less than fifteen seconds before spilling his guts.

Getting Murray to talk didn't require any torture at all. Ironically, for a member of SPYDER, Murray had severe arachnophobia. (As well as additional fears of snakes, dogs, rats, monkeys, otters, and dentists.) Cyrus had simply found a perfectly normal daddy longlegs crawling around the Pentagon and told Murray it was a genetically enhanced tarantula bearing poison that would make his brain explode. Murray promptly coughed up every last detail of SPYDER's operation to get rid of the chairman of the Joint Chiefs— as well as several hundred details about SPYDER's previous operations. In return, the government cut down his sentence. Instead of going to prison for life, he would only have to go for the next forty years.

Unfortunately, Ashley Sparks and Warren Reeves received no jail time at all. Both of them had disappeared without a trace. Cyrus himself combed Warren's dorm room for any sign of his connection to SPYDER, but found none. To everyone's surprise, Warren had done a masterful job of concealing his switch to the dark side. I assumed this meant someone else had done most of the work for him.

Of course there was a massive cover-up. No one wanted to reveal that an evil organization had almost taken over our nuclear arsenal. SPYDER remained a secret from the public at large—and most of the government as well. Instead, the presidential assassination attempt was pinned on Elmore Finch, who—it was claimed—had suffered a severe mental breakdown.

My friends and I were cleared of charges—and I was made out to be a hero. The official story went like this: I was a friend of Jason Stern's who happened to be passing through the West Wing when I spotted Elmore Finch with a bomb. I had bravely grabbed the bomb and thrown it into the Oval Office, saving the president and countless others, but the media had mistakenly reported that *I* was the assassin. The government had taken advantage of this, letting that story run to give Finch's accomplices the false impression that they weren't under suspicion, which had then allowed the government to catch and arrest those accomplices, keeping the world safe for everyone.

I even got a medal out of the whole shebang.

There was a big, fancy ceremony for it in the White House Rose Garden two days after my release from jail. My parents were invited, as were all of my friends from spy school. None of them got medals, though. The existence of spy school itself remained a highly classified secret, so their contributions to the cause couldn't be publicized. (They all got A's in Thwarting the Enemy, however.) The reason I was getting a medal had nothing to do with my help on the mission; it was to make it clear to the American people that I was no longer public enemy number one. Otherwise, alert citizens were going to keep reporting me to the police. (A day before the ceremony, an entire SWAT team had been mobilized when I went out to get a doughnut. Since then, I'd had to remain on campus, lying low.)

"Wow. Check out this crowd," Mike said. We were standing near the presidential podium in the Rose Garden, waiting for the ceremony to begin. "I haven't seen this many politicians in one place since the inauguration."

I scanned the crowd with him. It was surprisingly large. I had expected the ceremony to be small and intimate, but somehow it had grown into a huge event. There were hundreds of dignitaries, politicos, and their aides, all dressed in their finest suits. Both of my home state's senators and each of the congresspeople had come, then posed proudly with me before the press. The gaggle of reporters and camera crew that was usually stationed by the Eisenhower Executive Office Building had migrated to the Rose Garden to record the ceremony. A military band was playing. And, of course, there was the standard retinue of Secret Service agents. "I can't believe all these people are here for me," I said.

"They're not," Mike said. "They're here for the cameras. Like flies around a dead squirrel."

I noticed Zoe, Chip, and Jawa. They had grabbed seats in the front row.

Alexander Hale was close by, surrounded by his own personal crowd of admirers, none of whom had any idea how lousy a spy he was. One of Alexander's few real talents was socializing. I had no doubt that he was recounting his involvement in our mission in a way that played up his part in it. Everyone around him was hanging on to his every word.

My parents had a crowd around them as well. The days when the rest of the world had thought I was an assassin had been rougher on them than I'd even imagined, but now their spirits were sky-high. Politicians were lining up to shake their hands. My father noticed me looking at them and gave a proud smile.

Meanwhile, Cyrus Hale was off to the side, by the buffet. He had zero interest in talking to anyone else and was far more focused on getting as much free food as he could. I even spotted him stuffing some rolls in his pockets.

Sadly, Catherine Hale wasn't there. Since she was no longer married to Alexander and her status as a spy for MI6 was a secret, she couldn't swing an invitation. However, she had sent me a very nice note—in impeccable handwriting—congratulating me on my medal and saying that she hoped we would meet again someday when I wasn't a fugitive from justice.

One other person was noticeably absent. "Have you seen Erica?" I asked Mike.

"I came through security right behind her," he replied. "But I haven't seen her since. Knowing her, she's probably infiltrating a covert terrorist cell before the ceremony."

"Or maybe she's thwarting another assassination attempt so that I don't have one more than her," I suggested.

Mike laughed. "That girl's amazing, but she really needs to find some hobbies."

From a hidden speaker someplace on the grounds, a disembodied voice announced that it was time for everyone to take their seats, as the president would be arriving soon.

"Gotta go," Mike said. "Have fun. And make sure your fly is up. We're on national television here." With that, he gave me a pat on the back and hurried off to sit with Zoe, Chip, and Jawa.

I checked my fly. I had already checked it fifteen times, but still, it couldn't hurt to be safe.

"Stop playing with your pants," Jason Stern said. "You look like a pervert."

He'd come up behind me, along with Jemma Stern, Kimmy Dimsdale, and all their Secret Service agents, as they had orders to stand by the podium near me for the ceremony. Jason and I were stuck pretending to be friends for the press. Jason was putting on a nice show for the cameras, but in private he was still being a raging jerk every chance he got.

"Jason," Kimmy chided. "That's no way to talk to the person who saved your father's life."

"Yeah, thanks for that," Jason said sarcastically, as though he wouldn't have minded his father getting blown up. "You're my hero."

He smacked me on the back of the head as he set off for his place by the podium, well aware I couldn't retaliate. If I had ever tried to smack him back, the Secret Service would have dog-piled me in front of the entire nation.

"Don't pay any attention to him," Jemma Stern said. "He's just angry because Daddy wouldn't let him get a motorcycle."

Her friendliness caught me by surprise. The only time we had ever interacted was when I had caught her in the bathroom and she'd accused me of being a stalker. I was thinking that maybe she was impressed that I'd saved her father's life, but then she leaned in close to me and whispered, "Who was that boy you were just talking to?"

"Mike?" I asked. "He's my best friend."

"Do you know if he's dating anyone?"

Of course, I thought. Jemma Stern was the most eligible teenage girl in the country, so naturally she'd be interested in Mike.

"He's single," I told her. "I'd be happy to introduce you after the ceremony."

"That'd be great!" Jemma gave me a quick, friendly smile and headed off with Kimmy to join her mother.

In the front row, Jawa and Chip gave me the thumbs-up. Apparently, they had thought Jemma was flirting with *me*. Beside them, Zoe seemed annoyed, though she quickly tried to hide it.

Things had been weird with Zoe ever since I had learned of her crush on me. I wasn't really sure how to deal with it, and Zoe didn't seem to know either. So both of us had tried to pretend that it had never happened, which made things even more awkward. Zoe had barely even spoken to me at the reception, short of saying "Hi" and "Try the corn dogs."

It occurred to me that even though we had once again thwarted SPYDER, everything wasn't back to normal at all. There were plenty of unanswered questions: Where had Warren and Ashley gone? How many more secret agents did SPYDER have at spy school, or the CIA, or throughout the government? What would they be plotting next? And, most importantly, were they going to try to kill me again?

With a fanfare of trumpets, the band began to play "Hail to the Chief," the official presidential theme song. The president and his standard entourage of Secret Service agents emerged from the West Wing and headed our way.

Everyone respectfully stood at attention. Jason Stern did his best to make it look like he was doing this under duress, until his mother whispered something to him—probably a threat—and he pasted a plastic smile across his face for the cameras.

The president passed the ruined section of the Oval Office. Repairs had been paused for the ceremony, and the scaffolding was strung with red, white, and blue bunting to make it look good for the cameras.

I suddenly flashed back to the moments before the bomb had gone off. The moments when I realized I had been played by SPYDER, when I had been surrounded by the president and the chairman of the Joint Chiefs, and all the top brass of the military and Vladimir Gorsky. . . .

Gorsky.

I spun back toward the crowd, searching for Erica, desperately wanting to talk to her.

Only, she wasn't there with everyone else.

Instead, she was right behind me.

"What's wrong?" she asked.

I had to fight the urge to ask her how she had managed to get so close without me—or the Secret Service—noticing. Or how she already knew something was wrong. Instead, I said, "I don't think the chairman of the Joint Chiefs was SPYDER's only target with that bomb."

"Of course he wasn't. SPYDER also had the president there. And *you.*"

"I think they might have been going for Vladimir Gorsky, too."

The president was almost at the podium now. His family stood to one side, beaming lovingly at him. The ceremony was about to begin.

"Gorsky?" Erica asked skeptically. "Why would SPYDER want to kill him? Grandpa thinks they're working together."

"Well, maybe things aren't going so well with that. I saw Gorsky in the West Wing right before the bomb went off. The memory just came back to me. He noticed me—and he was *scared*. Really scared. At the time I thought maybe he was worried that I'd recognized him and that he was the mole, but now I realize that wasn't the case. *I* was the mole. And I think Gorsky knew it. When he saw me, he freaked out because he realized *he* was the target."

"So, in addition to wiping out the chairman of the Joint Chiefs, SPYDER also wanted to take out one of their major arms dealers?"

"Yes."

"Why?"

"I have no idea. Though I'm guessing it means they're up to something."

"SPYDER is always up to something."

"True. But this time we have a lead."

Erica stared at me for a bit, mulling this over, then

nodded. "Good thinking. I'll go tell Grandpa." She started to leave, then looked back and said, "By the way, you're welcome."

"For what?"

"You'll see." Erica gave me a slight smile, then slipped away to join the crowd.

The music stopped and the president stepped to the podium. A hush fell over the crowd. "Ladies and gentlemen, friends and family," he said, with his standard, impressive gravitas. "We have gathered here today to honor Benjamin Ripley for being the first person to ever regurgitate a wombat through a flugelhorn."

Well, he might have said that. I wasn't paying any attention.

I had *meant* to. In fact, I had planned to listen very closely to the speech so I could remember every word of it. It's not every day that you get the Presidential Medal of Freedom.

However, I was distracted by a few other things.

First of all, Erica had smiled at me and said, "Good thinking." Over the past few days, she had gone back to being her usual distant self around me. In fact, she had even been a little icier than usual, as though she was annoyed at me for taking advantage of her lowered defenses to ask embarrassing questions—or possibly embarrassed by the results. But now she had actually given me a smile and a compliment:

the same sort of thing that had made me jealous when she'd done it to Mike. And she had done it in public. In front of a whole crowd of people and television cameras. Which meant that, just maybe, the Ice Queen was thawing out.

Second, I was still concerned about what SPYDER was plotting. Were they actually trying to bump off Gorsky? If so, why? What was SPYDER up to now? And were Warren and Ashley a part of it?

But as important as both those lines of thought were, something else was distracting me from the president's speech even more. In fact, it was distracting everyone in the audience as well.

Jason Stern had wet his pants.

The moment the president began speaking, a large wet spot had bloomed right in the crotch of Jason's pressed khakis. Jason didn't seem to realize what had happened, but everyone else sure did. The entire crowd was gaping at him and, more often than not, trying to restrain their laughter. The camera operators subtly shifted their lenses from the president to his son. Through it all, Jason stood by the podium with his standard smug grin, completely unaware of what was going on.

I caught Erica's eye in the crowd. Even she was trying not to laugh. She also seemed quite pleased with herself.

I had no idea how she'd done this to Jason. Perhaps it

involved some sort of high-tech, time-released hydration pellets. Or maybe she had smuggled in a long-range water gun and scored a direct hit. But however she'd managed it, it had worked beautifully. Jason Stern, who'd been such a relentless jerk to me, was about to become a national laughingstock. The ceremony was on live TV, and my friends were already on their phones, doubtlessly posting photos online. Many adults appeared to be doing the same thing. Including a couple of congresspeople.

President Stern hadn't noticed yet himself, although he was starting to sense that something funny was going on. His speech became more and more stilted as he looked for whatever was distracting the crowd—until his eyes fell upon his own son. "Jason!" he gasped. "Have some decency!"

Jason glanced down at his pants, gave a yelp of horror, then slapped his hands over his crotch and bolted from the dais. Or at least, he *tried* to. Due to his haste—and the fact that he was trying to run with his hands clamped over his private parts—he tripped over a microphone cable and pitched headfirst into the buffet. The table promptly upended, and the enormous cake that had been baked for the celebration toppled over on Jason, smearing him from head to toe in buttercream frosting.

The camera handlers all recorded this as well. Every last moment.

No one could contain themselves anymore. Everyone, from the president to the Secret Service to my parents to Erica Hale herself, burst out laughing.

Thank you, I mouthed to Erica.

She gave me another smile in response.

Maybe Erica wasn't ready for a relationship quite yet. And maybe she never would be. I wondered if I'd go through my whole life waiting for another kiss from her—or if someday our stars would align.

But in the meantime, I knew one thing about Erica Hale for sure:

I was awfully lucky she was on my side.

February 17

To: CIA director █████████████

Re: Operation Pungent Muskrat recap

First off, I apologize for going rogue on this one. Unfortunately, as intel on this mission reveals, our highest levels of government remain corrupted by ████████████████. There was simply no other choice.

Admittedly, there were a few glitches in this operation. I accept full responsibility for Agent Ripley being used as a Bombay Boomerang and the subsequent destruction of the Oval Office. I understand that the president is still quite peeved about the whole thing. And, in a perfect world, █████████ agents Warren Reeves and Ashley Sparks would not have been allowed to escape.

However, if not for the performance of my team—including Ripley—things would have been far worse. We uncovered a plot to ███████ ████████████████████████████████ and thwarted it. And we captured two ████████ operatives to boot. While Elmore Finch is still holding out from giving information, I hope to get Murray Hill to tell us what ████████ has planned for the future—or even better, ████████████████████████████ ███████. Armed with this intel, I believe we can get the jump on ████████ for once, and therefore recommend we initiate Operation Tiger Shark. (I know we used that for a mission back in the 1960s, but damn it, I think it's about time we started recycling names. I'll be damned if I'm going to call this one Operation Flaccid Sparrow.)

Given their success on Operation Pungent Muskrat, I would highly recommend that Agents █████████████ and ███████████ be a part of this new operation as well.

Sincerely,

█████████████

TO SPY SCHOOL

POTOMAC RIVER

EISENHOWER EXECUTIVE
OFFICE BUILDING

LINCOLN MEMORIAL

TIDAL BASIN

ARLINGTON MEMORIAL BRIDGE

TO PENTAGON